ROMANCING THE RIFLEMAN

BOOK SIX IN THE ASTLEY CHRONICLES

COURTNEY MCCASKILL

HAZEL GROVE BOOKS

ALSO BY COURTNEY MCCASKILL

The Astley Chronicles

Book 1: How to Train Your Viscount

Book 2: What's an Earl Gotta Do?

Book 3: The Sea Siren of Broadwater Bottom

Book 4: The Duke's Dark Secret

Book 5: Let Me Be Your Hero

Book 6: Romancing the Rifleman

Book 7: A Laird for Lady Lucy (Coming Soon)

My Favorite Mistake: An Astley Chronicles Novella

The Weatherby Wallflowers

Book 1: A Wallflower Never Surrenders

Book 2: Snowbound with the Scoundrel

Book 3: One Bed for the Bluestocking (Coming Soon)

Book 4: How He Won His Wallflower (Coming Soon)

The Wicked Widows' League

Book 1: Scoundrel for Sale

Book 2: A Very Roguish Boxing Day

Other Books:

One Fine May (The Rake Review)

For more information, visit www.courtneymccaskill.com.

THE ASTLEYS OF HARRINGTON HALL

Edward Astley IV, Earl of Cheltenham
Georgiana Astley, Countess of Cheltenham

Edward Astley V, Viscount Fauconbridge, age 30
Harrington Astley, age 29
Anne Cranfield (née Astley), Countess of Morsley, age 27
Caroline Greville (née Astley) Viscountess Thetford, age 24
Lady Lucy Astley, age 22
Lady Isabella Astley, age 22
John Astley, deceased at age 2
Frederick Astley, age 17

First published in 2025 by Hazel Grove Books.

Romancing the Rifleman Copyright © Courtney McCaskill, 2025.

Excerpt from *A Laird for Lady Lucy* Copyright © Courtney McCaskill, 2025.

Kindle ISBN: 978-1-63915-046-5

eBook ISBN: 978-1-63915-047-2

Paperback ISBN: 978-1-63915-048-9

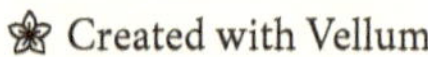 Created with Vellum

CHAPTER 1

London, England
April 1806

ady Diana Latimer pulled the polished rosewood door open and peered around its edge. The room behind it proved to be the library, and it was deserted. *Perfect.* Slipping inside, she shut the door behind her and leaned against it, pressing her hand to her heart.

The London Season had scarcely begun, and already she was sick of it. She had been raised by her Great-Aunt Griselda in an isolated house on the edge of Ilkley Moor. Growing up, there had been no glittering parties, no routs with a thousand guests crushed into a single mansion. There had been Diana, her great-aunt, a handful of servants, the pack of brown and white speckled pointers Aunt Griselda raised, and occasionally, when he was able to get away for a visit, her brother, Marcus. Her friends had been of the imaginary sort.

Such isolation had been necessary. Diana and Marcus's father had been a violent man. When Diana was two, he had killed her mother in a fit of rage by pushing her down the stairs. He had managed to escape punishment thanks to his status as a duke. Two years later, he returned to the family home and selected Diana as his new target.

That was when Marcus, who was nine years her senior, had managed to remove her to Aunt Griselda's protection.

But when Marcus inherited their father's title three years ago, he had brought Diana to London to take up a life befitting the sister of a duke. In Yorkshire, she had spent her days dressed in plain wool, tramping across the moors with her great-aunt and a pack of dogs. The only adornment to her gown had been the twelve inches of mud gracing her hem. They would shoot their own dinner and roast it over an open fire, and on the rare occasions when the English weather cooperated, they would sleep out under the stars.

And now, she found herself here, wearing a gown of delicate white silk and handmade lace that cost more than most men would earn in a lifetime. She had paired it with a necklace of aquamarines—a birthday gift from her brother, chosen because the pale blue stones perfectly matched her eyes.

Diana knew she shouldn't complain, knew there were scores of young women who owned only one set of clothes and had to struggle to scratch out a living working in the mills or sewing until their fingers bled. She knew just about every girl in England would give her eyeteeth to be the younger sister of a duke, and the richest heiress in all of England. But when she passed by a mirror and caught a glimpse of herself, it was always a shock to see a girl in silk and jewels staring back at her. A part of her still expected to see the shabby wool coat she had worn back in Yorkshire and a streak of mud on her cheek.

She also remembered how lonely she had been before coming to London. How she used to gaze at the empty night sky and issue a silent plea to the Almighty to send her a little company.

She had found it. And she had made some wonderful friends, especially the Astley twins, Lucy and Isabella.

But in retrospect, perhaps she should have been more specific when she was wishing upon a star and asked not just for some company but for some *intelligent* company.

Hence her need to steal away from the party for a moment of quietude. She found these huge London gatherings exhausting in general, and as the evening wore on, it became increasingly difficult to maintain a cordial veneer while surrounded by her ever-present flock of inane suitors.

Speaking of which… Diana turned back toward the door, pressing her ear against its panels. There were footsteps in the hall, accompanied by voices.

Male voices.

Someone was coming.

With skill born out of practice, Diana hurried across the library on tiptoes, identifying the perfect hiding place as she went. She deftly slipped behind the poppy-colored taffeta curtain just as the door swung open.

"Not in here, either," a man with a high, petulant voice said. "Where is she hiding?"

Behind the curtain, Diana frowned, wondering who their quarry might be.

"Come on," a different male voice, this one slow and dull, answered. "I'm sick of tramping through every room in this bloody house." She heard the soft slide of a drawer opening, followed by the muffled clatter of someone sifting through it.

"Look what we have here!" the second voice said. "Let's sit a minute and take advantage of Lord Richford's hospitality."

There were footsteps followed by the scrape of a chair against the hardwood floor. The pungent smell of cheroots confirmed the identity of the item they had discovered in Lord Richford's desk drawer.

"There," the second man said. "That's better. So, why does it have to be her, anyway?"

"I told you. I need an heiress."

Diana rolled her eyes. These two sounded like some of *her* suitors. Which was to say, insipid.

"Well, what's wrong with that friend of hers?" the second man asked. "She's just as pretty."

"Do you mean Lady Lucy?" the first man asked.

That got Diana's attention. Because she knew a Lady Lucy—Lucy Astley, her particular friend.

She reminded herself that there were three hundred people in attendance at this party, and it was likely that several bore the address *Lady Lucy*. It could easily be a coincidence.

"That's the one!" the second man agreed.

"She's rich, but she's not rich enough."

His friend chuckled. "Not rich enough? She has thirty-five thousand bloody pounds." Diana's heart started to race because that happened to be Lucy's exact dowry. Her father, Lord Cheltenham, was a wealthy earl, and there were vanishingly few young ladies in possession of a comparable fortune.

And if even Lucy was *not rich enough*, there was only one heiress in London capable of meeting this cretin's requirements.

Her.

"I told you," the first man growled, "I had a bad day at Boodle's."

His friend laughed incredulously. "I didn't realize it was *that* bad of a day."

Boodle's was the club where men went when they wanted to play deep. Something niggled in the back of Diana's mind. There had been a rumor about someone losing a terrific sum at the tables last week.

"I had a few bad days, all right?"

Hearing his voice, the man's name came to her in a flash —Joseph Cumberworth, fourth son of Baron Cumberworth. That would make his oafish friend Berkeley Blachford.

"I still say you should set your sights on Lady Lucy. I mean, what about...? You know. Her *arm?*" Blachford asked in a tone of voice that suggested he was wrinkling his nose.

Now, Diana knew without a shred of doubt that she and Lucy were the heiresses in question. She had been born without a right hand, and her right forearm was about half the length of its companion on her left.

"I don't give a damn about her arm," Cumberworth replied. "The real problem is that she's such a bitch."

It was fortunate that Diana had so much practice in hiding, which included staying perfectly still and silent, no matter how shocking the things she overheard might be. It was the one thing she could thank her father for. Because of him, she had spent countless hours standing behind a curtain or huddled on a shelf in a wardrobe during his drunken rages.

And so, she managed to hold her breath and not flinch when Cumberworth uttered the worst insult that could be used against a woman.

Cumberworth was still speaking. "At least things will be different once we're married. A man has the right to discipline his wife, after all."

Blachford didn't sound convinced. "But what about that brother of hers? He's a damned good fencer. And he seems like the type who wouldn't hesitate to run you through."

This might be the most intelligent thing Berkeley

Blachford had ever said. Diana didn't have a shred of doubt that Marcus would kill any man who raised a hand against her.

Of course, Blachford was overlooking a few pertinent facts. Diana was every bit as talented at fencing as her brother; she could skewer Cumberworth like a dish of *Veal à la Dauphiné* herself. To say nothing of the fact that Marcus would never allow a blackguard such as Joseph Cumberworth to marry her in the first place.

Cumberworth sounded unconcerned. "You have to be careful in how you do it. The trick is to avoid the arms, face, and any other place where someone might see a bruise."

"But won't she just tell him?" Blachford asked, sounding even more confused than usual.

"Not if she's sufficiently frightened," Cumberworth said confidently. "It's crucial that you terrorize your wife completely."

"*Oh.*" Blachford paused, as if giving this great thought. "I'll have to remember that."

There was a creak of leather as if Cumberworth were lounging back in one of the wing chairs before the fire. "It will be tiresome keeping her in line. But for a hundred thousand pounds, it'll be worth it."

Blachford warmed to this theme, and he and Cumberworth continued discussing how offensively opinionated she was. Diana listened with only half an ear. She was busy plotting her revenge. Eventually, she would tell Marcus, who wielded his social influence every bit as deftly as he wielded his sword. Overnight, Cumberworth would find himself cast out from all good society. Invitations would cease to be issued, and his former friends would cut him in the street.

But first, Diana wanted to toy with him. Perhaps she would grant him a dance in order to give him false hope. She would then proceed to forget his name. He would be Mr. Cumberland, then Mr. Cumberbatch, and then Mr. Cummerbund.

She would not stammer out an awkward apology when he pointed out her error. She was going to look him dead in the eye as she addressed him as *Mr. Cumbersome*, to better emphasize that his name was simply not worth remembering.

She was wondering if she could get away with calling him *Mr. Cucumber* when Cumberworth and Blachford's guffaws were interrupted by a new voice.

"Correct me if I'm wrong, but I believe you're speaking of Lady Diana Latimer, are you not?"

Every hair on the back of her neck stood up. Because she knew that voice.

It had been three years since she'd heard it, because he'd been away fighting with his regiment.

But that insouciant drawl belonged to her friends Lucy and Isabella's older brother, Harrington Astley. She was sure of it.

Behind the curtain, she scarcely dared to breathe. Because she *liked* Harrington Astley. Three years ago, she had arrived in London at the end of the Season, meaning that she'd only had a handful of conversations with him before the time had come to return to her brother's country house in Cornwall. By the time the following Season had started, he had left London to join his regiment.

But those few conversations had been excellent ones. She remembered him as being handsome, charming, and wickedly funny.

A lump rose in her throat. Thanks to her arm, she was quite used to people whispering about her behind her back. She had thick skin because otherwise, she would not have survived. Cumberworth and Blachford had earned her ire by speaking about her in such disrespectful terms. But she was not broken up about it.

Yet she found that if Harrington Astley were to agree, were to join in their mockery, that would wound her in a way few men had the capacity to do.

She held her breath as Cumberworth confirmed that she had identified his voice correctly. "What the devil are you doing here, Astley?"

CHAPTER 2

hat the devil are you doing here, Astley?

It was the very question Harrington had been asking himself.

He'd spent the past six months on a deployment to Germany with his regiment, the 95th Rifles. They had been part of a force tasked with reclaiming the king's ancestral homeland of Hanover. It had started off well enough. Napoleon had been busy farther south dealing with Austria, so they marched right in, along with their Swedish and Russian allies. They'd proceeded to sit there, freezing their arses off, all through Christmas.

But then, they'd learned that Napoleon had crushed the Austrian and Russian armies at Austerlitz. Their Russian allies had promptly retreated home to lick their wounds. Meanwhile, it turned out Prussia had betrayed them all weeks ago, signing a secret treaty with France. The prize Napoleon had dangled before the Prussians was, of course, the electorate belonging to his enemy, the King of England—Hanover.

With no allies left standing but the Swedes, they'd had no

choice but to flee back to the North Sea with the French dogging their heels. Harrington's regiment had been tasked with performing a rearguard duty, an exhausting combination of obstructing their pursuers and fleeing for their lives.

His men had done a damn good job of it, if he said so himself. There had been vanishingly few casualties during the long retreat. Then they'd packed themselves onto ships and fled back to England. The exercise had been utterly pointless, but at least it had not resulted in a great loss of life.

And then last week, some bigwig over at Horse Guards had requested he come up to London to receive a special assignment, so here he was, at this fancy party. It was disorienting to be here, sipping champagne and dancing a cotillion, when mere weeks ago, he'd been covered in mud and had bullets whizzing past his head.

But his family had been overjoyed to see him. That part had been nice. He'd spent most of the evening in the billiards room with his brother, Edward, and his friends Henry Greville and Peter Ferguson. Henry was a father now, if you could countenance it. He was married to Harrington's sister, Caro, who'd given birth to a baby girl late last year. They'd named her Georgiana after Caro and Harrington's mother.

He'd been heading back to the billiards room after a trip to the necessary when he heard voices coming from Lord Richford's library. He'd naturally stopped to eavesdrop, and that was when he heard it.

"I still say you should set your sights on Lady Lucy. I mean, what about…? You know. Her *arm*?"

That got Harrington's attention, first, because his sister happened to be a Lady Lucy, and precisely the sort of young lady men set their sights on—sweet, pretty, and rich.

It took a few seconds for the rest of the sentence to sink

in. Lucy's particular friend, Lady Diana Latimer, had been born missing a hand.

Lucy and Diana were surely the pair of young ladies under discussion.

Quietly, he stole up to the door, pressing his ear against a wooden panel.

"I don't give a damn about her arm," someone else replied. "The real problem is that she's such a bitch."

What the devil? First off, that wasn't the sort of thing one said about a lady.

But it wasn't even right. Diana Latimer wasn't a bitch. To be sure, she didn't suffer fools, and it was more than apparent that these were a couple of clowns. If they'd fared poorly with Lady Diana, Harrington was fairly certain it was their own damn fault.

The first man spoke again. "But what about that brother of hers? He's a damned good fencer. And he seems like the type who wouldn't hesitate to run you through."

He wasn't wrong. Lady Diana's older brother, Marcus, the Duke of Trevissick, was very much the running-you-through sort, and he was fiercely overprotective where his little sister was concerned.

He also happened to hate Harrington with a rare fervor, although that was neither here nor there. Considering how many schoolboy pranks Harrington had pulled on the duke during their days at Eton, it was a wonder he hadn't been run through by Marcus Latimer years ago.

The other idiot spoke again. "You have to be careful in how you do it. The trick is to avoid the arms, face, and any other place someone might see a bruise."

"But won't she just tell him?" his companion asked.

"Not if she's sufficiently frightened. It's crucial that you terrorize your wife completely."

Harrington gave the sort of laugh that was both soundless

and humorless. It was going to go *extremely* poorly for this wastrel once Trevissick found out about this. And Harrington meant to tell him. He wasn't about to sweep this under the rug. He quite liked Lady Diana.

'Quite like her?' Horseshit.

All right, in the interest of honesty, he more-than-liked Lady Diana. She was witty. Acerbic. Bloody gorgeous.

And *deliciously* strict in a way that made his pulse quicken.

But it was entirely out of the question. She couldn't marry without her brother's permission, and Harrington was the absolute last person on the face of this earth that Marcus Latimer would choose as the bridegroom for his precious, perfect sister.

Although the truth was, her dragon of a brother wasn't really the problem. What would *Diana Latimer* want with the likes of *him*? He was the family disgrace. He'd been paddled every single day during his time as a student at Eton. It had become a point of pride; once at suppertime during his final year, he'd realized that he had somehow gone all day without incurring the ire of Headmaster Davies. He'd promptly stood up on the table and launched into a rousing performance of "The Christening of Little Joey," and he meant the third verse, the one about all the things a fellow could do with his tongue to please his lady love. It had been sufficient to keep his streak going.

And those were just the things everyone knew about. Imagine if people knew about his worst flaw, the one he took such pains to conceal from the world. Only his closest friend, Henry, had managed to guess, but that just went to show what a decent sort of chap Henry was. Bless his soul, he hadn't breathed a word.

He did not delude himself into thinking that the rest of his loved ones would be as forgiving if they were ever to learn what a degenerate he really was.

He had only recently found something he was good for in life, and that was being cannon fodder for the British Army.

The point was, just because Lady Diana had laughed at a couple of his jokes a few years ago, it didn't mean he was remotely worthy of her. For Christ's sake, in addition to her many perfections, she was the richest heiress in all of Britain, possibly all of Europe! She could have literally any man she wanted.

It was worse than hopeless.

The first idiot was speaking again. "It will be tiresome keeping her in line. But for a hundred thousand pounds, it'll be worth it."

Keeping her in line. What a blithering idiot. Why would you even *want* to keep her in line? The way she had of looking down her nose at you like you were an absolute toad was one of his favorite things about her.

The two arse-heads were still blathering on about how awful she was, and what a chore it would be to marry her. Fucking shicers. It made his blood boil to hear it, but he knew what he ought to do was find a spot where he could watch the door. When the two idiots emerged from the library, he'd learn who they were. Then, he could march down the corridor, find Diana's brother, and tell him what he'd heard. Trevissick would handle it from there.

Of course, Harrington would help her brother if he wanted him to.

Which he most certainly would not.

That would be the right thing to do. Lie low. Make a plan.

But Harrington had never done the right thing in his life. So instead, he laid his hand upon the doorknob and strode into the library.

Two wide-eyed men turned to face him. Joseph fucking Cumberworth, and Berkeley bloody Blachford.

He might have guessed.

He gave them a winning smile. "Correct me if I'm wrong, but I believe you're speaking of Lady Diana Latimer, are you not?"

Cumberworth gave him a baleful look. "Astley, what the devil are you doing here?"

"Eavesdropping," Harrington answered cheerfully. Spying a decanter in the corner, he strolled into the room and poured himself a brandy. "So, you mean to marry Lady Diana?"

Cumberworth's eyes remained flinty, but he gave a curt nod. "Not that it's any of your affair. But yes. Yes, I do."

Harrington gave a low whistle. "That's an ambitious plan."

"Ambitious?" Cumberworth's eyes tightened. "Are you implying that I am not good enough for Lady Diana?"

"Oh, no. Not at all." Harrington paused for dramatic effect. "After all, why wouldn't the most eligible young lady in all of England want to marry a pox-riddled little bitch who's up to his ears in gambling debt?"

Cumberworth's cheeks reddened. "How dare you!"

Harrington raised a hand, ticking off the points against Cumberworth. "No gainful employment or income of any sort."

The redness had spread to Cumberworth's ears. "Shut it, you… you…"

"A fucking brute who's planning on beating his wife."

"This is none of your affair!" Cumberworth snapped.

"And all the physical attractions of a syphilitic potato," Harrington concluded.

"I ought to call you out!" Cumberworth roared.

Harrington smiled, unperturbed. He was, after all, a deuced good shot.

With his smart mouth, he had to be.

"I should be delighted," he said warmly. "I choose pistols. Shall we say tomorrow at dawn?"

Cumberworth was now performing the remarkable trick of being red with rage and a sickly shade of green at the same time. "Now, hang on a minute. I said I *ought* to call you out. Not that I *was* calling you out."

Harrington ticked another finger. "Cowardly, as well. What an absolute prince. It's a wonder the ladies don't fall into a swoon."

Cumberworth was back to scowling. "Well, it's not as if she's going to marry you, either."

Harrington laughed. "Certainly not. Lady Diana is *far* too good for the likes of me, to say nothing of the fact that her brother despises me."

Blachford, who had been watching their exchange in open-mouthed silence, spoke. "I say, Astley—if you don't want her for yourself, what do you care if Cumberworth wants to court her?"

"Because he just said he was going to *beat* her. And it happens that I like Lady Diana. She's clever, she's funny, she's nice—"

"Nice?" Cumberworth laughed incredulously. "She's a *bitch*."

Harrington raised his eyebrows. "She doesn't suffer fools, so if she doesn't suffer you, the implications are painfully obvious. And she's good friends with my sisters. So, if you'd like it to be pistols at dawn after all, just go ahead and call her that one more time." He gave Cumberworth a grin, not what you would call a nice grin, but judging by the way the man's shoulders slumped, Harrington figured it conveyed his message well enough.

Cumberworth rose. "I believe I've had enough of this *charming* conversation. Come, Blachford."

Harrington grabbed his upper arm. "Lord knows I won't miss your company. But let's make one thing clear before you go. You're going to stay the hell away from Lady Diana, and my sister, Lucy, too."

Cumberworth tried to shake him off without success. "Or else you'll tell her brother what I said, I suppose?"

"Oh, I'm going to tell Trevissick what you said as soon as I leave this room. I would leave town if I were you. If you think I'm a right cunt when I'm angry, wait until you see him."

Only now did Cumberworth seem to grasp the magnitude of his mistake. "Look, Astley, there must be some arrangement we can make. If I can get Lady Diana to the altar, I'll be a very wealthy man."

Harrington laughed. He was in the army, and he wasn't planning on resigning his commission. It was the only useful thing he'd managed to do in his twenty-nine years.

The men of the Rifle Brigade prided themselves on being the first ones in and the last ones out of every battle. Their casualty rate reflected this fact. Not that he was even considering Cumberworth's dishonorable offer. But really, what use did he have for the man's money? He'd likely be dead in a year, maybe two.

"Go to hell," Harrington replied.

Cumberworth's eyes were poisonous as he strode toward the door. "You'll regret this."

"I doubt it," Harrington said just before the door clicked shut.

CHAPTER 3

*H*eart pounding, Diana clutched the back of the curtain, listening to the now-silent room.

He had stood up for her. He had even threatened to call Cumberworth out, putting his own life at risk for the sake of her honor.

Tears pricked the back of her eyes not only for that, but because, based on the way Harrington had described her, he saw *her*. The *real* her. There were vanishingly few people who did. After her brother had saddled her with an absurdly large dowry, most of her suitors desired not her, but the hundred thousand pounds she came with. She'd asked Marcus not to do it. She'd argued that an ostentatious dowry would do nothing but attract fortune hunters. She would do just as well with a large dowry, but not a ridiculously large one, such as those her friends Lucy and Izzie had.

But Marcus was every bit as muleheaded as Diana, and he had this idea that the size of her dowry was a demonstration of the esteem in which he held his sister.

She knew his intentions were good. But the result was that she was surrounded by a flock of fortune hunters every time she set foot outside the house. Marcus had thought her dowry would make finding a husband easy, but paradoxically, it had made it nigh impossible. The constant scrum of fortune hunters scared off more honorable suitors who might be interested in getting to know her. She also found herself questioning every man's intentions, putting up defenses of her own that she had to acknowledge were probably discouraging good men along with the wastrels.

But Harrington Astley felt different. When she'd first made her debut, she'd thought him handsome, charming, and extremely witty. She hadn't had time to get to know him well before he had to leave London to join his regiment, but she hadn't been particularly upset about it. She had assumed she would meet dozens more handsome, witty men.

Except... she hadn't. It turned out that handsome, witty men were thin on the ground. Had she realized what a rare prize he was, she would have valued Harrington's company more highly during the brief interval she'd had it.

And, considering the way he had just defended her, she was feeling more warmly inclined toward him than ever.

And now he was back...

A newfound determination filled her. She was going to dance with him. Tonight. She had no idea how long he would be in London, but she was going to make use of that time.

If there was anything there, any possibility that the two of them would suit, she was going to uncover it.

The room had been silent for some time. It would be safe for her to emerge from behind her curtain.

Gathering herself, she slipped from her hiding place.

It turned out that the dark green jackets worn by officers of the Rifle Brigade were indeed an effective form of concealment, because she was halfway across the library before she noticed that the room was not quite so deserted as she had assumed.

Harrington's back was to her. Her heart squeezed as she noticed that his coat, which had fit his broad shoulders so beautifully the last time she saw him, was a trifle loose. The papers had reported that the retreat from Bremen had been a frantic affair, with his unit, the 95th Rifles, performing rearguard duty for its full duration. It was thanks to their efforts that the troops had returned home safely, and the reputation of the Rifle Brigade was very much in ascendance. Being a Rifleman was now considered to be every bit as modish as being in the Royal Hussars.

It seemed the reality was less glamorous. Harrington Astley's frame had been lean even before joining the army. She felt a lump form over her heart at the thought that he must've gone weeks without having enough to eat.

Gracious—it was not the time to grow all sniffly over his coat. Shaking herself, Diana took a careful step back, preparing to slip back behind her curtain.

That was when he began muttering to himself. "What a fucking toadstool. I hope he chokes on an onion. I hope a swarm of weevils takes up residence in his arsehole."

He was starting to get worked up, and began gesticulating with one hand. "I hope he steps in dog shit. I hope a cat throws up in his favorite boots. I hope he gets hogweed on his bollocks. I hope he trips and falls and lands on a cheese knife, and it goes straight up his—"

He spun around. It was not difficult to mark the moment he spotted Diana creeping back toward her curtain. He stopped mid-tirade, one finger raised in the air, mouth hanging open. Diana fancied that she would never forget his frozen look of horror.

Abruptly, he closed his mouth and dropped his hand. He sketched an awkward bow. "Lady Diana. I didn't realize you were, er…"

She found his discomfiture amusing, so instead of

hastening to reassure him, she arched an eyebrow. "Clearly not."

"I assume you heard"—he waved a finger in a circle—"all of that?"

"I did," she said, careful to keep her expression stern.

He cleared his throat. "I apologize for my language. I've, er… been in the army."

She crossed her arms and tilted her head ever so slightly. "And you did not use such language before joining the army?"

He cringed. "I must own that I did."

She managed to hold her stony expression for all of six seconds. Then, the corner of her mouth quirked upward.

The next thing she knew, they were both laughing. It was the kind of uncontrollable, tears-pricking, struggling-to-breathe, stomach-growing-sore laughter that one experienced far too seldom in life.

After the worst of it had passed, Harrington ran a hand over his face. "Oh, my *God*. I can't believe I said all of that in front of you. My mother would *kill* me if she knew."

Diana waved her hand. "Really, you oughtn't worry about it. Aunt Griselda says that much and worse on a regular basis, only she says it in Mecklenburgish."

Harrington grinned. "Just when I thought I couldn't like your aunt any better. How's she doing, by the by?"

"I am pleased to report that she is as hale and surly as ever." This was another point in Harrington's favor. Most men seemed to regard her unorthodox great-aunt as a cross to be borne. Harrington, on the other hand, found her delightful. At Diana's debut, he even asked Aunt Griselda to dance after she had commented that she enjoyed dancing but knew no one would ask her on account of her age.

Thinking back, that was the moment Harrington had truly captured her regard.

She shook herself. "But how are *you*? I didn't realize you were back in London."

"I only returned today. It was unexpected. My regiment is posted to Faversham, but I was called to London by somebody at Horse Guards. Seems they have a special assignment for me."

"Well, I, for one, am very glad that you have returned to us." Her voice quavered, and she found it difficult to meet his eye. Gracious, what was this? Diana wasn't normally the sentimental sort.

But she found that Harrington's safe return, combined with his defense of her to Joseph Cumberworth, had moved her.

Moreover, she had a feeling that this was important.

That, in spite of her reputation for being the ice queen who brushed men off like a speck of lint upon her gown, maybe, just maybe, this was a man she didn't want to flick away.

Harrington spoke into the silence that had descended between them. "So, if you heard my tirade, I take it you were also here when Cumberworth and Blachford were saying their piece?"

"I was. I was in the library when Mr. Cumberworth and Mr. Blachford entered. I sometimes find large gatherings such as this one to be taxing. It helps me to steal away for a moment of solitude." She gestured to the curtains. "When I heard them coming, I hid."

He cringed sympathetically. "I'm sorry you had to hear that."

She grinned. "At least I got to hear you call him a syphilitic potato."

He held both hands up. "If the shoe fits…"

"In this case, it fits like a glove. I had to bite my hand so I wouldn't laugh aloud."

"That's high praise." He was practically glowing, but his smile faltered. "Still, I hate to think of you standing behind that curtain while those blackguards abused you."

She shrugged. "I've heard worse. I wasn't sniffling into my handkerchief." Her lips twisted. "I was busy plotting my revenge."

He leaned forward. "Do tell."

She waved her hand. "Oh, nothing elaborate. I was merely going to give him false hope by agreeing to a dance, then proceed to call him every name I could think of other than his own."

He barked out a laugh. "Diabolical. I suppose I ruined it for you by threatening to inform your brother of everything he said."

She shrugged. "That's all right. Although Marcus's preferred form of revenge is boring in its predictability, I cannot deny that it is effective. I am sure I will enjoy watching Cumberworth get cast out of all good society."

"As consolation prizes go, it's not half bad," he agreed. He peered down at her a moment, biting his lip. She rather thought he was gathering his courage. "As you won't be dancing with him after all, perhaps you would do me the honor instead."

She inclined her head. "I should be delighted."

He offered her his arm, and they headed toward the door. As they were about to cross the threshold, something occurred to her. "But how remiss of me! I almost forgot to offer you my congratulations."

He gave her a curious look. "Congratulations? On what, surviving the retreat?"

She squeezed his arm. "No, silly. On your election to Parliament."

CHAPTER 4

*H*arrington tripped over the edge of the rug. In retrospect, it was a good thing Lady Diana had taken his arm, because for a second there, *she* was the one holding *him* up.

"I'm sorry," he said, stumbling to a halt. "What was that you said?"

It had sounded as if she had said something about Parliament, but he had obviously misheard. He hadn't been elected to Parliament.

It was patently obvious that he wasn't parliamentary material.

She looked up at him, surprise filling her pretty blue eyes. "Had you not heard? You emerged victorious in the special election."

He suddenly recalled what she was talking about. Their local M.P., a man named Andrew Milner, had recently been convicted of kidnapping. The matter was somewhat personal, as the person he had attempted to kidnap and ship off to New South Wales was Harrington's sister, Izzie.

The trial had been delayed for an age, but Milner had

eventually been found guilty, and now he was the one on a ship bound for Sydney.

The problem, according to Harrington's father, was that the frontrunner to win Milner's vacated seat, one Jacob Digsby, was "a man utterly without honor." Which sounded dramatic but boiled down to a horse race on which his father had lost money.

The Earl of Cheltenham's reasons for wanting someone else to win that seat may have been trivial. But, as Harrington's older brother, Edward, had noted, Digsby's brother owned a large sugar plantation in Jamaica, and he was staunchly pro-slavery. There were reasons to hope Digsby lost the election other than whether Battersea had been deliberately held back at Epsom.

But the man his father had proposed to stand against Jacob Digsby wasn't *Harrington*.

The mere notion was ridiculous.

"I believe you're thinking of my brother," he said.

She raised one eyebrow. It made her look haughty, which Harrington liked. "I assure you, I am not."

He laughed. "I think I would know if I was running for Parliament."

She shrugged. "According to the papers, you not only ran, but won."

His hands were growing clammy inside his gloves. "It was probably a typographical error. They printed *Mr. H. Astley* instead of *Mr. E. Astley*."

"They would have referred to your brother as Lord Fauconbridge, not Mr. Astley."

Shit. She was right.

"And besides," she continued, "the article specifically mentioned that you had been elected *in absentia*, as you were currently deployed to Hanover while serving as a lieutenant in the 95th Rifles."

Bloody hell. Now his hands were trembling. "There's been a mistake. Edward's the one my father wanted to run for the open seat. He said…"

He trailed off, struggling to remember. The truth was, he'd been extremely hungover when this conversation had taken place. It had been the eve of his deployment to Germany, so his friends, Henry and Peter, had taken him out for a night on the town.

Diana's blue eyes were piercing. "What, exactly, did your father say?"

Harrington screwed up his face, trying to dredge the memory from the recesses of his brain. "He said we didn't want Digsby for the seat, on account of him being a wastrel. But he knew someone who could beat him handily—his son, the most popular man in the county."

He looked at Diana, waiting for her to agree that this meant Edward. She blinked at him once… twice. "Which is you," she finally said.

"Which is *Edward*," Harrington insisted.

Diana crossed her arms. "I would agree, had your father said the most erudite man in the county, or the most respectable. But he said the most *popular*, which sounds like the fellow you could have a pint with down at the pub."

He hated that she had a point. He laughed nervously. "But he couldn't have possibly meant *me*. I mean, it's obvious, isn't it?"

Based on her blank expression, Lady Diana did not find it obvious. Which just went to show that she didn't know him as well as she supposed. "What happened next?"

"Er." Harrington racked his brain. "Edward said, 'I think it a splendid idea.' And then I noticed they were both staring at me, as if they were waiting for me to say something."

Diana gave him a pointed look. But surely, she wasn't

right. The notion that his father would want *him* to run for Parliament was absurd.

She prodded him with her elbow. "And what did you say?"

He squinted, trying to recall. "I said it was fine by me. Because the plan—for *Edward* to stand for Parliament—was a good one."

Diana rubbed her brow. "What happened after that?"

"My father already had the papers drawn up and ready to go. He had both Edward and me sign them."

"And what did the papers say?"

"I, uh…" This was the part he hated to admit. "I don't know. I didn't read them."

"Harrington!" Now she was laughing at him, but not in a mean way. "What do you mean, you didn't read them?"

"I assumed I was signing as Edward's witness!" He rubbed his eyes with both hands. "Oh, my *God*. How did this happen? This is *awful!*"

She waved her arm. "I fail to see what's so awful about it. I daresay you'll do a better job than half the idiots currently serving."

She obviously didn't know what a lost cause he was, and he certainly wasn't going to set her straight on that account. A part of him wanted Diana to think well of him, but the notion of her holding him in high esteem was also terrifying, because it was only a matter of time before he went and screwed things up, now wasn't it?

He sighed, checking his pocket watch. "I need to go. I promised Lord Kinwood I'd meet him in Lord Richford's study at half ten. But if you've any dances free, I'd—"

Diana seized his wrist in a surprisingly strong grip for a young lady who appeared so slight and delicate. "Lord Kinwood asked you to meet with him? Why?"

Harrington shrugged. "He wanted to speak to me about something or the other. Why do you ask?"

She cast a look toward the door as if to confirm that they were still alone, then dropped her voice low. "He's going to try to trick you into supporting his canal scheme. The one at Babbinswood."

Harrington gave a nervous chuckle. He had no idea what she was talking about. "A scheme, you say? I thought canals were good for commerce."

"They are, but this one is self-serving. Lord Kinwood owns five thousand acres around Babbinswood. There are a number of canals in the area, and more are under construction. Lord Kinwood seeks to connect his farm to this existing network, only he desires for the government to foot the bill."

Shit. He would have walked straight into that. Harrington rubbed his eyes. This only served to show how grossly unqualified he was to serve in Parliament. "I hadn't heard a thing about it," he admitted, his voice hoarse.

He chanced a glance at Diana, expecting to find her sporting her signature scornful expression. Instead, he found her regarding him steadily. "Of course, you haven't. You've been slightly busy holding off the French. You had weightier things on your mind than Lord Kinwood's stupid canal. Besides, where would you have even found a newspaper?"

Had she said it with even a trace of pity, he would have wanted to sink into the floor. But she said it so matter-of-factly, he almost believed her.

"Right." He shook himself. He was already five minutes late to meet Lord Kinwood. He needed to pull himself together. "What do I do?"

She leaned in close so he felt the whisper of her breath against his ear. "Ask him to name one stakeholder other than himself who would benefit from the proposed scheme. He's been throwing around some numbers, claiming the project would only cost six thousand pounds. That is based on a projected cost of two thousand pounds per mile of finished canal. Which is absurd." Her eyes blazed ice blue. "If he tries to argue with you, point out that the Royal Military Canal, which is nineteen miles long, cost a total of 234,000 pounds. Which puts the cost per mile at—"

"Closer to twelve thousand pounds," he interjected, then quickly wished he'd kept his mouth shut. This was Diana's cue to make a joke about how she hadn't realized he was capable of performing arithmetic.

It was true that Harrington had never applied himself in school. His brother, Edward, was the clever one. Everyone knew that.

But he wasn't the village idiot. He just played the part to perfection.

Instead of laughing, Diana gave a crisp nod. "Just so. And ask what goods, precisely, this canal would bring to market. That part of the country has a fair number of quarries and mines, and building a canal seems logical for the transport of heavy goods. But it is my understanding that this particular pocket has only farms, such as the one owned by Lord Kinwood."

Harrington nodded. "Right. No one to benefit other than Lord Kinwood. Twelve-thousand pounds per mile. And no heavy goods. I've got it." His heart was beating faster than it did when he was under fire, and he felt slightly queasy, but there was nothing for it, so he turned to go.

Diana seized the sleeve of his jacket, staying him. He turned and found her looking up at him with an obdurate expression that, strangely, suited her delicate features.

"You can do this," she said in a voice that brooked no argument.

He gave a nervous laugh. "I'll certainly try. But..." He

trailed off, figuring that sentence was best left unfinished. If she spent any meaningful time in his company, Lady Diana would notice his many failings soon enough. No need to go pointing them out.

She raised a haughty, expectant eyebrow and gestured for him to continue. It struck Harrington that, had she not been the sister of a duke, she would have made a marvelous headmistress.

He was unable to withstand that eyebrow. "But political negotiations aren't really my specialty." There. That didn't sound too bad.

The eyebrow lowered, only for its companion to go up. *Damn.* He'd always wanted to be able to do that eyebrow-arching thing but had never mastered the trick of it.

Diana, on the other hand? She could do it with *both* eyebrows.

"And what is your specialty?" she asked crisply.

"Um, you know…" He trailed off, struggling to think of a term he could utter in front of a lady. "Idle japes and mockery."

She lifted her chin. "Perfect. Lord Kinwood is an idiot. So, mock him." In a swift motion, she spun him around and gave him a push toward the door. A shudder went through him at her touch against the small of his back.

He was halfway down the corridor when he heard her call, "And Harrington?"

He turned, regarding her in the candlelight.

"I will be expecting a full report."

She turned on her heel and strode back toward the ballroom, leaving him standing alone in the shadowy corridor.

CHAPTER 5

As he strode into the study and called a greeting to Lord Kinwood, Harrington hoped he didn't look as ill as he felt.

The earl was about five years older than Harrington, in his mid-thirties. Their time at Eton had overlapped by a few years. Kinwood had reddish-brown hair and the stout, barrel-chested figure of a man who had been a sportsman in his youth, but now all that hard flesh was starting to go soft.

Harrington held out a hand. "Kinwood, you old canker. How've you been?"

He settled into the leather wingchair across from Kinwood's, accepting his offer of a brandy but declining a cheroot as he seldom partook. Besides, he was feeling nauseous enough as it was.

Kinwood made polite chit-chat for ten minutes, mostly about a horse he'd recently purchased, before coming 'round to the point. "I was surprised to hear you'd been elected to the House of Commons."

Harrington took a nonchalant sip of his drink, trying to

create the illusion that he hadn't been the more surprised of the two of them. "Were you?"

Kinwood laughed. "I'm not saying you're the last man I ever thought would stand for Parliament, but you're probably in my bottom five."

Harrington cast him a bored look, wishing he could do that eyebrow-thing of Diana's. "Is that so?"

Kinwood's expression turned earnest, as if he sensed that he had mis-stepped. "Look, Astley—I didn't mean anything by that. I'm sure you'll do a fine job. I was actually very pleased to hear that you'd been elected, seeing as we're old friends."

Old friends, my arse. Harrington took a long, slow sip of his drink, letting Kinwood stew. He turned toward the side table as he set down his snifter, careful not to look at his "old friend." "I take it there is some favor you wish to ask of me?"

Kinwood leaned forward, forearms resting against his knees and his cheroot dangling loosely from his fingers. "Not a favor, so much as an opportunity. An important bill will be coming up for a vote in a few weeks. I thought you might like the chance to sponsor it in the House of Commons. It'll be the perfect start to your political career. You see..."

Kinwood launched into it, and just as Lady Diana had suggested, it was a bit of canal in the middle of nowhere that served no discernible purpose other than to connect Kinwood's farm to the existing system. Harrington let him drone on, making the occasional encouraging sound.

"So," Kinwood concluded, "what do you think?"

Harrington leaned back in his chair. "How much will this cost?"

"That's the remarkable thing—I've had my man of business work up the numbers, and it should only come to around six thousand pounds."

Harrington made a sound of surprise. "It's only half a mile long, then?"

Kinwood laughed nervously. "Not that short. But it's just three miles."

"Funny." Harrington reached for the decanter and refilled both of their glasses. "The Royal Military Canal cost closer to twelve-thousand pounds a mile."

Kinwood chuckled again. "I think you might be misremembering the figures—"

"234,000 pounds," Harrington cut in. "Over a span of nineteen miles."

Kinwood swallowed, not seeming to have a ready answer.

Harrington continued, "What industries are in that area?"

Kinwood leaned forward, warming to his topic once more. "It's close to the Welsh border. There's a lot of iron and slate, coal, too—"

"In the *immediate* area," Harrington interjected. "I'm not asking about what's twenty miles away. I want to know what goods would actually be transported on this canal."

Kinwood's voice was tight as he replied, "A variety of farm goods."

Harrington gave him a baleful look. "And who owns these farms? Anyone other than you?"

Kinwood was silent. Harrington leaned forward, plucking the cheroot from Kinwood's hands and grinding it out in the crystal ashtray on the end table. "You're dropping ash all over Lord Richford's carpet." He placed it back in Kinwood's limp fingers, then stood.

Just before he reached the door, he glanced over his shoulder. "Oh, and Kinwood? Let me give you a little advice. Before you ask a man for a favor, it's best not to call him an idiot."

If Kinwood made a reply before he strode from the room, Harrington didn't hear it.

Harrington's heart was still pounding as he made his way back to the ballroom. Somehow, he had pulled that off! He hadn't made an utter numpty of himself.

It had even been—dare he say it—*fun*.

And, of course, it was only because of Lady Diana. He'd have been a complete wreck without her advice. Hell, even with her advice, he hadn't been confident in his ability to pull it off, but the fact that he'd managed was a tremendous relief.

He quickened his strides, eager to tell her how it had gone.

At the end of the corridor, his brother, Edward, came around the corner. A huge smile spread across his face.

Harrington did not return it. Grabbing his brother by the shoulder, he hauled him into the closest room, which proved to be a parlor.

"Harrington?" Edward asked. "Is anything the matter?"

Harrington shut the door behind him, then rounded on his brother. "You know damn right what's the matter! Why didn't you tell me?"

Edward blinked at him, confused. "Tell you what?"

"That I was elected to Parliament!" Harrington hissed.

The tension went out of Edward's shoulders. "Oh. That. I did write to you as soon as the votes were counted." He chuckled. "Given the situation in Germany, I suppose it is unsurprising that my letter never reached you. I'm sorry I didn't think to mention it earlier, but you've only been back for a couple of hours, and I must confess, it entirely slipped my mind. I was just so happy to see you!"

Harrington pinched the bridge of his nose. "I don't mean *today*. I meant, why didn't you tell me I was on the ballot?"

Edward looked confused, a rare state for the man who had been named Senior Wrangler, denoting the top student in mathematics at Cambridge. "Because… you knew?" he hedged.

"Of course, I didn't know!" Harrington snapped. "I thought *you* were the one standing for Parliament!"

Edward frowned. "But the papers we signed clearly said—"

"I didn't *read* them!" Harrington said as if this should have been obvious. "I'd been out drinking all night with Thetford and Ferguson. I could barely stumble down the stairs!"

Edward rubbed his temple. "*Harrington.*"

Harrington waved a hand. "I know, I know. I'm a dolt."

Edward held up a hand. "No. You're not. I just—Father said he wanted his son, the most popular man in the county, to stand for the seat."

Edward was staring at him as if this explained everything. Harrington was probably staring at him much the same way.

Finally, Harrington broke the silence. "That's you."

"That's *you*," Edward countered. "Had he said the most pedantic man in Gloucestershire, *that* would have been me."

Harrington frowned. "You're very well-liked. Everyone respects you."

Edward put a hand on his shoulder, steering him toward the sofa. "But not in the same way you are." They both sat, and Edward turned to face him. "How is it possible that you did not understand that Father was referring to you?"

"Because the mere notion is ridiculous. Me? In *Parliament?*" He laughed, waiting for Edward to join in.

But when he looked up, Edward was peering at him with a sad sort of bewilderment. "I don't find the notion ridiculous at all," he said softly.

Of course, he didn't. Because that was Edward. He persisted in believing the best of everyone, and, in spite of his outsized intelligence, seemed to have a particular blind spot when it came to his brother's many flaws.

"You should have seen the disaster I almost got into," Harrington said. "Lord Kinwood asked to speak to me."

Edward frowned. "He's pushing a canal scheme that's—"

"Entirely self-serving," Harrington supplied. "I was fortunate enough to bump into Lady Diana Latimer just before I spoke to him. She warned me."

"Then you told him you wouldn't support it?" At Harrington's nod, Edward brightened. "See? You did splendidly."

"Only because Lady Diana spoon-fed me the facts I needed to counter his arguments. On my own, I would have fallen for it."

Edward shook his head. "You're being too severe on yourself. You've been out of the country. Of course, you haven't been able to stay abreast of every petty domestic squabble. Now that you're back, I daresay you'll get up to speed more quickly than you think."

Harrington stared listlessly across the room. "I very much doubt it. I'm going to be awful at this. What was Father thinking?"

Edward's blue eyes were sincere. "You have positive qualities that you fail to appreciate. You're persuasive. Charismatic. And you're damn good at arguing a point." He gave a humorless laugh. "I just wish the point you were trying to argue wasn't what a failure you are."

"Yes. Well." Harrington put his hands on his thighs and pushed up to standing. "I suppose we'll see which of us is right."

Edward rose as well. "Me, of course. I'm always right." He grinned. "It's one of my most annoying qualities."

Harrington couldn't help but laugh. "Well, I hope I'm not the exception to your rule."

They returned to the ballroom together. A quadrille had just concluded, and Edward wandered off to find his next partner. Across the ballroom, Harrington spied Lady Diana making her way back to her great-aunt Griselda, who served as her chaperone.

Harrington hurried across the ballroom. Spying him, Diana cast him an expectant look. He gave her a small nod, trying to signal that everything was all right, then bowed over her hand. "Lady Diana, might I have the pleasure of the next dance?"

A dark, familiar voice came from just over Harrington's shoulder. "Her dance card is full."

Harrington turned to regard Diana's older brother, Marcus Latimer, the Duke of Trevissick. Harrington gave him a tight smile, which Marcus returned with a glower that could have curdled milk. Honestly, Harrington didn't blame him. Trevissick was good friends with Edward, and they had all been at Eton together. Harrington had been, for lack of a better term, a little shit. Whether it was nicking Trevissick's trousers and flying them from the flagpole or coating the soles of his boots in lard, hardly a week had gone by without Harrington pulling some sort of prank on the golden, perfect duke.

He really should apologize. And he would.

Just as soon as Trevissick would consent to speak with him for forty-five consecutive seconds, an event that it looked like would be taking place when hell froze over.

Another man came up and joined them. It proved to be Archibald Nettlethorpe-Ogilvy, better known as Thorpe, who was married to Harrington's younger sister, Izzie.

Thorpe inclined his head. "I have the next dance, but I would be happy to yield it." He gave a self-deprecating smile. "I feel quite certain that Lady Diana would rather dance with a dashing officer than a boring fellow like me."

"She would not," Trevissick said, seizing his sister's hand and placing it on Thorpe's arm.

~

Diana cast a poisonous glare at her brother. It was hardly the first time Marcus behaved in an overbearing manner when it came to what he perceived to be her best interests.

Nor, she felt quite certain, would it be the last.

"Perhaps," she said through clenched teeth, "you could allow me to manage my own dance card."

"Perhaps not," Marcus replied, glaring at Harrington.

Diana switched to Low German so they would not be overheard. "Marcus!" she hissed. "Stop acting like an arse."

He deigned to look at her, narrowing his eyes. "It is my duty as your brother to protect you," he replied in the same language.

Someone gave a not-very-ladylike snort. "Protect her," Aunt Griselda said, strolling over. "My Diana does not need your protection. I have raised her better than that."

Diana smiled at her aunt. Truly, she had done just that. Under Aunt Griselda's tutelage, Diana had learned not just to fence and shoot but to speak up for herself. Valuable lessons, indeed.

Beside her, Thorpe was smiling genially. "I honestly don't mind."

From off to her left, Diana heard a titter. "She's throwing him over," a feminine voice whispered.

"Honestly," another woman said, "who would want to dance with *him*?"

Diana sighed. Unlike most of the men in the room, Thorpe was in trade, running the iron forge founded by his grandfather. The fact that he was absurdly rich and could have bought and sold almost every man in that room ten times over only made his "betters" resent him that much more.

Diana knew that Thorpe didn't care. He had managed to

marry Diana's particular friend, Izzie, whom he had adored from afar for years. So long as he had Izzie's regard, what anyone else thought of him was immaterial.

Nonetheless, Diana was unwilling to expose him to ridicule. Izzie had informed her husband how much Diana hated balls because she was besieged by fortune hunters at every turn. Thorpe made it a point to ask her to dance, and their set was always a welcome respite.

She therefore said in a voice that carried, "I should like nothing better than to dance with you, Mr. Nettlethorpe-Ogilvy."

As she accepted his arm, she turned and met the eyes of the gossips. Jane Churchill and Charlotte Rawlings. Diana looked at them steadily, and Charlotte flinched.

Clever girl. Diana would deal with them both.

Later.

As she swept past Harrington Astley, she gave him a pointed look. She wanted to hear how his conversation with Lord Kinwood had gone.

He winked at her, and her heart tripped in her chest.

As she and Thorpe found their places in the set, Diana resolved that she would speak to Harrington Astley, one way or the other.

CHAPTER 6

The following morning, Harrington rose at half six.
After staying out late at the ball, he'd only managed a scant four hours of rest. Nevertheless, he awoke at his customary time and was unable to fall asleep again. It appeared that the army had ruined him for a life of sloth. Well, no matter—he was expected down at the army's central command, Horse Guards, in a few short hours, anyway.

A housemaid he passed in the hall recoiled in surprise as he came around the corner. And no wonder—it used to be a running joke in his family that he never rose before noon.

He was the first one down to breakfast. A footman poured him a cup of coffee and promised that his preferred meal, poached eggs and kippers, would be prepared at once. Harrington took a seat and reached for the morning paper. He supposed now that he was an M.P., he was going to have to start reading the damn thing.

After breakfast, he made the short ride to Horse Guards and presented himself at the front desk. The clerk rose and bowed. "Lieutenant Astley, thank you for coming so soon. If you will excuse me, I will let the secretary know you have arrived."

He disappeared into the offices, leaving Harrington to wonder which secretary he would be meeting. Probably the assistant to some general or another.

The clerk returned moments later and led him upstairs to a well-appointed chamber with pale green walls and a large, circular desk in the center of the room. Harrington blanched because he recognized the balding, grey-haired man standing behind it—William Windham, the Secretary of State for War and the Colonies.

He accepted Mr. Windham's proffered hand, resisting the impulse to tug at the stock around his neck, which suddenly felt unaccountably tight. What on earth had he done to draw the attention of the Secretary of State?

Mr. Windham gestured for him to take the solitary chair on the far side of the desk. The whole situation was reminiscent of the many times he'd been summoned before the headmaster at Eton. He tried to sit straight and still as he braced himself for what he assumed was going to be a dressing down.

"So, Lieutenant," Mr. Windham began, "I was surprised to hear about your recent election to Parliament."

Harrington bit back the words, *not half as surprised as I was.*

The Secretary of State continued, "May I ask why you did not inform your commanding officer that you were standing for office?"

"Oh, err..." Harrington grappled for a plausible excuse. "It seemed unlikely that I would win the election, considering I wasn't around to canvass for votes. I did not wish to raise false hopes, sir."

The Secretary of State regarded him for a beat, then nodded. "It happens that the timing of your return is fortuitous." He placed his fingertips on some papers lying atop the desk and pushed them toward Harrington. "There are a pair of Acts coming up for a vote next week that I think will be of interest to you."

Harrington accepted the stack of papers and read the words at the top of the page—*Pensions to Soldiers Act.*

He read in silence for around five minutes. After last night, he was wary, all too aware that people would be trying to trick him into supporting things he didn't properly understand.

But… there was nothing here that he disagreed with. The first proposed pensions for disabled soldiers. The next one would institute pay increases for soldiers who agreed to sign on for another seven-year term of service.

The proposals certainly seemed like good ones.

He looked up to find William Windham regarding him. "Well? Will you throw your support behind these Acts?"

"I will," Harrington said slowly. He cleared his throat. "I must confess, I'm hard-pressed to understand why anyone would vote against pensions for injured soldiers."

"Ah." Mr. Windham steepled his fingers. "War is exceptionally expensive. In addition to the cost of maintaining our own army and navy, our allies have become dependent on us to bankroll their military forces." He laughed darkly. "And certain parties insist on building and refurbishing multiple palaces, even during wartime." He cleared his throat. "I trust that you will not repeat that last remark."

Harrington nodded. He didn't disagree. First, the Prince of Wales had spent hundreds of thousands of pounds refurbishing Carlton House in the most extravagant style, only to turn around a few years later and commission a new royal residence at Brighton. The Pavilion at Brighton was still being built, but all indications suggested that it would cost every bit as much as Carlton House.

"In light of these expenses," Mr. Windham continued, "some of our members are looking to economize where they can. It is my belief, however, that we should not attempt to balance the budget on the backs of our wounded soldiers."

Harrington nodded. "I agree."

Mr. Windham leaned forward. "May I count on your support, then?"

Harrington released the breath he'd been holding. He was still nervous about putting a foot wrong.

But… pensions for wounded soldiers. That couldn't be a bad thing.

Could it?

"You may," he said, wondering if he was committing a great blunder.

Mr. Windham smiled broadly. "Excellent." He plucked another paper from his desk. "Here is a list of our fellow MPs who have been, shall we say, recalcitrant." He handed the sheet to Harrington. "See how many of them you can bring around. We're at least fourteen votes short at the moment. Try to secure more votes than that for a comfortable margin. And send me updates every day. I need to know where we stand."

Harrington rose and bowed, sensing that he had been dismissed. "Yes, sir."

He stepped outside feeling worse than he had before the visit. What the hell was he going to do now? If the Secretary of State couldn't drum up the votes to pass these pensions, how in God's name was *he* supposed to do it?

He swung up onto his horse and started toward home, cutting through St. James's Park. Half the men in Parliament never showed up. Why couldn't he be one of them? Goodness knew he'd never made a proper effort at anything in his life. It should have been what everyone expected, given his history. William Windham obviously didn't understand who he was dealing with.

The problem was the particular issue. How would he look the men of the 95th Rifles in the eye, knowing that better pay and pensions had been within his grasp, and he had responded with a shrug?

He had to do *something*, but he was hopelessly inept at this sort of thing. He needed help.

Edward. His brother would help him. He knew he would. And this was more Edward's area, anyway.

He would ask Edward to write him a speech. He couldn't do much better than that.

He also wanted to speak to Diana Latimer. She was close to his youngest sisters, Lucy and Izzie, and he knew from their letters that she had a keen interest in politics. She'd proved it last night, hadn't she, reciting the details of that canal scheme off the top of her head. She would have good advice for him. He had a feeling about it.

Or maybe you just want an excuse to talk to her again.

He had to admit it was true. The mere thought of speaking to her, of having her regard him with those still, ice-blue eyes, had him sitting up straighter in the saddle. But what of it? It wasn't as if anything would come of it. Trevissick had made it clear as cut crystal last night that he didn't want Harrington even dancing with his beloved sister, much less... anything else. And at this point, Harrington couldn't even define what *anything else* he wanted with Diana.

Well. That wasn't quite true. From early in their acquaintance, she'd captured his attention in a way no woman had ever done before. Specifically, from the moment at her come-out ball when a feeble-minded matron had made a snide remark about Diana's missing hand, and Diana had cut her to ribbons in front of the entire *ton*.

Most men wanted a woman who was as sweet as spun sugar. Not Harrington. He had a taste for the piquant, and it was Diana's tartness that set her apart from the dozens of pretty girls who populated the ballrooms of Mayfair. On that night three years ago, he'd had a dance with her—Trevissick had been worried she would be tongue-tied with nerves and had made it clear that the only reason he'd granted Harrington the supper dance was because he was the sort of tedious fellow who never shut up. Suffice it to say, the discovery that Lady Diana was every bit as sardonic as he was had fanned his spark of admiration into a raging inferno.

Ever since that night, she had been the woman fueling his fantasies, the one he pictured when he lay naked in his bed, stroking himself to completion. And no wonder—not only was she pretty, she happened to fit flawlessly into his most secret, most shameful fantasies. He could picture her now, standing over him, her expression stony. She would order him to undress, then reach for a—

"Hey! Watch where yer going, ye stupid toff!"

He shook himself, waving an apologetic hand at the driver of the wagon he had cut off. Clearly, this was not the sort of thought he needed to be entertaining in the middle of a busy street.

He was wasting his time. He was a wastrel. A waste of good linen, that was him. Good for only one thing, and that was cannon fodder.

He was always quick to make these jokes himself. Made it sting a little bit less if he was the one to bring it up. Showed everyone how little it bothered him.

But the bottom line was, it was all impossible. He would never so much as kiss her hand, much less do any of the things he'd drifted off to sleep dreaming about while he was lying on the frozen ground in Hanover. There was no point in trying to figure out whether he wanted to steal a solitary kiss out on a deserted balcony or pledge his troth, because none of it was ever going to happen.

But he needed to speak with her. Her mind was as sharp as a bayonet, and he knew with a terrible certainty that if he didn't do everything in his power to pass this damn act, he would regret it forever.

Now, he just needed to figure out how to steal a moment with the woman who was guarded more closely than the Crown Jewels.

CHAPTER 7

*D*iana had made plans to take part in the afternoon promenade through Hyde Park with Lucy and Izzie. This was Lucy's suggestion, as she liked nothing better than feeding the ducks. As Izzie was married, she could serve as their chaperone during outings such as this one—a great irony, considering Izzie was by far the most likely of the three of them to flaunt society's rules.

Diana arrived at Astley House and was admitted by the butler, Yarwood. In the yellow parlor, she was surprised to find not only Lucy and Izzie but Harrington as well. Although she had been hoping to speak with him, he had never accompanied his sisters on one of their afternoon outings before. Indeed, in the short time she had known him, he rarely seemed to be at home when Diana came to call on the twins.

Lucy sprang to her feet. "Harrington has volunteered to escort us to the park. Won't that be splendid?"

He had stood upon Diana entering the room and now shifted nervously from one foot to the other. "Who knows when they'll ship me out again. I figure I'd better spend time with my sisters while I can."

Lucy beamed, but Izzie's shrewd gaze traveled from Harrington to Diana and back again.

Diana inclined her head. "How delightful."

Diana had come in her brother's landau, an open-topped carriage that was perfect for the afternoon promenade. They piled in, with Lucy and Diana taking the forward-facing seat and Izzie and Harrington settling opposite them. There had been rain that morning, but now it was clear and cool. Diana had dressed for the weather by pairing her white muslin gown with a Kashmiri shawl the color of apricots.

Diana wanted to ask how Harrington's conversation with Lord Kinwood had gone, but as soon as the carriage door closed, he asked, "So, Izzie, when is your next book coming out?"

Izzie obligingly provided an update on her latest Gothic novel for the Minerva Press. It involved a young, orphaned woman who unexpectedly inherited a cottage. Naturally, this cottage was in the shadow of a ruined abbey that was not as abandoned as it seemed.

Diana, who had already read Izzie's story, sat back, pulling her shawl more tightly around her shoulders.

They soon arrived at the park. Rotten Row was the most tedious part of Diana's day. Failing to acknowledge an acquaintance was unspeakably rude and would generate a firestorm of gossip. *Did you hear that Lady Diana cut Mrs. Mapplethorpe this afternoon? Why, yes—and right in the middle of Hyde Park!*

She might have a reputation for being an ice queen, but even Diana wasn't that rude. As usual, everyone who was anyone wanted to show off their acquaintance with the sister of a duke, and so, Diana braced herself to acknowledge everyone in the park. "Mrs. Hurst," she said, nodding cooly. "Miss Reynolds. Lady Newcombe."

Her coachman was under strict instructions to keep the landau moving, so at least she was spared from having to stop and chat. But they'd only made it halfway down Rotten Row when a plague of fortune-hunters descended upon them. Unlike the social-climbing ladies, the fortune-hunters were on horseback, making them more difficult to shake.

"Lady Diana," Piers Pelham-Strangeways said, touching the brim of his hat. "May I say how lovely you look in that color?"

She was saved from having to answer by a bouquet of daffodils, which was thrust in her face. "Lady Diana," Winston Fitzherbert trilled, "would you do me the honor of accepting this very small token of my esteem?"

He was immediately interrupted by Humphrey Montague. "Lady Diana, dare I hope that you will be attending Lady Stanhope's ball this evening, and that I might secure the promise of a dance?"

The three of them began talking over one another. Diana slumped down in her seat, unable to get a word in edgewise, which was probably for the best, as the only words she wanted to utter were *sod off.*

Across the carriage, she caught Harrington's eye. The corner of his mouth was twitching.

He turned to the first of her suitors. "Pelham-Strangeways! It's been an age. Say, how's your rash?"

Mr. Pelham-Strangeways stiffened in his saddle. "I beg your pardon?"

Harrington grinned. "You know, the one on your—" He cleared his throat, making a circular gesture just above his own lap.

Mr. Pelham-Strangeways gave a nervous chuckle. "You seem to be confused, Astley."

Harrington leaned forward. "Oh, no. I remember it like it was yesterday. We were down at that gaming hell… What was it called again?" He tapped his chin as if deep in thought, then snapped his fingers. "The Fishwife's Tit, that's the one! You'd had… well. A few drinks, by the look of things. And you said it had been plaguing you ever since—"

Mr. Pelham-Strangeways's voice was shrill. "I don't know what you're talking about. You're obviously thinking of someone else. Good day, Lady Diana."

Harrington turned to her next suitor. "Fitzherbert, you old dog! I was thinking about you the other day."

Fitzherbert's eyes were darting around. "Were you?"

Harrington's smile was genial. "I was! My brother told me about the fascinating wager you recorded in the betting book at White's—"

"Oh, dear!" Fitzherbert cried. "I have suddenly recalled a pressing engagement." He dropped his daffodils so hastily that they tumbled to the floor of the carriage. "Lady Diana, a pleasure, as always."

Harrington turned to Humphrey Montague. "Monty! Fancy bumping into… Say, where are you going?"

They were doomed to wonder, because Mr. Montague had wheeled his horse around and was hying himself back toward Rotten Row.

Izzie beamed at her brother. "How I've missed you."

Diana murmured her agreement. Indeed, Harrington was an exceptionally useful fellow to have around. Why, he had vanquished her suitors in one minute flat!

He was handsome, amusing, and he valued her opinion. To say nothing of the fact that he was one of the few men of her acquaintance whom she did not find irritating. To be sure, he was not regarded as much of a catch, as he was a second son and not in possession of a fortune.

But what did she care about that? She had fortune enough

to last them a lifetime. She was the rare woman who could afford to choose a husband for his lively wit and finely turned leg.

As Harrington leaned down to listen to Lucy, Diana could not help but allow her gaze to sweep from his broad shoulders to his flat stomach and below. His legs were clad in skintight breeches, and Diana could not help but observe that there was no soft flesh there to tremble, in spite of the jostling of the carriage. Clearly, army life was not without its advantages…

They reached the banks of the Serpentine, and Diana ordered the coachman to stop. Harrington hopped down and handed his sisters out of the carriage.

As he helped Diana to the ground, he whispered, "I need to speak to you."

The corner of her mouth turned up. Even better. "I was hoping to speak with you as well," she murmured. "How did things go last night with Lord Kinwood?"

"Better than I could have hoped." His brown eyes were bright in the dappled sunlight beneath the trees. "Thanks to you. You see—"

"Hurry up, you two!" Suddenly, Lucy was there, seizing their arms and tugging them forward. "I thought we were going to walk by the water."

Diana shot Harrington a look. *Later.* He inclined his head in understanding. Lucy did not seem to notice that anything was amiss.

Izzie, on the other hand, was watching them with great interest. Diana detected no disapproval in her gaze; her expression was one of keen anticipation.

Which was arguably more frightening than if she had been furious about the prospect of Diana flirting with her brother, given that this was Izzie.

Striving for an air of nonchalance, Diana accepted

Harrington's proffered arm, and the four of them made their way toward the banks of the Serpentine.

Lucy broke off to admire a pair of swans. Izzie trailed after her twin, but not before casting Diana a speaking look.

After a moment, Diana leaned toward Harrington's ear and whispered, "So, did Lord Kinwood ask about the canal?"

He nodded. "Just as you said. He wanted me to sponsor the bill in the House of Commons! Made it sound like he was doing me this tremendous favor."

Diana hmphed. "The utter gall."

"But I was able to put him in his place with the numbers you gave me." He gave her a crooked smile, and time seemed to slow. "I can't tell you how grateful I—"

"What are you two talking about?" Lucy, who had abandoned the swans, was peering at them curiously.

"Nothing," Harrington said a little too quickly.

"Walk with me, Lucy," Izzie said firmly, striding over and hooking her arm through her twin's.

"Oh!" Lucy cried as Izzie propelled her forward. "But I—"

Izzie leaned in and hissed something in her sister's ear. Lucy stiffened, then glanced over her shoulder at Harrington and Diana, her mouth a perfect "O."

She said nothing more as Izzie marched her along the banks of the river.

CHAPTER 8

*I*zzie had obviously told Lucy that she and Harrington were engaged in a flirtation. Diana found she didn't mind. Perhaps he had no designs on her and was merely using her for political advice.

But she had decided that she wanted to flirt with him, and she didn't much care who knew it.

Harrington chuckled, seeming unperturbed. "Good old Izzie."

The corner of her mouth curled up. "Subtle, as ever. So"—she looped her arm through his and started after the twins at a discreet distance—"tell me what happened with Lord Kinwood."

He recounted the conversation, and she chuckled when he came to the part where he advised the earl not to call a man an idiot before asking him for a favor. "Well done, you!"

He smiled, but his expression was rueful. "It turned out all right in the end. But I would have floundered without your advice."

She studied him a beat. "I take it that the conversation has left you feeling uneasy?"

He tore his eyes from hers. "You could say that. I'm in over my head. I'm not up to speed on the issues of the day."

She considered her words carefully. "Staying abreast of the issues is a full-time job. That is why most politicians, especially those with other responsibilities, as you do to your regiment, employ a secretary. My brother certainly does."

He laughed bleakly. "That's a good strategy, if you can afford it. Which I can't."

She squeezed his arm. "I think you are being overly severe on yourself. You've been thrown into this rather suddenly. But you will find your bearings. Give yourself a chance."

He didn't look convinced. "Well, I made it out of the frying pan last night. But I seem to have leapt straight back into the fire. I mentioned last night that I had received a summons from Horse Guards…"

He told her about his meeting with William Windham and how the Secretary of State had asked him to drum up votes for the Pensions to Soldiers Act.

"I was hoping to ask your opinion about Windham. Is he a scoundrel, like Kinwood?"

"He's not," Diana said at once. "He's a good man, but…" She paused, considering how best to describe the Secretary of State. "He's an academic at heart and is sometimes out of his depth when it comes to Parliament. His ideas are lofty, but often impractical, and he has no talent for political machinations. But I don't think he is the sort to deliberately mislead you as Lord Kinwood attempted to do."

He pulled some papers from his coat pocket. "These are the acts he's asked me to support. I didn't see anything objectionable about them, but I'd like to hear your opinion."

I'd like to hear your opinion. The words were as sweet to her ears as honey on her tongue. Who gave a fig about marrying a lord? Diana found she much preferred this man, who valued her thoughts.

They paused in the dappled shade of a tree, ignoring the lovely view of the Serpentine beside them, while Diana pored over the proposed acts. After she finished reading, she looked up. "This seems fine to me."

His eyes flared with hope. "Do you really think so?"

"I do." She looped her arm through his, resuming their stroll. The twins were well out of earshot. In the distance, she saw them peering back at them, curious about what she was getting up to with their brother. *If only they knew...*

Harrington exhaled. "That's what Edward said as well. If both of you think it's all right, I can't do better than that. Now I just have to figure out how to persuade the holdouts to support our side."

"Indeed. What is your strategy?"

He pulled another sheet of paper from his pocket. "Mr. Windham provided me with a list of opponents to the bill."

They stopped again, and Diana began scanning his list.

"I've asked Edward to write me a speech," he offered.

"No," she said at once.

He looked adorably flustered. "I know any speech I put together wouldn't be any good. But if Edward writes it—"

"I'm sure it would be brilliant. But do you know who is very good at delivering high-minded speeches? William Windham." She gestured to the list of names he had handed her. "Those who can be swayed by logic and reason already support this act. There's a reason he turned to *you*. Look."

She turned the list of names toward him. "How many of these men do you know?"

"Around half." He took the list from her and pointed. "I was at school with Webster and Chapman. Doyle was a few years ahead of me, but I know him a little bit. As for Knatchbull and Williams, I've run into them at"—he coughed —"places I'd best not mention."

Considering he had not hesitated to mention such an

exalted establishment as The Fishwife's Tit, it was safe to assume this must be a shocking place, indeed. She made her voice light. "All the better. If you have some information about these men that they would prefer not become common knowledge, you can use that."

His mouth was twisted to the side. "Is that really the way things are done? It seems rather… unsporting."

She jabbed him in the arm. "Not half so unsporting as refusing to grant pensions to disabled soldiers. Unsporting!" She scowled. "You sound like *Marcus*."

He grinned. "That's probably the first time anyone has ever compared me with your brother. I must insist that you relieve my curiosity by telling me how so."

She waved her arm. "He is always droning on about the *rules of engagement* and the *gentleman's code* when we fence. But I learned to fence from Aunt Griselda, and do you know what she taught me?"

He looked delighted. "What?"

"That the *gentleman's code* is a mere fabrication. There is only what works and what doesn't. It would be a cold comfort to die at the hands of a highwayman, knowing that I followed the *rules of engagement* when I should have gored him in the eye. And I don't see how this is any different."

He was back to cringing. "No?"

"No," she said firmly. "You might not be one for delivering lofty speeches, but that doesn't mean you can't be effective as a politician. You have your own set of skills." She gestured back toward the landau. "You routed that pack of fortune-hunters in one minute flat, and you did it with your wit. I think you should employ a similar approach when it comes to swaying the men on this list to your cause."

He frowned. "So, I should be… obnoxious and annoying?"

She tossed her head. "So long as you're obnoxious and annoying for a good cause."

That earned her a smile. "I do have a certain talent for it. Why should I hide my light under a bushel?"

She gave him an approving nod. "That's the spirit. Although…" She tapped her lip, considering. "There is a time to employ the stick and a time to employ the carrot. Many of the men on this list would like nothing better than to claim you as a friend. In addition to your personal charisma, you are the son of an earl and an officer in the Riflemen. I don't know if you are aware, but your regiment has become all the rage since your impressive rearguard action in Hanover."

"Have they?" Harrington looked genuinely surprised. "It was not a glamorous business, believe me."

"I am sure that is true. Nevertheless, they have. It was a rare spot of good news on the war front." She waved her arm. "On land, anyway. I suspect you will find that green jacket lends you more cachet than you anticipate. And if you're going to be in politics for the next twenty years, it will behoove you not to go around burning bridges. So, use the carrot where you can, and the stick where you must."

He pursed his lips, considering her words. "That sounds suspiciously like wisdom."

She smiled brightly as she looped her arm through his. "How good of you to notice. Come, we'd best catch up with your sisters. Goodness knows what lurid theories Izzie is formulating about what we're up to."

"Oh, I don't know." He tilted his head toward hers. "I quite enjoy Izzie's lurid theories."

Their laughter was interrupted by a voice from the river. "Lady Diana! Oh, Lady Diana!"

She turned to look, her guard back up in an instant. The sight that greeted her was Rafe Westbrook, one of her more odious suitors, steering a rowboat toward the shore. Rafe was considered a Corinthian, always up for a boxing match or a race in his highflyer. He was handsome enough, with thick dark hair, green eyes, and broad shoulders. But he liked to play deep, and rumor had it that his gaming debts were in the neighborhood of twenty thousand pounds. And even worse, Diana once overheard him mocking Priscilla Jenkins, both for being a bit plump and for having a lisp. Diana scarcely knew Priscilla, who was widely regarded as a wallflower.

Still, the remark had done nothing to endear him to Diana.

Rafe was grinning at her. "If this isn't fate smiling down on me." He stood, holding out a hand. "Allow me to take you on a tour of the canal."

"No, thank you," Diana said coolly.

Ignoring her demurral, Rafe spread his arms wide. "Don't be shy. It's a glorious day! What better way to spend it than on the water?"

It was on the tip of Diana's tongue to answer that she'd rather spend it in the company of a man she could stand. But she bit the sharp words back and said, "I find I am not in the mood for boating. Good day, Mr. Westbrook."

She was turning away when she felt him seize her wrist from behind. Diana stiffened. How *dare* he!

Harrington's voice was sharp. "She said no, Westbrook. Release her. Now!"

Although Diana appreciated his protestations on her behalf, they were unnecessary. She had been raised by Aunt Griselda, after all. Executing one of the first techniques her great-aunt had taught her, she twisted her wrist so its thin edge was aligned with Rafe's joined fingertips, then thrust her hand down as hard as she could.

She slipped from his grasp easily. Her sudden move had the happy effect of causing his boat to pitch perilously forward. Rafe managed to right himself, but only by stepping to the left. This, in turn, caused the boat to list in the opposite direction, and he tumbled over the side.

Abruptly, she realized her error—she was about to get soaked by the splash. As soon as the thought crossed her mind, strong hands seized her about the waist. Harrington swooped her around so that he stood between her and the river. She felt his body jolt as cold river water sprayed across his broad back. No more than a drop or two touched her.

Time seemed to slow down. He was standing so close, hunched protectively over her, she could feel his breath against her brow and smell his scent, which was of cinnamon. She became conscious of the feeling of his hands, so much larger than her own, around her waist. She rarely allowed a man near her and felt instinctively defensive when most men put their hands on her waist for something as mundane as a dance. But Harrington Astley's hands on her body felt... right. As if that was where they were *supposed* to be.

Gracious, his thumb had even settled on the underside of her breast—accidentally, she felt sure, but still. Strangely, she did not mind...

His eyes were heavy-lidded and focused on her lips. "Diana," he breathed, and it occurred to her that if she slid her arms up, she could wrap them around his neck and pull his head down to hers.

He squeezed her waist, drawing her close...

... which caused his thumb to press into the soft swell of her breast.

His eyes flew open. He must have realized where his hand had landed, because he jerked his hands off her and took a stumbling step back. "S-sorry! I didn't mean to grab your... your..."

"It's all right." Diana seized his hand so he wouldn't back

all the way into the Serpentine. "I know you were only trying to shield me."

Rafe came up sputtering. Izzie and Lucy called out as they jogged along the riverbank, recalling Diana to the fact that they were in the middle of Hyde Park, surrounded by dozens of interested onlookers.

Rafe spat out a mouthful of river water. "What the hell, Astley?"

Diana rolled her eyes. How like a man, to be unable to admit that a woman had felled him. "He didn't have the slightest thing to do with it."

Izzie and Lucy arrived on the scene. "Diana, are you all right?" Lucy cried, clasping her hand.

Izzie took a different approach, placing a half-booted foot on the prow of Rafe's rowboat and giving it a push.

Rafe sputtered protests as it drifted off into the middle of the Serpentine. "How dare you, you—"

"You'll want to be careful how you finish that sentence," Harrington cut in. "You fancy yourself a bit of a boxer. If you insult his wife, I'm sure Thorpe would be happy to settle things in the ring."

Rafe gave a soggy gulp. Thanks to days spent lifting cannons at his family's iron forge, Izzie's husband was built like an ox and had a hard time finding partners willing to spar with him at Gentleman Jackson's.

Casting Izzie a dark look, Rafe swam after his boat, and at last, they were rid of him.

Lucy was still clucking over Diana. "I'm fine," she hastened to reassure her. "It's neither the first nor the last time one of my purported suitors has been overly forward." She laughed bleakly. "Just another Tuesday in the park."

"How about you, Harrington?" Izzie asked. "I think you bore the brunt of it."

He waved this off. "Eh. Believe me, this jacket has seen worse."

Diana's heart was still racing as they made their way back to the landau. Harrington had almost kissed her! Surely that meant that he felt something more for her than mere friendship.

Equally stunning was the revelation that, for the first time in her life, Diana had not wanted him to stop.

Of course, it was for the best that they had been interrupted. Rotten Row was not the place for a romantic tête-à-tête. The mere fact that they had been seen walking together would provide grist for the *ton's* gossip mill for the next week.

But if they could find a better place, a secluded balcony, or a moonlit garden…

They had come to the landau. A thrill coursed up Diana's arm as Harrington took her hand to help her into the carriage.

Lord Pearson was hosting a ball three days hence. As she settled back against the squabs, Diana found herself looking forward to the prospect for the first time in several years.

CHAPTER 9

Harrington rose early the following morning and set out to execute his mission.

He started at Castle Court Tea and Coffee House, an establishment he had heard was popular with MPs because it carried a large selection of newspapers. Unfortunately, it appeared to attract the wrong sort of politicians, as none of the men diligently perusing the news of the day were on Harrington's list of idlers. He passed an hour perusing the latest edition of *Cobbett's Political Register*—something he had never imagined himself doing—then set off in search of a new strategy.

Harrington didn't know a damn thing about the habits of the men on his list. But he did know who to ask. His friend from Oxford, Peter Ferguson, was head of his family's business importing textiles from India, his mother's home country. Peter had an encyclopedic memory which he applied diligently when it came to his potential customers. He had intelligence on everyone—whether they paid their bills on time, what fashions they preferred, and how they could best be beguiled into making a purchase.

He dropped by the showroom of Ferguson's Fine Draperies on Leicester Square. Unsurprisingly, Peter was busy charming a dowager marchioness into purchasing an expensive Kashmiri shawl, but they arranged to meet at the chophouse around the corner for luncheon.

Harrington decided to spend the interval imposing himself upon his friend, Henry, and his sister, Caro so that he could meet his new niece, Georgiana. Little Georgie was the spitting image of her mother, had a bright giggle, and adored batting at the red tassels hanging from the sash of his Rifleman's uniform. Harrington informed Caro and Henry that they could not have done any better.

Henry decided to accompany him to the chophouse. As they stepped outside, Henry said, "Your birthday is coming up in a few weeks. Do you think you'll be in town? Or will the army have found somewhere to send you by then?"

"I don't know. They could send me anywhere, but for now, they seem eager to make use of my new position in Parliament."

"Good." Henry shot him a grin. "I've got a few things planned. We'll start in the afternoon over at Bentinck's property just outside of town. He has the perfect setup for trap shooting—your favorite. We'll stay the night at his villa, and Peter's going to send his French chef to prepare us a real feast." Henry gave a low whistle. "You should see the wines he's purchased for the occasion. I have no idea how he's getting them during wartime." Henry glanced at him, and his eyes held a trace of nervousness. "How does that sound?"

It was on the tip of Harrington's tongue to say *different*. Because for many years, the birthdays of Harrington, Henry, and the rest of their friends had served as a convenient excuse for a night of extreme debauchery, inevitably ending in a house of ill repute.

But each year, the number of revelers dwindled.

Harrington's friends either married or started the sorts of careers where they needed to have a care for their reputation, or both. Harrington hadn't much cared until Henry had been the one to marry. Henry was his best friend. He couldn't possibly celebrate his birthday without Henry in attendance.

But that meant that the nature of the celebration had to change. Harrington didn't mind, precisely. It wasn't as if he wanted to visit a bawdy house with the man who was now married to his *sister*. The mere thought made him shudder. Besides, Henry marrying had brought home the fact that the rest of his friends were moving on, were growing up, while Harrington was still living the life of a young buck even as he reached an age at which most people no longer considered him young. Henry's wedding was the event that had spurred him to join the army, and looking back, he could see that he had needed the push.

And yet, part of him missed those wild parties of years past. It wasn't that Harrington found their new festivities unappealing. Everything Henry had suggested, from the trap shooting to the feast, sounded bloody brilliant.

But out of all his friends, Henry was the only one who had somehow figured out Harrington's secret, who knew what he really liked in bed. This meant that every year on Harrington's birthday, they didn't wind up at just any bawdy house. More often than not, they found themselves at an establishment specializing in flagellation.

It was one thing if it was Henry's choice. Harrington could laugh it off as some mad lark schemed up by his friend. He was just going along with it! It wasn't as if he really *liked* that sort of thing.

Except... he did like that sort of thing. He had discovered as much on his first day at Eton, when he and Henry were paddled soundly for sneaking a goat into Headmaster Davies' private quarters on a dare. To his surprise, Harrington had sprung a cockstand during his caning.

He hadn't thought too much of it at first. He'd been a twelve-year-old boy at the time. *Everything* caused him to spring a cockstand. The sound of a girl laughing. His trousers, rubbing against him from an unexpected angle. Neatly stacked melons in a market stall. It was a wonder he ever *didn't* have a cockstand in those days.

But, given how much trouble Harrington got into, and how many paddlings he received as a result, it became impossible to ignore the fact that his cock jumped to attention each and every time. Not that Headmaster Davies inspired those sort of feelings in him! *Yech.*

But when he imagined that it was one of the pretty barmaids down at The George Inn wielding the birch, the ones who wore low-cut dresses and smiled at all the boys when they walked through the door… Well, he'd learned that he'd best not do that while the caning was taking place unless he really wanted to embarrass himself in front of the other boys. But if he imagined one of those barmaids spanking him later, when he'd found a private spot to stroke himself to completion, it made his resulting orgasm ten times more intense.

He'd come to discover that his proclivities weren't that unusual, at least, not for schoolboys. Every year, there were a handful of boys who had the same reaction to getting paddled. They would even joke about it sometimes.

But it was one thing to be a bit oversexed when you were fourteen. *Everyone* at Eton was oversexed. Enjoying a spanking was one of a number of behaviors that you could get away with during your school days, but not later in life.

So, it wasn't necessarily scandalous that Harrington had liked being paddled back when he was young and foolish, nor was it surprising that Henry had noticed. But he was supposed to have grown out of this strange perversion years ago, and it was the fact that he hadn't that was shameful.

Henry would never judge him. Harrington trusted Henry implicitly. And those scant handful of birthdays Henry had planned for him had been the best sexual experiences of his life, even though he hadn't trusted those women enough to tell them precisely what he wanted them to say and do. He'd just pretended he was going along with it on a whim, because he was game enough to try anything once. He definitely did not have a precise script that he secretly wished they would follow, one he'd been fantasizing about for roughly half of his life—what an absurd suggestion!

And so, even though he knew he was too old for such things, that it was past time for him to grow out of it, Harrington couldn't help but feel morose at the thought that, without those birthday parties, he would never have the chance to experience what he really liked in bed.

Ah, well. Such was life.

Henry was still looking at him expectantly.

Harrington squeezed his shoulder. "That sounds outstanding."

Relief washed over Henry's face. "Does it really?"

"It truly does. Thanks for putting something together for me. Means a lot."

Henry nodded. "Good. Good. I'll ask all our usual crowd. Put together a list of any new friends from the army you'd like to include, and I'll make sure they receive an invitation as well."

They came to the chophouse. As they stepped inside, Harrington recalled that he had bigger problems than his birthday party. How he hoped that Peter would be able to help him solve them.

CHAPTER 10

*P*eter had already secured a table in the corner of the chophouse. They ordered joints of meat, and the waiter brought them a round of ale.

"Cheers," Peter said, raising his glass. "It's good to have you back."

"Hear, hear," Henry said as they clinked their glasses.

Peter sipped his drink and set it aside. "So, what did you want to ask me?"

"I need a favor. You've no doubt heard that I was elected to Parliament." Harrington paused, waiting for one of his friends to crack the inevitable joke about what a fucking surprise that had been.

Neither of them did. Peter and Henry were both looking at him expectantly.

Clearing his throat, he spread the list of recalcitrant MPs out on the table. "William Windham has asked me to drum up some votes for a couple of acts. Pensions for disabled veterans, better pay for soldiers, that sort of thing. This is a list of holdouts. I need to know where to find them so I can attempt to bring them around."

Peter pulled a pair of spectacles out of his pocket, placed them on his nose, and began poring over the list. As Harrington had expected, he was familiar with most of the names.

"Charles Sutton is a member at Boodle's. He plays brag, but not very well. He's rumored to be in debt to Lord Fletcher to the tune of seven hundred pounds. Stephen Chichester fences. At Angelo's, I believe. As for Francis Barrett..."

Harrington flagged down a waiter and asked to borrow a pencil so he could scrawl some notes in the margins.

Peter showed no signs of slowing. "Quentin Carstairs is a member at White's, as is Colin Rhys-Jones. You'll find Julian Deverill hanging around the Drury Lane Theatre. Rumor has it that he is desperate to make Cressida Beauregard, who is presently doing a turn on stage as Ophelia, his mistress, but Mrs. Beauregard is skeptical of his ability to support her in her preferred style. Which she absolutely should be—the man hasn't paid his tailor in almost a year. Let's see... you'll find Anthony Leveson-Gower at—"

"Tattersall's!" Henry burst out. He grinned. "I actually knew one."

Peter kept going for another five minutes. It really was remarkable that he could keep all of that in his head.

Finally, he came to the end of the list. "I don't know much about David Crawley, but Bertram Newcombe is the particular friend of Lord Pearson and will no doubt be attending the ball he's hosting on Friday."

"Brilliant," Harrington said, writing quickly. He paused. "You didn't say anything about Walter Davenport or Edmund Elliot."

Peter had paused to take a sip of his ale. As he set down his glass, a wicked grin stole across his face. "That's because they both owe me money. Leave those two to me. By the time

I get through with them, they're going to be *delighted* to support this Pensions to Soldiers Act."

"Bless you." Harrington slumped back in his seat as the waiter deposited a joint of beef in front of him. He took up his knife and fork. "Truly, Peter, I don't know what I'd do without you."

"It's no trouble," Peter said, tucking in to his rack of lamb. "How are you finding life as an MP so far?"

"Not so good." He told them about his near-miss with Lord Kinwood. "I'd have made a complete and utter hash of it if not for Lady Diana's advice. And now, I'm expected to sway all these men." He paused, part of him not wanting to admit to any weaknesses, but then decided, what was the point? Everyone already knew he was pretty much good for nothing. "If you want to know the truth, I'm in over my head."

Henry had laid down his knife and fork and was listening intently, which Harrington did not entirely appreciate. "Give yourself a chance. You just need a little time to get your sea legs. You mustn't expect yourself to know everything on day one, especially as you've been out of the bloody country."

"I agree," Peter said. "You're going to do better than you think."

"I doubt it," Harrington muttered, slicing a parsnip.

"Take it from someone whose livelihood hinges on persuading people to buy very expensive things," Peter said. "The first step is being likable. And you are *extremely* likable. There are dozens of MPs who are honorable, diligent, and erudite who couldn't sell an umbrella in a rainstorm. What they wouldn't give to have a tenth of your easy nature."

"You make me sound like the beloved family spaniel," Harrington muttered.

"Don't discount it," Peter insisted. "It takes a range of

skills to succeed in politics. You already have some of them in spades. The others you will develop with time."

"I hope you're right." Harrington was having a hard time believing it, but he had to admit, Peter was bloody clever. The man spoke nine languages. Nine!

But he was obviously trying to placate him.

Although… so long as he had Peter's ear, he might as well get his advice. "Diana said something similar. She thought the fact that I'm an officer in the Riflemen might also work as a point in my favor. Apparently, we're fashionable."

"She's absolutely right," Peter noted. "What else did she say?"

He summarized her advice, about using the carrot where he could and the stick—his biting wit—where he must.

Peter speared a potato. "I have always considered Lady Diana to be one of the most intelligent women of my acquaintance. She has proved it once again. Sound advice, all of it."

Henry pushed his plate aside. "Speaking of Lady Diana."

Harrington felt a tingling sensation spread across his cheeks. God, he hoped he wasn't blushing. "What about her?"

Henry made a not-particularly-successful attempt to look nonchalant. "It sounds like you've been spending a fair amount of time in her company."

Harrington reached for his glass. "Hardly. Her brother ran me off the second he saw me. I'm lucky to have exchanged four words with her."

He was taking in a mouthful of ale when Peter said, "And what about the rumors that you almost kissed her in broad daylight, in the middle of Hyde Park?"

Harrington barely managed to swallow his drink. He came up coughing, and Henry gave him a couple of thumps on the back.

"I… *what*? That's… that's ridiculous. It was all Rafe Westbrook's fault."

Henry and Peter exchanged a look. "Is that so?" Henry asked.

The words tumbled from his mouth. "He was trying to make Diana get in a rowboat with him. Wouldn't take no for an answer, and he had the temerity to grab her. But then"—Harrington couldn't help but laugh, remembering—"she did this thing with her arm." He punched his fist downward, demonstrating. "I'll bet her Aunt Griselda showed it to her. It had 'Aunt Griselda' written all over it. And she sent the idiot tumbling right into the Serpentine."

"Really?" Peter asked.

"Yes, and the point was, when I saw that she was about to get splashed, I did what any gentleman would do. I moved her out of the way and stepped in so I took the brunt of it. It was entirely innocent, I swear."

Both of his friends looked baldly skeptical. "Well," Peter drawled, "it certainly sounds as if you've been spending *hardly* any time in her company."

Henry was even less discreet. "She's his type."

"She's exactly his type," Peter agreed.

"He's had a weakness for her ever since she cut Lady Pritchard to shreds at her debut ball," Henry observed.

Peter opened his mouth to agree, but Harrington cut him off. "Will you two shut it? It's completely impossible. At the Richford ball, Trevissick wouldn't even let me *dance* with her."

Peter looked at Henry. "Note that he doesn't deny liking her. Merely that her brother wouldn't allow it."

Harrington decided a change of tactics was in order. "You're the one who said she was one of the most intelligent women of your acquaintance. Why don't *you* court her? You'd actually stand a chance in hell."

Peter paused, wiping an errant drip from the side of his glass. "I actually proposed to Adelaide last week."

This was not entirely surprising. Peter had been courting Lady Adelaide De Courcy for the past year. Harrington hadn't realized things were that serious, but of course, he'd been out of the country for the last six months.

Lady Adelaide's father was the Marquis of Siddington, a highly placed diplomat. Much like Peter, she had grown up abroad, primarily in Vienna and St. Petersburg, and she spoke a half-dozen languages.

"Congratulations," Henry said, raising a hand to flag down the waiter. "This calls for a toast."

Peter grabbed Henry's arm, pulling it down. "Not so fast. She hasn't given me an answer yet."

Harrington scowled. "She hasn't *what?*"

Peter shrugged. "It's an important decision. She asked for some time to consider it."

Harrington snorted. "If she hasn't figured out that you're a fucking prince, it doesn't say much for her intelligence."

Henry's expression was pinched. "I hope this doesn't come out wrong, but I am surprised to hear that you decided to propose. Perhaps I have formed the wrong impression, but I have not observed a great deal of ardor on either side."

Peter seemed unbothered. "Paradoxically, that is one of the things I like about her. I'm seeking a practical arrangement. I work long hours. The last thing I need is a wife who would expect me to dote on her day and night. I need someone sophisticated. Worldly. I need to host a wide array of business associates in my home. I need a woman capable of planning impressive gatherings, who will not be cowed entertaining some of the most influential men in Europe." He gave a philosophical shrug. "Lady Adelaide meets all of my requirements."

Henry was shaking his head. "Peter. Good *God*. We're

talking about your *wife*. You're going to spend the rest of your life with this woman!"

Peter tilted his head. "Not necessarily. Should the relationship become untenable, I could certainly afford to set her up in her own household."

Henry groaned. "*No*. What is *wrong* with you? You haven't even married the woman yet, and you're already planning for the failure of your marriage!"

Peter still looked unperturbed. "I'm being realistic. How many people do you know who are truly happy in their marriage?"

"I can think of one." Henry pointed to his chest. "*Me*. Do you have any idea how happy I am being married to Caro? I am—" he paused, gesticulating wildly—"*absurdly* happy."

"Honestly, it's disgusting," Harrington confided. "I was at their house earlier today, and I was forced to endure the sight of my little sister pinching his arse!" He shuddered at the memory.

"And do you know whose marriages are every bit as disgustingly happy as Caro's and mine?" Henry jabbed a finger against the table. "Every single one of Harrington's siblings. Thorpe is so happy being married to Izzie, I worry he might burst from it. Hell, even Trevissick is happy being married to Ceci. I didn't realize he was capable of smiling."

Peter spread his hands. "Well, that seems to apply to people who have married into the greater Astley clan. And I have proposed to Adelaide. So, I suppose I will have to adjust my expectations accordingly." He signaled to the waiter. "Now, if you two are done badgering me, I have work to do."

"As do I. Thanks to you." Harrington patted his breast pocket. "I'm going to see how many of these men I can track down this afternoon."

Henry sighed. "Even I have horses to train."

Peter snatched the bill and paid the waiter in one smooth motion.

Henry stood. "Thank you for getting lunch. *Again.* One of these days, you're going to have to let me treat you."

Peter rose, reaching for his hat. "Yes, well, for some inexplicable reason, I like you two."

They parted at the door. As Harrington headed to his first stop, he could feel his beefsteak roiling in his stomach. The time for talking and planning was over. The only thing left to do was to go out there and try his hand at being a politician.

As he headed toward White's, Harrington could not help but observe that he was every bit as anxious as he'd been two months ago when the French army had been actively shooting at him.

CHAPTER 11

ucy and Izzie arrived at Latimer House at teatime.

This was usually a good time for a private visit as Diana's sister-in-law, Cecilia, her great-aunt, Griselda, and her nephew, Alaric, were all in their respective rooms, taking a nap. Cecilia because she was heavily pregnant with the next member of the Latimer brood, Aunt Griselda because she was eighty-five years old, and Alaric because he was not yet two.

They gathered in the sitting room connected to Diana's bedroom, which was decorated in rich shades of emerald green and gold. Ellery, their beloved family butler of more than twenty years, personally delivered the tea tray.

As soon as the door clicked shut behind him, Izzie pounced. "What's going on between you and Harrington?"

Diana accepted the cup of tea Lucy had poured for her. "He had a particular question he wanted to ask me. William Windham has asked him to throw his support behind a pair of acts coming up for a vote, relating to soldiers' pay and pensions. Mr. Windham wants your brother to drum up some votes, and he asked for my advice about how best to go about it."

Lucy's face fell. "Then… you don't like him?"

Diana sipped from her cup, considering her answer. The conversation was a bit awkward, as Harrington was the twins' brother.

But Izzie and Lucy were her best friends. Although Diana was very good at deflecting questions with an icy stare, she found that in this case, she didn't want to.

"I do like him," she admitted. She held up her hand as Lucy squealed, and a familiar arch look came into Izzie's eyes. "I don't want to overstate the situation. My acquaintance with him has been short. But I would like to spend more time in his company, to see if there is potential for something more than friendship."

Lucy clapped her hands and bounced in her seat. "That's *wonderful*, Diana!"

"It really is," Izzie agreed. "I can't recall you liking another man even this much."

It was true. There were a great many men who wanted to marry her for some combination of her dowry and her status as the sister of a duke.

But Harrington seemed to regard the notion of marrying her as impossible. Which made a certain amount of sense, as her brother despised him.

But the point was, as far as Harrington Astley was concerned, her fortune was out of reach and any time he sought to spend in her company was because he *wanted* to. Because he actually enjoyed her acid wit and admired her intelligence.

A tantalizing prospect, indeed.

"So," Diana said, plucking a madeleine from the plate, "tell me more about your brother."

"Harrington is *wonderful*," Lucy said.

"He acts the part of the scapegrace." Izzie waved her own madeleine. "And to a certain extent, he is. But he would do *anything* for the people he cares about."

"He does have a reputation for being a bit wild," Diana noted. "Do you think he will make a good husband when he finally settles down and marries?"

The twins exchanged a look. "I do," Izzie said.

"I do as well," Lucy added.

Izzie bit her lip. "In my opinion, the reason Harrington has pursued, shall we say, fleeting attachments, is not because he is incapable of being faithful. It's because he believes deep down that no woman would want a permanent alliance with *him*."

"That's it exactly," Lucy agreed.

Diana frowned. She had been pursued by any number of men with far fewer personal attractions than Harrington Astley. Most of them had a level of self-regard entirely disproportionate to their shortcomings. "Why would he feel that way?"

The twins exchanged another one of those speaking looks. "It's largely because of Edward," Lucy said at last.

"Edward?" Diana asked. "You mean, Lord Fauconbridge? I thought they were close."

"They are," Izzie hastened to reassure her. "Please, don't mistake me. Edward has never been unkind."

"That's not in Edward's nature," Lucy added.

"But..." Izzie waved a hand, formulating her words. "Edward was so bright and so focused on doing well in school."

"*Too* focused on doing well in school," Lucy added darkly.

"Harrington decided from an early age that he could never measure up," Izzie explained. "And so, he chose a different path."

"And didn't try in school at all," Lucy said sadly.

Izzie nodded. "This in turn caused him to conclude that he was an idiot, and worthless, and that no woman would want him, when really, none of those things are true."

Diana leaned back in her chair, considering. "That certainly tracks with what I've observed. He could scarcely believe your father wanted him, rather than Edward, to stand for that seat in Parliament. I was actually the one who first informed him that he had been elected, and his reaction was somewhat panicked."

The twins shared another pregnant glance. "I can't say I'm surprised," Lucy said.

"Well," Diana said, setting down her cup, "this is certainly good information for me to have. Thank you for informing me."

Izzie set her teacup aside. "Speaking of useful information to have, now that we have established that you will be marrying my brother—"

"Izzie!" Diana laughed. "We have established no such thing."

Izzie ignored Diana's protestations, as Diana had known she would. "Are there any questions you wish to have answered prior to your wedding night?" Izzie paused dramatically, giving Diana a lurid look. "Questions of an *intimate* nature?"

Diana considered. There were decided benefits to having a married friend. Izzie had already explained, in detail, what went on between a man and a woman in the bedchamber. Whenever she did marry, Diana would be going into her wedding night with far more information than the typical bride.

And Izzie had done more than describe the basics of the marital act. Before she married Thorpe, she had commandeered a book of scandalous prints from its hiding place beneath Harrington's mattress and presented it for Lucy and Diana's perusal.

Diana had found the pictures shocking. Aunt Griselda bred her own hunting dogs, so Diana had already understood the basic mechanics of copulation. But seeing those naked men and women tangling together had been a thousand times more startling than watching a pair of dogs rut. Some of them showed a woman putting her mouth on a man's most intimate parts, the mere thought of which made Diana blush. And the notion that *she* might want a man to do the same to *her* was inconceivable.

As astonishing as the images were, Diana could not deny that they were also... stirring. After Izzie's wedding, she had encouraged Diana and Lucy to keep an open mind toward those images of the couples kissing one another between their legs, assuring them that the act was exquisitely pleasurable. After a few years spent pondering the matter, Diana felt more curious than horrified. Armed with her newfound knowledge about the workings of her own body, she had experimented late at night in her bed and found that caressing the areas shown in the prints did, indeed, bring about a delightful result. She could now easily imagine that a man putting his mouth on that little spot between her legs might bring about the sort of bliss that radiated from the couples shown in the book.

She would go so far as to say that she was eager to try it. And since his return, when she lay in bed at night, touching herself, the man she liked to imagine she was engaging in those acts with was Harrington.

There were other pictures in that book for which the appeal was less clear, including the image Harrington had marked by folding down the corner of the page.

It depicted a man bent over while his lover spanked him with a birch. But far from finding the experience painful, the man had an expression of bliss on his face, and was reaching down to rub his own cock, which was fully erect!

It was possible that the corner had been folded down by accident, perhaps as Harrington hastily shut the book and shoved it back into its hiding place. But Diana could not help but notice that when the book was opened to this particular page, it lay flat very easily.

She didn't know for sure. But she had to wonder—was this what he liked? Being spanked? Diana could not fathom why someone might enjoy such a thing. But this was likely due to her own ignorance. It was also mortifying to picture a man placing his lips between her legs, yet Izzie had assured her she would enjoy that particular act very much. She supposed it was one of those things you could not truly understand until you had experienced it for yourself, and she therefore tried to reserve her judgment.

She felt a pang of guilt that she knew anything about Harrington's more intimate preferences. Her only goal in looking at the pictures had been to gain general information. She had not intended to invade his privacy, but that was precisely what she had done.

She was startled from her reverie by someone shaking her arm. She blinked and found Lucy smiling at her. "Diana? Are you even attending?"

Izzie looked amused. "And here I thought I was the one whose mind was always a thousand miles away. What were you thinking about?"

She could hardly answer, *Your brother, with his head between my legs.* "Nothing!"

Izzie gave Lucy a significant look. "She's blushing."

"She was definitely thinking about Harrington," Lucy said. "And what were we discussing? Ah, yes—the marriage bed."

Now Diana could feel her cheeks burning. "I wasn't... I mean, I... er..."

"She's usually such a good liar," Izzie observed.

"She is," Lucy agreed. "And I don't think I've ever seen her blush before!"

"You're the one who introduced the topic," Diana grumbled.

"True," Izzie said, unrepentant. "So, do you have any questions?"

"None at this time," Diana said crisply. "I do believe you have already provided me with as much information as it is possible to absorb through mere description."

"It sounds as if she's eager to move on to hands-on practice," Izzie observed, causing Diana's cheeks to flame even hotter.

"We both want to be bridesmaids at the wedding!" Lucy added cheerfully.

Diana sighed. "I'll keep that in mind."

Diana endured a few more minutes of teasing before the conversation blessedly moved on. But she was distracted. As she couldn't stop thinking about Harrington, she at least attempted to direct her thoughts toward more decent subjects. She wondered how he was faring in his quest to sway the politicians on his list to his side. By the time the twins departed, she was more anxious to speak to him than ever.

CHAPTER 12

*U*pon entering White's, Harrington enquired after his quarry. Quentin Carstairs wasn't there, but a footman informed him that Colin Rhys-Jones was in the billiards room. Harrington scarcely knew the man, in spite of their being around the same age, as Rhys-Jones had attended Harrow and Cambridge, whereas Harrington had been at Eton and Oxford. But much to Harrington's astonishment, Rhys-Jones and his friends responded enthusiastically when Harrington asked if he could join them.

Everyone wanted to hear about his experiences in Germany. Which, in truth, had mostly consisted of sitting around in the cold for weeks, waiting for something to happen, followed by a frantic march to the sea. But Harrington managed to come up with a couple of interesting anecdotes from the retreat, and if Rhys-Jones and his friends formed the impression that he had held back out of a becoming sense of modesty, he wasn't about to correct them.

Two hours later, when the party was breaking up, Harrington pulled Rhys-Jones aside and mentioned the two acts Willim Windham had asked him to support. And wouldn't you know it, Rhys-Jones nodded solemnly, clasped Harrington's shoulder, and informed him that he would be glad to.

The following two days passed in a whirlwind. He fenced with Stephen Chichester and played brag with Charles Sutton. He attended the theater and assured a drunken Julian Deverill that the buxom Cressida was a fool for rejecting him. He spent an afternoon at Tattersall's with Henry, who agreed to work with a recalcitrant filly Anthony Leveson-Gower had recently acquired. After that, Leveson-Gower was delighted to support the Pensions to Soldiers Act.

Not everyone said yes, of course. And he didn't manage to track everyone down in the limited time he had. But by the time he strolled into Lord Pearson's ball on Friday night, he had brought around nineteen of the men on his list.

He spotted one of his final targets, Bertram Newcombe, a portly man forty years his senior with whom he shared only a passing acquaintance. Much to Harrington's surprise, Newcombe greeted him enthusiastically and dragged him off to Lord Pearson's study for a glass of port. It turned out that Newcombe had been a military man himself and had served with some distinction in the War of American Independence. Although he purported to want to hear about Harrington's recent exploits, he spent most of the conversation waxing nostalgic about his own days with the 59th Regiment of Foot. Harrington couldn't help but notice that Newcombe refilled his own glass four times in the course of an hour.

Sensing an opening, Harrington leaned forward. "Have you perchance heard about the act that's coming up for a vote tomorrow? The Pensions to Soldiers Act?"

"Pensions to S-soldiers?" Newcombe slurred. He waved his hand sloppily. "Haven't heard a blessed thing about it."

"It's a worthy cause. You see…"

Newcombe didn't take much convincing. "Of course, they must have pensions! Of course!" he repeated, belching.

Harrington had a feeling that, in spite of his professed support, the odds that Newcombe would remember this conversation tomorrow, much less drag himself down to the Palace of Westminster in time for the vote, were slim to none. "Perhaps I could save you the trouble of going down there and cast a vote for you as your surrogate?" Harrington suggested.

"Yes," Newcombe said, reaching for the decanter. "That would be s-splendid."

Harrington rifled through Lord Pearson's desk until he found paper and pen. "I'll write out a note for you to sign, explaining your intentions. Just so everything is clear."

Newcombe scrawled his signature, and Harrington's heart sang. He had actually done it! He knew it was just a bit of luck, that by some happy chance the Riflemen had become all the rage at the perfect moment, and his success was only due to the green coat gracing his shoulders.

But still, he felt bloody good about himself for once in his life.

He listened to Bertram Newcombe's increasingly slurred stories for another fifteen minutes before the man fell asleep in his chair. Harrington slipped out, asked the footman in the hall to keep an eye on him, and went in search of the person with whom he most wanted to celebrate.

Striding into the ballroom, he almost bumped into Peter Ferguson. "Have you seen Diana?" he asked without preamble.

Peter gave him a speaking look. "*Diana*, is it? It happens that I was just going to claim her for the next dance."

"Can I have it?" Harrington asked, not bothering to act coy. "Please?"

Peter's eyes turned sympathetic. "Of course."

"Except…" Harrington peered across the ballroom. As usual, Marcus Latimer was looming over his sister, watching her like an immaculately dressed hawk. "You'll have to go and fetch her."

Peter gave him an incredulous look.

Harrington dropped his voice low. "Her brother will never let her go off with me. You go and claim her for the dance, and I'll take your place after you've lined up."

He could tell Peter was holding in a laugh, but all he said was, "All right."

Harrington watched from the edge of the ballroom, bouncing on the balls of his feet. He couldn't wait to tell Diana how well he had done.

He watched Peter bow over her hand. As he escorted her across the room, Peter leaned down and whispered something in her ear. He made a subtle gesture to the corner where Harrington stood, no doubt asking her if she had any objections to dancing with him instead.

Diana looked up, and her eyes found his across the ballroom.

Then, she did it.

She smiled.

It was one of those glowing, light-up-your face sorts of smiles, and it knocked him right back on his heels. Diana Latimer rarely smiled. She wielded a stony expression as effectively as she wielded her sword, using it to keep the fortune-hunters of London from laboring under the delusion that they had wormed their way into her good graces.

But now, she was smiling like *that*? Because she was going to dance with *him*?

It made him feel ten feet tall.

She and Peter found places toward the bottom of the line of dancers. Harrington waited until the orchestra struck the opening notes, then he strode across the ballroom and clapped Peter on the shoulder. Peter surrendered his place at once, squeezing Harrington's arm as he took himself off.

Then, it was just him and Diana.

Well, and fifty-some-odd other dancers.

Not that he could see any of them. He only had eyes for her.

As they circled each other, Harrington tilted his head toward her ear. "I did it."

It was a country dance, and a quick one at that, so she didn't have time to say anything before the steps forced them apart, but she managed to squeeze his forearm. When they came together again, she asked breathlessly. "You got the votes?"

He didn't have time to respond, but he nodded from his spot in the opposite line of dancers. When it was time for them to dance another turn, he managed to say, "I started with Colin Rhys-Jones."

After another ten turns, he had only managed to impart a tiny fraction of the story of how he'd brought Rhys-Jones around.

By then, they had almost reached the bottom of the line of dancers. Soon, they would have to dance their way back to the top.

To his right, the balcony doors loomed, open and inviting.

As they came together again, Harrington made a quick decision. He took Diana's hand, but instead of dancing the expected turn, he tugged her toward the balcony doors.

She went with him without hesitation. As they ran out into the night together, the beautiful sound of her laughter washed over his ears.

Now *this* was more like it.

Diana had never been whisked out onto a balcony by a handsome man before. Gracious, up until recently, she had never even encountered a man whom she would want to do the whisking!

Yet, here she was, dashing out the French doors, hand-in-hand with Harrington under a sky littered with… clouds. It was probably too much to hope for a blanket of stars. This was England, after all.

Still, it felt *magical*. And, on the bright side, the light drizzle was keeping everyone else inside.

He drew her into a little nook in the corner, positioning her closest to the wall. Diana knew he had done it so she would be out of the weather, but she could not help but note that it had the additional advantage of being out of view of the French doors. He did not release her hand, and she found she did not want him to.

She was prickly by nature, freezing most of her suitors with a glare before they could get close enough to touch her. But holding hands with Harrington Astley felt natural. It felt… *right*.

She squeezed his fingers. "Tell me."

The words tumbled from his lips. About how he had charmed Colin Rhys-Jones during a game of billiards and Charles Sutton over a hand of cards. About how he was now chums with Stephen Chicester and Julian Deverill and a dozen other men.

Finally, he patted his pocket. "I doubt Newcombe will have sobered up sufficiently to show up for the vote tomorrow. But he agreed to let me vote as his surrogate. I got it in writing and everything. So, that's twenty men who have promised to support the Pensions to Soldiers Act!"

She beamed up at him. "That's *brilliant*, Harrington. I knew you could do it!"

He looked so happy, and she was so delighted that *she* was

the one he had wanted to share this moment with, she didn't even think.

She threw her arms around his neck.

Before she had time to worry that he might not welcome the gesture, his hands came around her waist. He lifted her off her feet and spun in a circle, twirling her around and around. Their laughter mingled together, bouncing off the balcony's flagstones, causing her heart to swell to the point of bursting.

After a perfect eternity that was probably only a few seconds, he set her down. His smile was fond as his hand came up to frame her face. "Diana," he whispered.

Her breath hitched. His fingers curled behind her ear, sending a shiver down her neck. Slowly, ever so slowly, he tilted his lips toward hers.

Her eyes fluttered shut as she slid her arms down across the planes of his chest.

That was when a dark voice came from the French doors. "What the *hell* are you doing to my sister?"

CHAPTER 13

*D*iana muttered a curse.

It was a *bad* one, and she knew Harrington heard it, because he grinned.

But as Marcus stormed across the balcony and yanked her out of his arms, his face turned solemn again.

Marcus's eyes were icy with fury. "How dare you lay your filthy hands on her!"

She shook herself. "Marcus! Stop. He didn't do anything wrong."

"Didn't do anything—" Her brother rounded on her, incredulous. "I *saw* him, Diana! Saw the way he was *forcing* himself on—"

"He wasn't forcing himself on me!" she snapped. "*I* was the one who hugged *him!*"

Marcus's nostrils flared. "Have you forgotten who he is? This is the man who once put snakes in my boots. Who started so many vile rumors about me, I cannot count them on both hands. Who *stole* the only miniature I have of Mother and didn't give it back for *six weeks*! I thought it was *gone*! I thought—"

"I'm especially sorry about that one," Harrington said, stepping forward with his palms held out. "I'm sorry for all of them, if you want to know the truth. But thinking about that one, knowing what happened to your mother…" He swallowed, and his expression was stricken. "I feel deeply ashamed, and I'd like to express my—"

"*Silence!*" Marcus shouted, casting Harrington the sort of glare that could turn a man to stone. "You expect me to believe that you're sorry? At the very moment you come dangling after my sister?" His laugh was vindictive. "How very convenient."

"No, really, I am sorry. And it's not what you think." His gaze fell on her, and his expression turned sorrowful. "I know Diana would never be interested in the likes of me."

"She most certainly would not," Marcus snapped. "And that's *Lady* Diana to you."

Diana wrenched her arm from Marcus's grasp and rounded on her brother. "Why don't you let *me* decide whom I grant permission to call me by my first name? Who I dance with, who I—"

"Because I. Know. *Better!*" Marcus hissed. "I know he is in possession of a certain amount of wit and charm. But I have known him for almost twenty years. I know the true measure of his character!"

"You knew him when he was twelve years old," Diana shot back. "I will grant you, his behavior at the time was appalling. But that was more than fifteen years ago. People change, Marcus. And if you would consider the man he is today—"

"I cannot *believe* you are defending him!" Marcus snapped. "That you would choose *him* over *me*, after everything I have…"

His voice broke, and her brother, who was never less than absolutely confident, trailed off, looking down.

"Marcus." Diana took two steps forward and seized his arm. "Don't think of it that way. Just because I hold Lieutenant Astley in high regard does not mean I don't love you."

"Doesn't it?" Marcus asked softly. "Because…"

The click of shoes on the flagstones caused them all to look up. Edward Astley was crossing the balcony with brisk strides. "You're causing a scene," he said without preamble. "Gossip is spreading like wildfire across the ballroom that Harrington and Lady Diana repaired to the balcony together, and whatever they did out here was bad enough that you two are coming to blows over it."

Marcus muttered a curse. Coincidentally, it was the same one Diana had used earlier.

Edward seized his brother by the shoulder. "Harrington and I will exit through the gardens." He nodded toward a door at the far end of the balcony. "That will lead you into the morning room, should you wish to slip out unnoticed."

"I think we should all return to the ballroom together and act as if nothing is amiss," Diana said. "After all, the truth is that we didn't do anything improper, and the doors were open the entire time. We can brazen it out."

Edward paused. "That… is a good idea." He looked pointedly at Harrington and Marcus. "Especially if you two can manage to act as if you're the best of friends."

"I can do it," Harrington offered.

Marcus remained silent a beat before grumbling, "I can do it, too." He smirked at Harrington. "As friendly as I ever look, that is."

Diana took Marcus's arm. Harrington came up on his other side, slinging an arm around his neck. Edward walked beside his brother.

As they came into the ballroom, Marcus leaned in and whispered something to Harrington. It was most likely a death threat, but Harrington laughed as if it were some hilarious joke.

She glanced up at her brother. He was smirking at Harrington. She had to admit, it was cheerful *for Marcus*, and the expression was probably more convincing than if he'd walked in grinning like an idiot.

Harrington whispered something she couldn't make out in Marcus's ear, slapped him on the back, then drifted off across the ballroom with his brother.

Diana caught a trio of matrons gaping at her while a fourth whispered something behind her fan. She gazed at them steadily and arched an imperious eyebrow. In unison, their eyes went wide. One of them took a step back as if she'd been physically struck.

Diana donned a smirk to rival her brother's. It was good to know she hadn't lost her touch.

CHAPTER 14

When Diana went to speak to her brother the following afternoon, she brought reinforcements.

She knocked on the door to his study. "Come in," Marcus called. Diana held up a finger, requesting that her companion wait a moment before making her entrance, then opened the door.

She found him seated behind his desk with his one-and-a-half-year-old son, Alaric, on his lap. Marcus had a pile of papers and an open ledger in front of him, and Alaric, who was his spitting image, had his own stack of papers, which he was scribbling on with a pencil.

Marcus frowned upon seeing her, but Alaric's face lit up. "Aunt Diynah!"

She came around the desk and kissed his golden head. "Good afternoon, my little prince."

His nursemaid appeared in the doorway. Diana had selected this time because she knew it coincided with Alaric's nap. "Shall I take him, Your Grace?"

"Yes. Thank you, Maureen." Marcus ruffled Alaric's hair, his expression turning fond. "Rest up, my boy. We have more ducal business to attend to this afternoon."

Alaric hugged his papa around the neck, then left with Maureen. Diana took the chair opposite Marcus. "We need to talk."

He scowled. "I was afraid you would say that."

She might as well come out and say it. "I am strongly considering setting my cap for Harrington Astley."

Marcus looked as if he'd drunk vinegar. "You cannot mean that."

"I do." She waved her arm, struggling to find the words to make him understand. "I like him, Marcus. Very much."

He shut the ledger he'd been reviewing with a snap. "You will meet someone else whom you like even more."

She sighed. "That's just it. I don't think I will."

He looked at her then, and his eyes held a twinge of concern. "Of course, you will. Why would you say such a thing?"

"Because it's been three years since I made my debut, and I haven't met anyone else that I like even a little bit." She gave a humorless laugh. "Most of the men who swarm around me are interested in nothing but my fortune."

He inclined his head in acknowledgement. "I had to put up with the same thing for many years. But eventually, if you sift through enough silt, you will find a diamond. I did."

"I think I have as well," Diana countered. "And that diamond is Harrington Astley."

Marcus's scowl snapped back into place. "He is fool's gold, at best. And not every man courting you is a fortune hunter. What about the Duke of Hunwicke?"

Diana gave him a baleful look. "He is forty years my senior and plagued by gout."

Marcus frowned, but he couldn't argue with that. "Well, how about the Marquess of Beasley? He's young and handsome."

Diana snorted. "I have had more stimulating conversations with Inge."

This was not a ringing endorsement, as Inge was one of Aunt Griselda's hunting dogs.

Marcus's lips thinned into a line, but he soldiered on. "Then what about Viscount Ryburn? He's young, handsome, *and* intelligent."

"And completely disinterested," Diana shot back. "I'm not sure how you failed to notice, but his efforts at flirtation have been directed not at me, but at *you*."

Marcus froze, and she marked the moment he realized she was right.

Not that he was prepared to admit as much. He narrowed his eyes. "You're not supposed to know about such things."

She rolled her eyes. "Thank goodness I do. What a disaster that match would have been! My point is, I have done everything you asked. I have considered every suitor you suggested. And I haven't felt so much as a sliver of interest in any of them." She leaned forward. "Not until Harrington returned."

He rubbed his brow. "We'll keep looking. We'll find someone else."

"I'm not so certain." She looked at her brother with real sympathy. Because even though he could sometimes be an overbearing arse, she knew the reason he was an overbearing arse was because he loved her, and because he wanted desperately for the next phase of her life to turn out better than her early years.

Marcus was nine years her senior, and he had always viewed protecting her as his responsibility. The period when

Diana had been forced to live under the same roof as their father had been brief, less than a month, and the servants had largely succeeded in helping to keep her hidden from the cruel, violent former duke. But she knew that Marcus regarded the fact that it had happened at all as a personal failure, and he did not consider the fact that he had been the one to rescue her, to coerce his father into allowing her to go and live with Aunt Griselda, as an absolution for this lapse. Almost twenty years had passed, and he was still anxious to make sure nothing bad ever happened to her again.

Knowing all of this made it possible to love Marcus even when his attempts to protect her crossed the line into controlling her.

She regarded her brother across his desk. She needed to get this next part right. "I was aware that you were Harrington's favorite target for pranks while the two of you were at school. But I had somehow formed the impression that you saw him as a nuisance. I did not realize that he had... wounded you."

Marcus looked away. "Your initial impression was correct," he answered, his voice tight. "Other than that one incident with Mother's portrait. But he did return it, once he realized that I..." He broke off, clearing his throat. "I was several years older than Harrington, and at the top of the proverbial ladder. He was an annoyance, but I did not spend my nights weeping into my pillow. In truth, I scarcely spared him a thought." His eyes, as brittle as ice chips, found hers. "But the fact remains that he is a wastrel, and I want better for my sister than the likes of him."

Diana held his gaze. "Let's see, shall we?" She turned to face the door. "Ceci? Would you come in, please?"

Marcus groaned, rubbing his eyes with the heels of his hands as his duchess entered the room. "Not you, too."

Ceci, who was heavily pregnant, grasped the arm of the chair next to Diana as she lowered herself into the seat. Marcus sprang to his feet and was around the desk in a flash. He made sure his wife was comfortably settled before returning to his chair.

"The truth is," Diana said, "having grown up a stone's throw from the Astley family's estate in Cheltenham, Ceci knows Harrington better than either of us. I thought it only logical that we should ask for her opinion."

A gleam came into Marcus's eyes as he turned to his wife. "Indeed. Please regale us with stories of Harrington from your youth. I believe one of them involves a toad."

"At least three of them involve toads." Ceci ticked them off on her fingers. "On my pillow, in my sewing basket, and my personal favorite, inside my glass of water." She shuddered. "When I say I have kissed some frogs, unfortunately, I mean it literally."

Marcus turned to Diana, his smile triumphant. "Do you see?"

"But…" Ceci interjected, a note of steel in her voice.

Marcus wrinkled his nose. "But?"

Ceci shifted in her seat, no doubt trying to find a comfortable position. "But these were minor infractions in the grand scheme of things. When the stakes were high, Harrington showed his true colors."

Marcus's brow remained low. "Explain."

Ceci turned to Diana. "The summer I turned thirteen, there was a boy in town who liked to mock me. I've never been what you would call willowy—"

"You are stunning and gorgeous, and any man who says otherwise will be meeting me at dawn," Marcus said darkly.

Ceci cast a fond smile at her husband. "Thank you. But I am sorry to report that not everyone shares in your opinion. That summer, the boy in question bestowed upon me a new nickname." She grimaced, as if the memory was still painful. "Cecilia Cheno-*width*."

Diana winced in sympathy at this unkind variation of Cecilia's maiden name, Chenowith.

Marcus's chair skidded across the floor as he surged to his feet. "What is his name?"

Ceci raised a hand, her expression placating. "It was a long time ago—"

"I *insist* that you tell me." Marcus paced across the room to the hearth in four quick strides. He raised a hand before the mantelpiece, then closed it into a fist, as if he had barely suppressed the impulse to grab one of the Dresden porcelain figurines atop it and hurl it into the fire.

Ceci smiled fondly at her husband. "I appreciate your desire to defend me. But I assure you, there is no need. It is my understanding that this young man trained as an apothecary and set up his practice in Worcester." She gave a little shrug. "I can't imagine that our paths will ever cross again."

"They most certainly will not," Marcus muttered darkly as he resumed his seat and seized one of the blank sheets of paper Alaric had been using to scribble. Diana watched him scrawl down the words *apothecary*, *Worcester*, and *ask Fauconbridge*.

Diana rolled her eyes. Typical Marcus. At least Lord Fauconbridge would talk some sense into him.

Ceci cleared her throat. "One day, Harrington stumbled upon me crying behind the stables. I didn't want to tell him what had happened, but he eventually wormed it out of me. And do you know what he did?"

"What?" Marcus asked in a clipped voice.

"He wrote a play about it, of all things. You see, a company of traveling players had come to Cheltenham for the high season, and there was a contest in which they would present a work written by one of the local youths at the summer festival. Harrington wrote a brilliant comedic scene in which a moonstruck young man makes a fool of himself trying to gain the attention of a pretty young lady through mockery." Ceci laughed, remembering. "He didn't use our names, but he wrote it in such a way that all the local residents knew to whom it referred. He portrayed my tormentor as a pathetic dunderhead."

Ceci paused to dab her eyes with her handkerchief. "In the end, 'I' threw him over for a man who turned out to be a prince in disguise—a nice bit of irony, considering I went on to marry a duke. My antagonist became a laughingstock overnight, and wouldn't you know it, he never said a word to me again."

At some point during Ceci's story, Marcus had slumped down in his chair with his arms crossed over his chest. He did not look thrilled about the fact that Harrington was the hero of this particular story. "Hmph."

Diana turned to face her sister-in-law. "What, then, is your overall impression of Harrington?"

Ceci directed her answer toward her husband. "He could certainly be annoying at times. But when it was important, he never let me down, and I am pleased to count him as a friend."

Marcus's expression was distinctly sulky. "I'm still not convinced he is worthy of you."

Diana leapt in. "But you'll give him a chance to show that he is."

Marcus scowled, but he muttered, "I suppose."

Diana sprang to her feet, eager to seize this small victory and make her exit before he could change his mind. She came around the desk and kissed her brother on the cheek. "Thank you, Marcus," she whispered.

As she hurried from the room, Ceci cast her a significant

look. *Don't worry,* it said. Her sister-in-law would soothe the savage beast.

Diana smiled as she stepped out into the corridor. Her next opportunity to see Harrington would come in two days, at a picnic being hosted by Lord and Lady Morsley.

She could scarcely wait.

CHAPTER 15

The following morning, Harrington reported to Horse Guards in response to another summons from William Windham. The vote had taken place the previous day, and both acts the Secretary of State had asked him to support had passed by a comfortable margin. For once in his life, Harrington wasn't dreading the prospect of going before his superior. He'd done a deuced good job, if he said so himself.

He was once again escorted into the room with the large, circular desk. Windham rose and came around the desk, then proceeded to pump Harrington's hand and thank him for his good work.

Hoping that would be it, Harrington leaned toward the door, but Windham gestured for him to sit. "You have been of great use to the government on this initiative." His brown eyes bored down on Harrington. "I hope you will prove to be equally effective in accomplishing your next task."

Next task? *Fuck.* Harrington was reminded why he had never made any effort in school. Letting on that you were competent led to nothing but trouble.

But he could hardly deny the Secretary of State, so he said, "What did you have in mind, sir?"

Windham peered at him. "What I am about to tell you is a matter of national security. I only entrust this information to you because you are a member of Parliament. I trust you will hold it in the strictest confidentiality."

Bloody hell. How had it come to this? He was *Harrington Astley.* One of the worst-behaved students in the history of Eton. He was the last person who should be trusted with state secrets!

He shifted in his chair. "I'm not sure I'm comfortable being privy to such sensitive information."

Windham inclined his head. "I understand your reticence, especially as you are so new to your role as MP. I'm afraid it is necessary. You see, you are in a unique position to accomplish the task I am about to set before you."

"Really?" *How the hell was that possible?* The only thing he could think of that he was in a unique position to accomplish was making an arse of himself.

But Windham's face was sincere. "Indeed. I believe that during your deployment to Hanover, you befriended a young Swedish duke."

"You mean Carl Frederick?" Harrington blurted. Which was an idiotic thing to say, because who else could it be? Swedish dukes weren't exactly thick on the ground. Harrington thought of Carl Frederick as a captain, which was his rank in the army. But he knew he was also somehow related to the Swedish king—his second cousin once removed, perhaps? And that he was the duke of the Swedish province of Värmland.

It was funny that Windham mentioned Carl Frederick, because Harrington had received a letter from him just that morning. It seemed Carl Frederick was in Britain on a diplomatic errand and had rented a country house just outside of London. He had invited Harrington to come out for a few days to attend an impromptu gathering.

Windham leaned forward, interlacing his fingers. "Precisely. He has invited you to attend a house party he is hosting."

Harrington sat back in his chair, stunned. "How did you know that?"

Windham waved a hand. "This is another thing that I must ask you to keep confidential. The Royal Mail has a secret division charged with... keeping the government abreast of matters of state interest."

"At The Royal Mail?" Harrington gaped at him. "You're saying that they... open and read people's mail?"

"They open and read people's mail," Windham confirmed. He pointed a finger at Harrington. "You are to tell no one of that."

"Right." Harrington ran a hand through his hair and noticed it was shaking. He was in so far over his head right now. How did Windham not understand that he was speaking to the man who was once arrested for being so drunk, he didn't notice that the wall he was pissing against belonged to the offices of the Bow Street Runners? It hadn't helped that the incident had taken place at three in the afternoon, rather than three in the morning. Fortunately for Harrington, Peter had made a handsome donation of new firearms to the Bow Street Officers, and the charges had been dropped.

Still, the point was, he was not the sort of man you entrusted with state secrets. "But... The letter I received from Carl Frederick hadn't been opened. It was still sealed."

Windham brushed this off. "The men employed in this particular office are experts in opening and re-sealing letters in such a way that makes it impossible to tell that the letter has been tampered with."

"I… I see." Harrington tried to stop squirming in his seat. "So, what is it you want me to do?"

Windham's expression grew pained. "I'm sure that during your time in Hanover, it did not escape your notice that Sweden's king is…" He waved a hand, trying to come up with a diplomatic way to describe Sweden's eccentric monarch.

Harrington appreciated his struggle. On the one hand, King Gustav IV Adolf was Britain's staunchest ally, the only head of state who hadn't stabbed his erstwhile allies in the back or promptly folded when Napoleon marched on Germany.

On the other hand, the king's assertion that the six thousand troops Sweden had garrisoned in Stralsund could stand against Napoleon's *Grande Armée* was not what you would call realistic. To make matters worse, the king persisted in addressing the man who had proclaimed himself emperor as *Monsieur* Bonaparte, an insult that had moved him to the very top of Napoleon's list of enemies.

"A bit of a fruitcake?" Harrington offered.

Windham cleared his throat. "Just so. Although, once again, I trust you will keep that comment confidential."

Harrington inclined his head. "Of course."

The Secretary of State clasped his hands before him on the desk. "In spite of his idiosyncrasies, King Gustav remains a potential ally, and a valuable one at that. We are currently attempting to build a new coalition to challenge Napoleon, and it would behoove us to know which way the wind blows." At Harrington's blank look, he continued, "We have considered the possibility that King Gustav was disappointed by Britain's choice to retreat from Hanover, rather than stand and fight, as he wished to do."

"Stand and fight?" Harrington surged to his feet. "That would have been *madness*. Napoleon had 180,000 men! Maybe if Emperor Francis hadn't given that idiot, General

Mack, command of the Austrian army, all because he told him what he wanted to hear—that Austria's forces could stand against the *Grande Armée* when they weren't trained and weren't even *armed*—"

Windham held out both palms, placating. "Please—"

Harrington was unable to stifle the words spilling from his mouth. "And if Prussia hadn't double-crossed us, and Russia hadn't jaunted back to the safety of their ice-encrusted—"

"*Lieutenant.*" Windham spoke the word sharply enough that Harrington managed to stop his rant.

"I'm sorry, sir." He rubbed the back of his head, embarrassed.

The Secretary of State gestured for Harrington to resume his seat. "There is no need to convince me. You are correct on every point." He gave Harrington a wry smile. "I'm sure the issue feels very personal, given that you were the one abandoned by our allies in the field."

Harrington cleared his throat. "Just so, sir."

"But our concern is that, in spite of the eminently reasonable points you have raised, King Gustav might see the situation differently."

"And so, you'd like me to speak to Carl Frederick about it." Harrington put his hands on his thighs, preparing to stand. "I'd be glad to."

Windham held out a finger. "I would not say that we want you to *speak to* Carl Frederick about it, precisely."

Harrington wasn't sure where this was going, but he had a feeling he wasn't going to like it. "Oh?"

"The young duke is a clever man who will, naturally, tell us what we wish to hear. His correspondence, on the other hand, may contain the king's… unvarnished opinions."

Harrington laughed nervously. "I thought you were already opening and reading his correspondence."

Windham cringed. "We are. But we missed a letter. Carl Frederick was overheard mentioning it to one of his advisors. He referred to it as containing, 'state secrets.'"

"Oh, God." Harrington leaned his elbows on his knees, burying his face in his hands. "And you want me to... steal it?"

Windham waved a hand. "Not at all. We would prefer for you to make a copy and bring it to us. That will arouse far less suspicion."

Harrington squinted at him. "But won't it be in Swedish?"

Windham shrugged. "Yes. But I'm sure you'll figure it out. The house party isn't for a few days, after all."

Harrington gaped at him. So, he was supposed to learn *Swedish*? That was the actual plan? And that was assuming he could even find the bloody letter.

Harrington tugged at the stock around his neck, which felt unaccountably tight. "How will I know which one is the right letter?"

"Our associates at the Royal Mail have a guess. Although they do not have the capacity to open all the duke's correspondence, they have been cataloguing each piece of mail he receives. Upon further review, one of those unopened letters was sealed with an old crest associated with the Swedish crown, dating back to the period when it was in the hands of the House of Mecklenburg."

"M-mecklenburg?" Harrington stammered. Hope blazed inside of him. Because... Diana's Aunt Griselda had been born on the Continent. Her last name was *Saxe-Mecklenburg!*

He couldn't find Mecklenburg on a map to save his life. But he was damn sure Diana could. And from the sound of things, Mecklenburg and Sweden were more closely connected than he had realized.

She spoke a half dozen languages, didn't she? Maybe she even spoke Swedish...

Harrington looked squarely at the Secretary of State. "I will do my best. Tell me exactly what I'm looking for."

A half-hour later, he stepped outside. The day had dawned bright and sunny, which was incongruous, given the despair welling in his heart. He was still convinced that he was doomed to almost certain failure.

But thanks to Diana, there was a sliver of hope.

He needed to speak with her. His sister, Anne, and his brother-in-law, Michael, were hosting a gathering tomorrow at their villa a few miles outside of town. Diana and her family were bound to have received an invitation.

He would need to find a way to have a private word with Diana. As he mounted his horse, he mused that getting her alone would probably prove just as difficult a task as stealing the letter from Carl Frederick.

CHAPTER 16

$\mathcal{D}$iana peered out the carriage window as they approached Lord and Lady Morsley's villa. It was a lovely property an hour's drive north of London. Since their wedding four years ago, Lady Morsley had given birth to two black-haired, blue-eyed boys named Michael and Colin. Knowing that his wife cherished the work she did for the Ladies' Society for the Relief of the Destitute, the charitable society she had founded, Lord Morsley had purchased this property so that she could be within easy reach of London without exposing their children to the sooty air and infectious maladies that plagued the capital. Although it did not compare to their family seat, Ravenswell, they had about four acres that included a small garden, a manicured sweep of lawn, and a little copse of trees at the top of the rise that provided a pleasant view from the house.

The earl and countess were planning a picnic along with some friendly sporting competitions. That most likely meant lawn bowls and shuttlecock, but Diana had brought her sword and fencing costume, just in case.

Lady Morsley greeted them at the door and informed

them that everyone was gathering in the back garden. Diana saw that many of the guests had already arrived. Aunt Griselda had brought along a trio of her brown and white speckled pointers, and Michael and Colin came toddling up to pet the dogs. Aunt Griselda produced a ball from her pocket, and the boys, including Alaric, ran off toward the lawn.

Ceci looped her arm through that of Lady Thetford, and they began a leisurely stroll through the garden. Marcus went to join his friend, Lord Fauconbridge.

Diana was looking around for Izzie and Lucy when someone stole up next to her.

She smiled when she saw it was Harrington. "Lieutenant Astley, you startled me."

He grinned. "Sneaky fellows, us Riflemen." He dropped his voice low. "I need to speak with you."

"Oh?" She arched an eyebrow. "More political machinations?"

He froze. His face looked slightly green, and Diana didn't think it was due to the sunlight reflecting off his officer's jacket.

She seized his forearm. "What's wrong?" He didn't answer right away, so she continued, "Has William Windham given you another assignment?"

"He has." He somehow managed to infuse his chuckle with despair. "I thought the last one was just about impossible, but this one…" He trailed off, squeezing his eyes closed.

"What is it?" she whispered, curiosity ablaze.

He cringed. "Do you by any chance speak Swedish?"

Now her interest was truly piqued. "I do. Why do you—"

"Lieutenant Astley. Good afternoon."

Diana glanced up to see Marcus hovering like a great

golden mother hen. She cast him a warning look while Harrington returned a polite greeting.

Marcus gave her an almost imperceptible nod. "Lovely day for a picnic," he said in a clipped voice.

"It is, indeed," Harrington agreed.

An awkward silence ensued. Diana appreciated that Marcus was trying to be civil. But she could not help but wish he would be civil from a distance. She and Harrington were merely talking, and they were doing so in broad daylight, surrounded by twenty people. Even the notorious sticklers who served as patronesses at Almack's could find no fault.

Marcus cleared his throat. "I did not mean to interrupt. Please, continue your conversation. What were you discussing?"

"Politics," Diana supplied.

Marcus nodded tightly. "Excellent. As you know, I am a member of the House of Lords, so it is a subject of interest to me as well."

Diana bit back a groan. Marcus obviously did not plan on going away anytime soon. "Lieutenant Astley was recently rallying votes in support of the Pensions to Soldiers Act."

"I was, indeed," Harrington said. "Your sister was kind enough to advise me regarding my strategy."

Marcus glanced back and forth between them, his lips turning into a slight frown. "But that vote has already taken place. Surely the lieutenant is no longer in need of your advice."

Diana hesitated a beat too long. "True."

Marcus eyed Harrington suspiciously. "Yet you were discussing it again?"

Harrington cleared his throat. "Not precisely."

Marcus's eye twitched. "Then what, may I ask, was the topic of conversation?"

Harrington tugged at the stock around his neck. "I am not at liberty to say."

"Not at liberty to say?" Marcus snapped. "I should like to know what you mean by that."

"Marcus!" Diana switched to German. "We discussed this. You promised you would give him a chance."

Marcus answered in the same language. "How am I supposed to give him a chance when his behavior is so obviously suspect?"

"There is nothing suspect about his behavior," Diana countered. "We were merely talking!"

Marcus remained unmoved. "A likely story!"

The words must have sounded harsher in German than they truly were, because Harrington stepped between them, his brow creased. "Don't talk to her that way."

Marcus rounded on him, scowling. "Oh, that's rich, coming from you."

Harrington bristled. "What are you suggesting?"

Marcus took a step forward. "That you are in no position to criticize the propriety of *my* behavior!"

Harrington's hands clenched into fists. Diana could almost feel the frustration rolling off him in waves. "It's not like that. I didn't say anything untoward."

Marcus made a sweeping gesture with one hand. "Then what, exactly, were you discussing?"

"I cannot tell you," Harrington bit out. "I promised to keep the matter in confidence."

Marcus's voice started to rise. "Any topic that is appropriate for my sister's ears you can have no qualms in speaking of before her brother."

Now, Harrington looked annoyed. "Well, I can't! Now, if you would be so kind as to sod off for five bloody minutes—"

"This is your notion of appropriate language to use in front of a lady?" Marcus snapped.

Diana rolled her eyes. "Really, Marcus, you used that very word at breakfast this morning. And Aunt Griselda says the equivalent every time she opens her mouth. I'm hardly going to fall into a swoon."

Marcus's nose curled. "That is not the point. The point is—"

He was interrupted by a feminine clearing of the throat. Lady Morsley stood before them, flanked by Izzie, Lucy, and Izzie's husband, Thorpe. She smiled anxiously, clearly eager to diffuse the tension. "I believe everyone has arrived. Shall we play a few games before lunch?"

"That's a fine idea, Anne," Harrington said. He glanced at Marcus, his brown eyes sparking. "In fact, why don't we lay some odds on the outcome?"

Marcus met his glower. "What are you suggesting?"

"A tournament," Harrington proclaimed. "The winner shall receive a boon from one of the other participants."

Marcus stepped forward so they were standing mere inches apart. "And what *boon* did you have in mind?"

Harrington didn't flinch. "Your sister."

Other than Lucy's gasp, there wasn't a whisper of sound as everyone in the party stared raptly at the two men.

Diana felt a flush rising to her cheeks as several pairs of eyes shifted to her. It wasn't really a declaration, but it certainly sounded like one.

She lifted her chin. Let them stare. And let them conclude that she and Harrington were courting. If she had her way, they soon would be.

Harrington blinked, seeming to realize the extreme impropriety of what he had just said. "That is… I should very much like to have the pleasure of Lady Diana's company during the picnic." He turned to face her, sketching an elegant bow.

Marcus smirked, practically radiating confidence. "Fine. But you'll have to get through me. At swords."

"Targets," Harrington countered, miming the shooting of a gun with his hand.

Just like that, they were nose-to-nose and snarling once more. "Swords!" Marcus spat.

"Targets!"

"Swords!"

"Targets!"

"My gracious!" Lucy laughed awkwardly. "Perhaps we should play shuttlecock instead."

"No!" both men snapped in unison.

Lucy winced, and Thorpe cast a reproachful look at Harrington and Marcus. "I should be glad to play shuttlecock with you, Lady Lucy."

Harrington shot his sister an apologetic look. Lucy laughed, waving it off. "Thank you, Thorpe. Let's have a game after luncheon. After all, we don't want to miss the show."

"Swords it is," Marcus said, attempting to bowl over everyone, as usual.

"We'll draw straws," Harrington countered.

Marcus's lip curled, and Diana knew her brother well enough to know that he was really, truly angry. But he snapped, "Fine!" and stalked off.

Lord Fauconbridge cut two blades of grass. He held them out for Harrington and Marcus to inspect, then turned his back, arranging them in his cupped hands. "Trevissick will draw. Close your eyes."

Marcus did so, fumbling until he managed to grasp one of the ends sticking up from Fauconbridge's fist. He pulled it out, revealing the long straw.

Her brother's smile as he turned to Harrington was

vindictive. "Fetch yourself a mask, Astley. You're going to need it."

CHAPTER 17

*F*encing. It would be bloody, fucking, *fencing.*

Not that Harrington was terrible with a sword. He was an officer in the 95th Rifles, thank you very much. He carried a sabre into battle and drilled with it regularly.

But Trevissick was on an entirely different level. He'd been fencing obsessively ever since he was a small boy, because—as Harrington and the rest of the world had learned when the duke was forced to testify at a trial a few years back—his father was a violent piece of shit who used to beat his mother. Trevissick had formed the idea that he could protect her in spite of being all of nine years old if he could gain enough skill with a blade.

Harrington knew he'd already lost. The real battle had taken place when they'd drawn straws. Had it come to targets, he would have won. Easily. He'd been shooting about as obsessively as Trevissick had been fencing, and for about as long.

But no. It had to be *fencing.*

The servants brought out a rack of swords, some canvas

jackets, and mesh masks. As Harrington shrugged into a jacket, his friend, Henry, came over. Which was perfect, because just what Harrington needed—for someone to make a crack about how he *clearly* wasn't interested in Diana, just as he'd said over lunch the other day.

He should have given his friend more credit. "I've volunteered to fence so we'll have four for the tournament," Henry said, taking off his own coat. "We've agreed to three rounds, unless someone draws ahead by ten touches, in which case, the bout will end. I drew Fauconbridge in the first round, which leaves you to take on Trevissick." He reached for one of the padded jackets. His eyes were sympathetic as he added, "I very much doubt I'll get past your brother, but if I do, I'll do my best to give Trevissick what for."

Harrington squeezed his shoulder. "Thanks, Henry."

Surely enough, Edward, who was a damn good fencer by virtue of the fact that he was one of Trevissick's regular sparring partners, eliminated Henry with ease. That brought up the most anticipated match of the day.

The duke didn't bother donning one of the mesh fencing masks, which was both insulting and an accurate assessment of their respective skill levels. Harrington put one on because he wasn't a complete idiot. He glanced around as they took up their positions, but he couldn't find Diana in the crowd. It stung that she hadn't bothered to stay and cheer for him, but, upon further reflection, maybe it was for the best that she wasn't going to witness his annihilation at the hands of her brother.

The bout went every bit as badly as Harrington had anticipated. He felt the button on the tip of Trevissick's sword spearing him in the chest before he even had a chance to blink. He improved a bit after that and managed to prevent the duke from scoring the next touch for all of fifteen seconds. But he didn't score any touches himself, and the bout ended ingloriously near the beginning of the second round when the score reached ten to zero.

His smile was tight as he removed his mask, but he offered his hand to the duke, trying at least to be a good sport. Trevissick's smirk was triumphant.

Harrington excused himself and stalked over to Edward, who was about to don his mesh facemask. "Can you beat him?" he asked without preamble.

Edward's expression was pained. "Probably not. I've never done so before."

"Try," Harrington said tightly.

Edward squeezed his shoulder. "I'll do my best."

Trevissick again did not feel the need to don a facemask. Edward did a damn sight better than Harrington had, but that only meant that the final score was ten to two instead of ten to zero. After shaking hands, he jogged over to Harrington, wiping sweat from his brow. "I'm sorry, brother. I tried."

Harrington thumped him on the back. "I know you did. Thank you."

Trevissick's face glowed with triumph. "It seems that I have won a boon from one of my competitors. Let's see, from whom shall I claim it?" He tapped his chin as if considering the matter seriously. "Ah, yes—Lieutenant Astley."

God, but this tasted like vinegar. But Harrington inclined his head. "What would you have from me, Trevissick?"

The duke's eyes gleamed. "For you to never come near my sister, ever ag—"

"Not so fast, Marcus."

The words had not been spoken loudly, but they held an unmistakable air of confidence. Every head swiveled toward the house.

Diana strode across the lawn. She had changed into a

snow-white fencing costume, which was similar to a man's ensemble—a padded jacket and slim white trousers—with the addition of a loose skirt that fell midway down her shins to allow for both movement and modesty.

She slashed her sword through the air in a jaunty salute. "You have one more challenger."

CHAPTER 18

Diana regarded her brother in the dappled sunlight. She had wondered how he would react to her flagrant attempt to subvert his will.

He looked more annoyed than angry. But he also looked confident. And why shouldn't he? They were evenly matched.

But he wouldn't win this time. Diana was determined.

And she had a *plan*.

"Three rounds," Marcus said crisply. "The bout will end if one of us goes up by ten touches."

"That won't happen," Diana said coolly.

Her brother's lips twisted into a reluctant smile. "No. Finally, some proper competition."

Marcus stalked over to the rack of swords and picked up a mask. Diana took one as well and pulled it on. She performed a few lunges to warm up.

They took up their positions and saluted one another. Marcus went into a classic French guard, with his sword pointing toward Diana's heart and his left arm raised behind him.

Diana, on the other hand, adopted a German guard known as the Ox. It was a stance seldom taught in the British fencing schools, with her wrist high, at the level of her forehead, and her sword angled downward. Behind his mask, she saw Marcus's eyes narrow, and she knew he was wondering what she was about.

He soon found out. During her childhood on the moors of Yorkshire with Aunt Griselda, Diana had had nothing but time. Time to fence, time to think, and time to read every book in their library three times over. This included a half-dozen fencing manuals written in Italian, French, and German.

One of those German books described a duel. The victor, it said, fought in a position of very high *prime*, just like the one she had assumed. He focused not on the attack, but on an endless series of flipping cuts and parries, delivered from the wrist. It was an exhausting technique, "as much a trial of endurance as of skill," as the book had put it, and the slightest lapse of concentration would be her downfall.

But Diana knew that it put her at an advantage. She had been born missing her right hand, meaning that she had to do everything, absolutely everything, with her left.

That meant that her left side was *strong*. It had to be.

And she was risking everything on the conviction that she had the strength in her sword arm to outlast her brother.

It took Marcus only a moment to notice what she was doing. "Attack, damn it!" he growled in German.

Diana did no such thing. She focused all her attention on flicking his blade to the side, flicking it *hard*, the better to wear him down, again and again. She was biding her time, waiting for him to falter.

And falter he did. After a few minutes, she saw it. The slightest wobble in his sword point. An uncharacteristic gracelessness to his movement.

Without warning, she slashed as hard as she could, knocking his sword to the side, and lunged. Her blade bent as the button buried itself in her brother's padded coat.

The onlookers burst into cheers. Marcus ripped his mask off, scowling, a sheen of sweat on his forehead. "That's only the first round. We've two more to go."

Diana inclined her head. She had not expected this to be easy.

In the second round, her attention faltered, only for a fraction of a second, but that was all the opening Marcus needed to execute a *balestra*, skipping into a lunge with perfect form and skewering her in the left breast.

They retreated a few paces, both breathing hard. Anticipation was thick in the air because whoever scored the next touch would be the winner.

After a moment, they resumed their stances, and then, it began. Diana tried to focus on Marcus's sword, to block out the cries of encouragement from her friends. It was probably for the best that only she and Marcus understood German, because the things Aunt Griselda was shouting were not considered suitable for mixed company.

He almost got through on a couple of occasions, and she found herself back on her heels, barely managing to deflect his blade. But she recovered, reset her stance, and continued her relentless series of parries.

Cracks started to form in her brother's technique. His wrist action, always crisp and impeccable, began to slow. Diana wasn't doing much better, truth be told. Her forearm was aflame, and she could feel her grip on her sword starting to fail.

But the one thing that never wavered was her determination. She would *not* give up, would never quit, no matter how much it hurt, or if she couldn't bend her wrist for the next week. As much as she wanted to win an interlude with Harrington, this was about more than that. This was her way of showing her brother that he couldn't push her around, couldn't dictate the terms by which she would live her life.

So, she fought on through the pain.

And when her brother made an uncharacteristically graceless feint, she attacked. She dropped into a *passata-sotto*, lunging so low to the ground that she had to rest the tip of her right arm on the grass for balance. With the last of her strength, she thrust her sword up toward his exposed stomach. She couldn't make out much of Marcus's face through his mask, but she registered the shock in his posture as the tip of her blade struck home.

Raucous cheers surrounded her. Izzie and Lucy reached her before she could rise, almost bowling her over in their exuberance. They helped her up and she peeled off her mask. Her face was coated in sweat, and she could feel frizzy curls breaking out at her temples.

She held her breath as Marcus removed his mask, wondering how he would react to his public defeat. Would his face show rage? The icy disdain he usually reserved for others? Or what was perhaps worse, disappointment?

But when he pulled his mask off, she found his lips were twisted wryly, his expression one of pride. "That was *brilliant*, Diana. You have become such an outstanding fencer." He crossed to her in three strides, laying a hand on her shoulder. "I'm *so proud* of you."

Her smile was warm, at least, by Latimer family standards. "Thank you, Marcus."

There was a smattering of applause. Once it died down, Diana lifted her chin. "And now, I believe I am owed a boon." She turned her head, smiling as she found Harrington in the crowd. "Lieutenant Astley. Might I have the pleasure of your company during the picnic luncheon?"

Beside her, Marcus rolled his eyes. Diana ignored him. She couldn't seem to look at anything but Harrington's beaming face.

He placed a hand over his heart as he sketched an elegant bow. "I should be delighted."

CHAPTER 19

Harrington all but skipped as he rushed around, conferring with Anne's servants and making arrangements for his interlude with Diana. Soon, a half dozen footmen were carrying the items he requested—a blanket, pillows, and an assortment of delicacies—up the slight hill at the edge of the lawn. The location would be perfect—within sight of the party so that no one could complain that any improprieties were taking place but removed enough for a private conversation.

Finally, Harrington begged the final item he needed from his mother. Tucking it beneath his coat, he strode over to Diana, who was downing a glass of lemonade in thirsty gulps.

He bowed deeply and offered his arm. "My lady?"

She looped her arm through his but didn't look at him. As they made their way up the hill, she dabbed her temple with a handkerchief. "I probably look a fright."

"You've never looked more beautiful. Not even on the night of your debut, when I thought you were the most gorgeous sight I'd ever beheld."

This wasn't empty flattery, but the truth. Although he couldn't believe he'd said it out loud. He normally tried to conceal the extent to which he yearned for Diana.

But really, how could he hold it in? She'd been bloody magnificent. He'd always heard how talented she was at fencing, but he'd never had the chance to see her in action before today. She had reminded him of a falcon in flight—swift, light, and agile. And, when the time came to strike, deadly.

Throw in the notion that the thing she was fighting so fiercely to possess was *him*, and it was no wonder he was done for. Watching her, he had been overcome by the fantasy that *he* was the one she was fencing against. She would drive him back, disarm him, and pin him against a wall. Then, she would order him to pleasure her. He had all but worked himself into a lather picturing her holding her sword at his throat as he drew up her skirts and fell to his knees between her trembling thighs…

Ahem. This was not the train of thought he ought to pursue, leastwise, not unless he wanted to give Diana a real eyeful should her gaze stray to the placket of his trousers.

But the point was, Diana Latimer was completely, utterly breathtaking. What chance did a poor sod like him stand?

She peered at him out of the corner of her eye, looking startled by his compliment, but not displeased. "Is that so?"

"It is," Harrington said solemnly.

She regarded him, the corner of her mouth twitching upward. "You, Lieutenant Astley, are full of surprises."

They had reached the picnic blanket. Diana tried to sit primly with her legs curled to her side, but Harrington would have none of it. He arranged the pillows behind her and helped her to lounge back against them. He offered her wine, but she indicated that she would prefer lemonade, as she was still thirsty from the fencing. He also made sure he had an assortment of fruits and cheeses readily at hand.

Then, he pulled the item he had borrowed from his mother—a frilly, pink fan—from beneath his jacket, opened it with a flourish, and began fanning her.

She laughed. "Harrington! What are you doing?"

"You won me. I'm your war prize." Still fanning her, he plucked a grape from the tray and popped it in her mouth. "Isn't this what I'm supposed to do?"

She finished chewing the grape before answering. "I wouldn't know. I've never had a war prize before."

"You'll just have to take my word for it, then." He waggled his eyebrows. "I would have you rest your head on my lap if I didn't know that your brother would come flying up the hill to disembowel me."

She peered toward the house. "He'll probably come flying up the hill to disembowel you, regardless."

"Hmm." Harrington followed the direction of her gaze. Surely enough, Trevissick's expression was murderous.

Turning back to Diana, he brushed a curl off her damp brow. "Thank goodness I have you to protect me."

He fed her a piece of cheese on a water biscuit. She laughed, brushing crumbs off her chin, and sat up. "I believe there was something you wanted to discuss with me."

"Oh, there is. It's actually rather urgent. But now that we're here, I can't seem to muster the energy to do anything but flirt with you shamelessly."

Her pale eyes were bright as she leaned forward, placing her hand on the cuff of his jacket. "Believe me, I am enjoying your shameless flirtation."

Harrington's heart did this burbly thing inside his chest. Because this was the first time he had been certain that Diana wasn't just being droll or sarcastic but was specifically *flirting*. And she was doing it with *him*!

It was her turn to pick up a grape and pop it in *his* mouth. Her thumb grazed his lower lip, which really took the sting off the next word she said. "But."

He frowned. "But?" he asked around a mouthful of grape.

Her smile was fond. "I find you have piqued my interest to such a degree, I must order my war prize to explain why you asked if I speak Swedish."

He gave the most elegant bow he could manage while seated on a blanket. "My lady's wish is my command." He paused, rubbing the back of his head, unsure where to begin. "Would you believe I've been asked to spy on the King of Sweden?"

He explained everything, starting with the fact that the Royal Mail opened important-looking letters. Which he had been asked to keep a secret, but really, what was he supposed to do? "Then, Windham mentioned that the reason the letter had slipped through was because it had been sealed with an old signet ring, from the House of—"

"Mecklenburg," Diana guessed in unison with him.

"Precisely. That's what made me think of you. I mean, how on earth am I supposed to find this letter? I don't even know what the crest of the House of Mecklenburg looks like." He cursed beneath his breath. "I should have asked Windham while I had the chance."

"There have been several variations over the years, but it will be some combination of a black bull and a gold griffin." She tapped her chin, her expression thoughtful. "It's been several hundred years since the House of Mecklenburg had any claim to the Swedish throne. But I can confirm that over the years, there have been a number of marriages amongst the royal houses in that part of the world. That's the reason Aunt Griselda speaks Swedish and was able to pass it on to me."

Harrington laughed, suddenly nervous. "So, what you're saying is, you're related to the King of Sweden?"

She shrugged. "Probably. Distantly, mind you. I know Aunt Griselda is first cousin to the King of Denmark. I believe that's my closest brush with royalty."

Oh, God. What was he thinking? He'd always known Diana was a thousand miles above him, as unattainable as a star in the sky. But the truth was somehow even worse. She wasn't just a princess in his imaginings; she was literally descended from royalty!

What was he doing, fanning her, popping grapes in her mouth, and allowing himself to dream?

It was hopeless. Completely, utterly, hopeless.

Diana nudged him with her shoulder. "What?"

"S-sorry," he spluttered. "Just, er. Thinking about the challenge ahead."

"Of course. So, what do you want me to do? Teach you a little Swedish?"

"That would be a good start," Harrington said in a choked voice.

They had a servant bring out a portable writing desk. Diana sketched a few likely crests that might have been used on the letter, then wrote out a list of words that might indicate a royal letter—king, uncle, nephew, that sort of thing.

After a half hour, Harrington threw down his pencil. "It's no use. I'll never even find the bloody thing."

Ignoring his blasphemous language, she placed her hand on his forearm, which he enjoyed, even as he reminded himself that nothing would ever come of it. "You're picking it up very quickly. But I agree, it's unlikely that you can gain any real fluency in a few scant days."

He rubbed his eyes with the heels of his hands. "God, I

wish there was a way to take you with me. I feel like maybe, just *maybe,* we could find it together."

She made a sympathetic sound. "I wish so, too. But, of course, an unmarried lady could never accompany you to… to…"

She trailed off. Suddenly, her eyes went wide and her mouth fell open. Harrington watched as her spine straightened, one vertebra at a time.

When she spoke, her voice was quiet, yet completely resolute. "There's only one solution." She turned to face him, her expression inscrutable. "We'll have to marry."

CHAPTER 20

$\mathcal{D}$eep down, Diana knew that suggesting that she and Harrington marry was a terrible idea.

But she wasn't about to let such a trifling concern stop her.

She might not know this man nearly well enough to be contemplating holy matrimony. But she did know this much about him—that he didn't like her because she was the sister of a duke, or a distant cousin to kings. He had not requested the pleasure of her company because of her enormous dowry, nor was he in awe of the perfectly coifed, bejeweled girl who twirled through the ballrooms of London. In fact, all those things that served as enticements to most men, he seemed to regard as impediments to a potential union. Just look at how he had clammed up when she mentioned the most tangential relation to the King of Denmark!

No, Harrington liked her when she was glistening not with diamonds, but with sweat. Instead of fleeing in horror when she performed the horrifyingly unladylike act of entering a fencing tournament—and worse, besting all the men—he had proclaimed that he had never found her more attractive. And he didn't mind that she was clever and sharp-tongued; much to the contrary, he admired it! He was *desirous of her opinion!*

And the reason all of that mattered was because that was the real Diana. She was so sick of the London Season and all of its fussy entertainments. Of it taking two hours to get dressed every night. Of being poked and prodded and polished every time she wanted to leave the house until she resembled a doll, rather than a living, breathing woman.

But if Harrington liked her with a sword in her hand, she would wager he'd like her just as much with a gun, traipsing across the moors, a pack of Aunt Griselda's pointers at her heels, and her hem coated in six inches of mud. She could, in fact, picture him there with her! He loved to shoot, after all.

And that wasn't all—she could imagine waking up beside this man and eating breakfast together off a tray in bed, their heads bent together over the morning papers, plotting his next political move.

If he wanted to continue his career in the army, she could even go with him. Many officers' wives followed the drum, after all.

In conclusion, she was *almost certain* that Harrington was the man she wanted to marry.

She also knew that he would never ask her. The notion that he wasn't good enough for her had somehow become fixed in his mind, making him blind to the possibility that he was what she wanted.

She could not convince him with words. Her only recourse was to show him how good they could be together. What she needed was a convenient excuse for the two of them to marry.

And she wasn't going to get a better excuse than this one.

She regarded Harrington steadily. As she had expected, he was gaping at her as if she had suggested he resign his commission in the army, purchase a trained monkey, and take up a career in street performance. He blinked at her once… twice… three times, then shook his head. "I think I must've misheard."

"We'll have to marry," she said again. "It's the only way I can attend the house party with you—as husband and wife."

"But marriage…" He gave a nervous laugh. "Isn't that a bit… serious?"

She made her face very solemn. "It's for king and country."

"But you don't want to marry me. I'm just"—he gestured to his torso—"cannon fodder."

Diana seized his hand. "Don't even joke about that," she said, her voice soft but fervent. "You are so important to so many people."

It felt nice to be holding his hand. He seemed to like it, too, because he threaded his fingers through hers. "To my family, I suppose."

"Of a certainty. But they aren't the only ones."

"My soldiers," Harrington said, his voice gruff. "The men of the 95th Rifles."

Diana leaned forward. "And?"

"And the ones I helped get pensions. By passing that act."

"To be sure." She stroked her thumb over the back of his hand. "But there's someone else."

His eyes looked hesitant, as if he were terrified to even speak the words. "Are you saying I'm important to you?"

Her pale blue eyes were steady on his. "Yes, Harrington. That's exactly what I'm saying."

She seized a fistful of his coat just as his hand came up to trace the outline of her jaw. And her face tipped up as his lips strained toward hers, and—

"What the *hell* are you doing?"

Harrington blinked, looking too dazed to pull back right

away. Marcus grabbed him by the collar and yanked him to his feet. He staggered before managing to gain his balance, his eyes never leaving Diana.

Ah, well. They were off to a bad start, but it was never going to be easy convincing Marcus. She would just have to brazen it out. "You may be the first to congratulate us, brother. Lieutenant Astley and I are to marry."

She had expected Marcus to explode. But instead, he looked… baffled. "I think I must have misheard."

"That's what I said!" Harrington exclaimed.

Marcus squinted at Harrington. "What are you talking about? You're the one who proposed!"

Harrington held his hands up, palms out. "Not me. I would never presume."

"Then…" Marcus's gaze swung from Harrington to Diana. "Does that mean *you* did the asking?"

A fraught silence descended over the picnic blanket. Diana lifted her chin. "It would be more accurate to say that I informed him."

Marcus's expression turned smug because those were the precise words he had once used in admitting that he had *informed* Ceci they were going to marry, rather than asking her. This degree of high-handedness was clearly an intrinsic failing particular to the Latimer siblings. She had never let him live it down, and Diana knew he would return the favor.

But Marcus had bigger fish to fry at the moment.

"And why, dear sister, did you *inform* Lieutenant Astley that the two of you were going to wed?"

"Look, Trevissick." Harrington dropped his voice low, eying the stream of guests making their way up the hill. "It's not what you think. I have to ask you to keep this in the strictest confidence."

He explained to her brother in hushed whispers about the

house party and his assignment to find the letter from King Gustav.

Marcus's scowl deepened. "Do you mean to tell me that you two don't want to get married at all? That this is nothing more than a ruse to retrieve this letter?"

"Precisely!" Harrington cried in the same breath Diana said, "I wouldn't say that."

Harrington's head jerked around. "*What?*"

Marcus was already speaking, so she merely shrugged.

"That is the most idiotic scheme I have ever heard!" he snapped. "I forbid you two to marry for such ridiculous—"

"Who's getting married?" Lucy asked brightly.

Marcus stiffened as he realized that the entirety of the party had trooped up the hill to get a better view of the unfolding scene. "No one!"

"Harrington and I," Diana said casually, looping her arm through his.

"Oh!" Lucy clapped her hands, bouncing on her toes. "This is the *best* news! We're going to be *sisters!*" She ran over and enveloped Diana in a hug.

"No!" Marcus snapped. "No wedding. Absolutely not!"

Aunt Griselda crossed her arms. "Who are you to tell Diana who she can or cannot marry?"

Marcus rounded on her. "Surely you don't think Diana should marry him?"

"Have you seen him with a gun? He is a very good shot." Aunt Griselda flicked her hand toward Harrington. "If she is bound and determined to marry a man, I don't think she could do much better."

Diana's lip twitched. As far as Aunt Griselda was concerned, this was the highest possible praise.

"Well," Marcus snarled, "your opinion is not relevant, nor is Diana's. She is not yet twenty-five and therefore cannot marry without the permission of her legal guardian."

Diana could see the triumph written on his handsome face.

But Aunt Griselda only laughed. "There is something you seem to have forgotten, nephew. *You* are not Diana's legal guardian." Her eyes were every bit as flinty as Marcus's. "*I* am."

CHAPTER 21

Ten minutes later, Diana had her ear pressed to the door of Lord and Lady Morsley's study. Harrington hovered just above her.

On the other side, Marcus and Aunt Griselda were arguing in German.

It turned out that years ago, when Marcus managed to wrest her from their father's grip, Aunt Griselda had been appointed her legal guardian as Marcus had been just thirteen years old.

Had her overbearing brother recalled this fact, he would have had it changed years ago. But it had slipped his mind, and here they were.

"What are they saying?" Harrington whispered.

Diana listened for a beat. "He explained that you are being sent on a secret mission, and that it is our true motivation to marry." *Not really.* But she would ignore that for now. Harrington was skittish enough about their proposed arrangement as it was. She pressed her ear to the door. "She is not deterred."

Her brother began shouting, and Diana pulled back, wincing. "He says, er…"

"I understood that word," Harrington said brightly. He made a faux scandalized face as Marcus uttered an impressive string of profanity. "And most of that, too. While I was in Hanover, I had some of the officers of the King's German Legion teach me a little German."

Diana pursed her lips. "And the first words they taught you were curses and oaths?"

He shrugged, his expression one of faux innocence. "They say you should start with your most frequently used vocabulary. I've actually been studying French for the past three years, ever since I joined the army. And I started learning Spanish last Christmas." He leaned forward, eyes sparkling. "All countries I hope to invade someday."

Diana couldn't help but grin. This was another reason she wanted to marry Harrington—he could make her laugh even in the tensest situation. "Let's hear your French, then."

He swept her with a lascivious look. "*Seriez-vous, par hasard, apparenté à Giuseppe Bussandri, le chef de la rébellion dans la région italienne de Piacenza? Parce que vous êtes à l'origine d'un soulèvement au sud.*"

Diana elbowed him in the ribs, but she was laughing. "Your French is both excellent and completely atrocious."

He bowed. "Thank you. That was precisely my aim."

Raised voices came once more from behind the door. "Fine!" Marcus snapped. "But mark my words, I will never forgive you if Diana comes to grief as a result of this folly!"

Hearing the thump of his boots against the carpet, she grabbed Harrington's arm. "Hurry! He's coming!"

They scurried down the corridor. As soon as they came to a door, Diana yanked it open, and they slipped inside.

It proved to be some kind of closet, apparently used by the household staff. Some rags hung from a pegboard on the wall, and a mop and broom leaned against the corner. The room was dominated by a large wooden crate, leaving no room for them to stand.

Harrington climbed atop the crate, seizing Diana by the waist. Without thinking, she scrambled into his lap, then pulled the door closed behind her.

She held her breath as the door to the study opened. The muffled sounds of Marcus's boots against the carpet grew louder, but she could scarcely hear them over the pounding of her own heart. Neither of them moved as her brother passed by the door and proceeded down the corridor.

The danger having passed, Diana slowly became aware of her position. She was still sitting on Harrington's lap. Only a bare sliver of light entered the cramped room from a slit at the bottom of the door, but the darkness made her exquisitely conscious of everything she could feel. His hands, big and warm about her waist. His breath, sweet and tart from the lemonade they'd shared earlier, stirring the hair at her temple. His thighs, hard as iron, beneath her legs. And... oh, gracious... his thighs weren't the only thing that had hardened. She could feel a telltale bulge pressing against the outside of her thigh. She knew precisely what *that* was, ironically, from perusing Harrington's own book of erotic prints.

Her heart was tripping over itself, and her limbs felt heavy. Some mad impulse had her reaching for his face. She felt a jolt go through her as her curious fingers found the stubble of his jaw. It was so different from her own delicate skin, rough and smooth at the same time. It was fascinating. *Masculine.*

"Diana," he breathed.

In the dark, she could not have said if she was the one to lean forward, or if it was him. Most probably it was both. But suddenly, they were kissing.

Diana had never kissed a man before. Frankly, she had never met a man she wanted to kiss. This was not to say that any number of fortune-hunting fools had not attempted to compromise her. But the few who were not deterred by her icy glare quickly learned that she was not the sort of girl to flutter and fret and fly into a panic. No, she was the sort of girl to calmly stab a man in the thigh with her diamond-encrusted hairpin if he grew too free with his hands.

But she had no desire to make Harrington stop. His lips were surprisingly soft, a dizzying contrast with the hard lines of his jaw. Even this gentle contact had her pulse tripping over itself and her body trembling.

Then, he slid his hands up her spine and pressed her body against his chest. He groaned at the contact, and she was glad to know she wasn't the only one who was so affected. His hands continued their leisurely journey north, then his fingers threaded into her hair.

Gently, he tilted her head, positioning her where he wanted her. Then, his tongue traced the seam of her lips, and she opened for him on a gasp.

So, *this* was what the fuss was all about, this dizzying, delicious pleasure. Diana had no idea what she was doing, but it felt natural to tangle her tongue with his, so she did. Harrington responded with a groan, so she took it she wasn't doing too badly.

It wasn't merely the pleasure of his mouth on hers. His hands, so big and strong, were touching her with an intoxicating combination of eagerness and reverence, as if he had dreamed of this moment for years and could not believe his dream was actually coming true. He traced her jawline and the column of her neck, then took a moment to appreciate the sweep of her collarbone. His fingertips inched lower but then paused, as if he were unsure if he should continue.

Diana answered his unspoken question, stretching up and pressing her breast into his palm. He moaned as if in agony and brought his other hand up so he could cradle both of her breasts. Her bosom was not what you would call ample but based on the thundering of his pulse beneath her fingertips, he did not seem displeased by what he had found.

He wasn't the only one who was curious. Up until this point, Diana had been clinging to his neck, but she allowed her left hand to drift across the width of his shoulders. Gracious—Harrington had always tended to be more lean than hulking. But there wasn't an ounce of fat on him, and she could feel well-defined muscles even through the thick wool of his coat.

She traced her fingertips down his chest and felt his stomach turn to iron. She couldn't deny that she was exquisitely curious about the bulge pressing insistently against her thigh.

Harrington tore his mouth from hers, his breath coming in pants. "Diana," he gasped. "*Please.*"

She inched her hand lower, and lower still, until her fingers were just on the edge of that fascinating bulge. She summoned her courage, and—

Light flooded the closet as someone wrenched the door open. "What the *hell* are you two doing?" Marcus snapped, grabbing Diana by the arm and pulling her off Harrington's lap and out into the corridor.

She yanked her arm free. "Nothing you and Ceci didn't do prior to your wedding, I daresay."

Marcus opened his mouth to argue, then seemed to recall that he didn't have a leg to stand on. Diana should know—her bedroom was just down the hall from Marcus's, and he and Ceci had not been particularly quiet about it.

Having nothing he could say in his defense, he directed his glower toward Harrington. "Stand up."

Harrington cast a significant look down at his own lap. "I'd recommend giving it a minute or two. Some things a man doesn't wish to see from the fellow who's about to marry his sister."

Marcus ran a hand across his face. "This is one of the worst days of my life. *Fine*. Meet me in Lord Morsley's study in three minutes." He turned his attention on Diana. "You are coming with me."

Diana expected a lecture. But Marcus was silent as he marched her to a parlor at the front of the house and left her in the care of Lady Cheltenham and the rest of the Astley clan. At least *they* were excited about her impending wedding.

CHAPTER 22

There was nothing to cool a man's ardor like Marcus Latimer levelling a speaking glare your way, especially when the message contained within said glare was, *I am going to disembowel you with a rusty blade.* And so, Harrington was ready and waiting for the duke when he returned to the study.

Trevissick didn't waste time with pleasantries. "Aunt Griselda is correct. She is Diana's legal guardian, and she has made it clear that she will not refuse her permission. I therefore cannot stop the two of you from marrying."

Harrington's head swam. He couldn't believe any of this was happening. Kissing her in that closet had felt like a fever dream. Surely, he must have imagined the eagerness with which she'd kissed him back, the greedy touch of her hand on his body, the way she had pressed her breast into his hand.

And the notion that *he* was going to marry *Diana Latimer* seemed so obviously impossible that he wondered if someone had slipped something nefarious into the lemonade. He felt unbearably happy and as if he might cast his accounts, simultaneously and in equal measures.

The duke was still speaking. "We have never got along."

"Which is my fault," Harrington said quickly. "And I would like to apologize. I was ghastly."

Trevissick responded by rolling his eyes. "Rest assured, even had you not pulled a litany of childish pranks, I would not have liked you, regardless."

That brought Harrington up rather short, but really, how could he argue? What was there to like? Edward was the clever one, the responsible one, the one who never let his family down. Harrington, on the other hand, was nothing but a wastrel. A waste of good linen, that was him. Good for nothing but cannon fodder.

Diana's words echoed in his head. *Don't even joke about that.* He knew she was the clever one, but he wasn't sure she had the right of it there. Experience had taught him that it was always best to make the joke yourself, before someone else got the chance. To show the world how little you cared.

And the tightness in your throat, the way you worried you might have to wipe your eyes after she said that? Is that a mark of how little you care?

But she didn't know the awful truth. She thought she did, no doubt. But she imagined that his indiscretions ranged from schoolboy pranks to drunken carousing to the pedestrian sort of sexual depravity.

Unfortunately for both of them, there was nothing pedestrian about Harrington's sexual vices. If Diana had an inkling what he really liked, she would have slapped him across the face, rather than kissing him in that closet...

Harrington shoved that thought aside. "Of course. Your sister, on the other hand, seems to be laboring under the delusion that I'm a decent sort of chap."

"Precisely. What is more, you left to join your regiment

mere weeks after she made her debut. The two of you scarcely know each other." The duke drew in a breath, wrinkling his nose as if what he was about to say was extremely distasteful. "This will come as a shock, but yesterday, I gave Diana permission to spend more time in your company. To see if the two of you might be compatible."

"Really?" At the duke's crisp nod, Harrington continued, "That was downright decent of you, Trevissick."

"It was against my better judgment," he snapped. "But I am trying not to be tyrannical where my sister is concerned. Regardless, this"—he gestured between himself and Harrington—"is happening entirely too fast. I am not unaware of how heady the early days when you are first falling in…" He trailed off, seemingly unable to countenance the possibility that the thing his beloved sister felt for his mortal enemy could be described as *love*. "When you develop an infatuation," he amended. "You can only picture your happy future. The possibility that things could sour is the farthest thought from your mind. But sour they often do. And that is why I want to give Diana options."

"What kind of options?" Harrington asked. There certainly weren't many. 'Til death do us part was about as final as you could get.

"An annulment," Trevissick said crisply. "Should Diana change her mind, we will leave the door open for her to dissolve this impulsive union."

"I would never deny her," Harrington said. Because really, what was more understandable than Diana wanting to be shot of him? "But if we go to that house party together, it won't matter what papers we sign. Everyone will regard Diana as ruined."

Trevissick leaned forward over the desk, his expression furious, as if Harrington had spoken ill of her. "I do not give a single damn what 'everyone' thinks! I want my sister to be happy. She will always have a place in my household and my full support. And if anyone dares to breathe a word against her, they can meet me with swords at dawn!"

Harrington held up his hands. "Of course. Well, I'll readily agree to that. If, after the house party, Diana wants nothing to do with me..." His throat contracted, which was ridiculous. After all, this was the most likely outcome. He knew that. "I'll sign anything she wants," he said, the words coming out less steadily than he would have liked.

"There is one more thing that is necessary to make an annulment possible," the duke said stiffly.

Harrington cleared his throat, praying the conversation would end soon. "What's that?"

"The marriage cannot have been"— Trevissick's face contorted into a portrait of disgust—"*consummated.*"

Oh. Right. Of course, that was a condition for any annulment. He knew that.

It didn't stop his cheeks from burning, though. "R-right," he stammered. "I, uh. I expect we'll be sharing a room at the... you know. The house party."

"You will not," Trevissick countered. "I will write to Carl Frederick explaining that you and Diana require separate bedrooms, on account of your atrocious snoring."

"I don't think I snore," Harrington muttered. After all, he'd spent six years sleeping in Long Chamber at Eton with close to a hundred other boys. The odds that they wouldn't have mocked him relentlessly for that were about as good as a snowball's chances in hell.

The duke's glare was poisonous. "You do now."

Harrington waved a hand. Really, what was the point of arguing? "Fine. Say whatever you need to say. I won't argue."

"There's one thing more."

Harrington gave a bitter laugh. He'd already agreed not to

lay a hand on his own wife! What more could Trevissick possibly ask of him? "What's that?"

The duke's eyes were deadly serious. "You must swear—"

Harrington rolled his eyes. "Fine! I swear, she'll come back from that house party a virgin."

"—on your brother's grave," the duke amended.

"On my...?" Harrington gaped at him. He had to be referring to John, the second youngest of the Astley siblings.

When Harrington was twelve and John two, a fever had swept through the house. He hadn't been that sick, but it had been a close thing for several of his siblings. Freddie, who had been just six months old, had nearly died, and Lucy hadn't been able to move from her bed for a month.

And John, bright, bubbly John, who'd had the biggest smile in the world, and who Harrington had absolutely adored, had fallen into a feverish sleep one night and never awoken.

It still hurt to think about it, even all these years later. It wasn't just that Harrington didn't know what to say to the duke's callous request. He couldn't seem to physically force any words past the lump that had formed in his throat.

Seeming to grasp what a vicious thing this was to ask, the duke softened his voice. "I know it is harsh. But this is the only way I can be satisfied that you will not fall into temptation."

Harrington swallowed. He could do this. After all, nothing was really at risk. He had just sworn he wouldn't sleep with Diana during the house party, which meant he wasn't going to do it. His word was good.

Not that Trevissick seemed to appreciate this.

"I swear," he said hoarsely, "upon the grave of my little brother, John..." He had to stop and clear his throat. "That when your sister returns from Carl Frederick's house party, her maidenhead will be intact."

Trevissick clasped him on the shoulder, and for the first time Harrington could recall, the duke was looking at him with something other than disdain. "Thank you."

The duke left the room, and Harrington found himself alone, feeling strangely hollow, considering he was about to marry the girl of his dreams.

CHAPTER 23

There was no conversation inside the carriage as it bounced toward Burkhill Manor, the country house the Duke of Värmland had rented to serve as his temporary home. Marcus had insisted on accompanying Diana and Harrington as far as he was permitted to go, so here he was, serving as third wheel to what should have been a happy pair of newlyweds.

Not that Diana felt much like a new bride. She and Harrington had been married by special license two days prior. The ceremony had taken place in the turquoise parlor of Latimer House. The bashful elation with which Harrington had spoken his vows, his eyes never wavering from hers as he pledged to love and honor her, was everything Diana could have hoped for.

But as Harrington leaned in to kiss his new bride, Marcus grabbed Diana by the arm and pulled her away, leaving him standing alone before the makeshift altar, pursing his lips awkwardly into the empty air. Harrington had borne this stoically, glancing down sheepishly as if he had been the one at fault for presuming he would be permitted to kiss his own bride.

There had been no wedding breakfast. Marcus had latched onto the ridiculous notion that she would want to have the marriage annulled after spending five days in Harrington's company, and that this was nothing more than a temporary measure. After the wedding, the Astleys, including Harrington, had returned to Astley House, leaving Diana alone in a cold, empty chamber on her wedding night.

Diana was so furious with her brother that she had not spoken to him in three days. She could not wait for the carriage to arrive so she could finally have a moment alone with her husband.

At last, the red-brick façade of Burkhill Manor came into view. It was a medium-sized country house built in the Queen Anne style. It was rectangular in shape and adorned by flat pilasters and a white stone cornice ringing the house's perimeter. A tiny fountain burbled inside the circular drive, creating a very charming prospect indeed.

Marcus began droning on about how they were not to be caught in any compromising situations that could prevent the marriage from being annulled. Diana ignored him. She had, after all, heard this particular lecture any number of times over the past three days.

As soon as the carriage stopped, Diana opened the door and climbed out, waiting for neither the footman nor Harrington to assist her. Harrington scrambled out behind her, and at last, they were rid of her brother.

She smiled up at Harrington, looping her arm through his. "Alone at last! And just in time—if I had to spend five more minutes in my brother's company, I fear I would have committed a crime for which I would face, at a minimum, transportation."

He chuckled, but said nothing, perhaps sensing that,

while it was one thing for her to grouse about her brother, he would do better not to insult him. "Thank you for doing this."

"It is my pleasure." Or at least, it was about to be. *Her wedding night.* A thrill of anticipation shot down her spine. This was a part of her marriage that she was very much looking forward to.

They stepped inside the foyer just as a handsome young man came jogging down the stairs. He wore a dark blue officer's coat with a gold collar and a blue sash. "Lieutenant Astley," he said warmly, clasping Harrington's hand before turning to Diana. "This must be your new bride."

Diana dropped into a curtsey. Carl Frederick didn't so much as blink at her missing hand. Not that this came as a surprise—although he was a royal duke, he was also a military man. Diana preferred the company of officers because, unlike most members of the *ton*, they had seen something of the world and did not seem to regard her missing hand as noteworthy, much less scandalous.

As Harrington made introductions, Carl Frederick bent over Diana's hand, properly stopping an inch shy of her glove. When the duke turned to Harrington, his eyes were bright. "I can see why you were so eager to wed that you could not wait for the banns to be called."

Harrington rubbed the back of his head. "Oh, er…"

Carl Frederick laughed. "Come! You must be tired from your journey. I will show you the way." He turned toward Diana as he led them up the stairs. "I received the letter from your brother about your need to have separate rooms."

Diana attempted a breezy laugh, hoping she didn't sound as annoyed as she felt. "My brother is as fussy as a mother hen. There is no need to go to any trouble on my behalf. I should like nothing better than to share with my new husband." She cast a fond smile toward Harrington, but his eyes were fixed on the stairs.

"Oh, it is quite all right," Carl Frederick said. "I have hit upon the perfect solution! This house has a master suite." He opened a door and ushered them into a corner bedroom with a fine view of the grounds. The walls were adorned with a dignified dove-grey wallpaper decorated with white quatrefoils. The room was large enough to contain a canopied four-poster bed with dark blue hangings and a spacious seating area by the window.

"And look over here." Carl Frederick opened a side door with a wink. It led to another bedroom, identical in layout to the room in which they stood, except the wallpaper was rose-pink instead of grey and the bed hangings were the color of claret. "It is ideal, is it not?"

Harrington frowned. "I appreciate this, Carl Frederick. I really do. But we couldn't possibly turn you out of the master suite."

"I insist," Carl Frederick said. "I am already settled at the other end of the house, and my room has the most charming view. I would be loath to leave it. Besides, newlyweds should receive certain… considerations."

Harrington opened his mouth, but Diana stepped in front of him. "And we appreciate that. So very much. My husband and I will be quite happy here."

Carl Frederick beamed. "Wonderful. I have adopted your English country hours so dinner will be at seven. I will leave you two to get settled."

The duke departed with a bow, leaving Diana and Harrington alone. She considered her strategy. The servants would be arriving any minute with their trunks. Diana's lady's maid, Veronique, had accompanied them from London. But, like most junior army officers, Harrington had grown accustomed to dressing himself and no longer employed a valet.

This meant that, while Veronique would be fussing around Diana's room, unpacking her things, Harrington's bedroom would be free of servants.

All she had to do was make it clear that she would not object to holding their wedding night at half two.

Whirling around, she looped her arms around his neck. He did not lower his head, so she began pressing kisses against his jaw. "We have some time."

"T-time?" he stammered.

"Time," she confirmed. "Before dinner. To be *alone*."

From the wild look in his eyes, you would have thought that he was the skittish virgin and she the experienced rakehell. "A-alone?" His voice was half an octave higher than its usual register.

"Of course!" She laughed. "You can't tell me you haven't thought about it." She leaned forward, rubbing her stomach against the bulge that had sprung up behind the placket of his trousers, and made her voice sultry. "That you aren't thinking about it right now."

He jerked back as if he'd been stung. "I, er... I think I hear the servants. With my trunk. I'd best go and unpack!"

He hurried back to his room. Diana tried to follow but found the glossy white door shut firmly in her face.

Her shoulders sagged. That was strange. He was clearly interested in consummating their marriage, physically, at least.

So why had he fled as if terrified?

She didn't know, but she meant to find out.

~

Harrington pressed his back against the connecting door to Diana's room, breathing hard. Damn, but the next five days were going to be torture. The woman he'd been infatuated with from the moment he first spoke to her was on the other side of that door, and by all appearances, she was not only willing but *eager* to make love with him.

And here he was, having sworn on his little brother's grave that he wouldn't touch her.

Shaking himself, he spun around. The connecting door between their rooms did have a keyhole, but there wasn't a key in the lock. He dashed around the room, checking in drawers and on tables, but he couldn't find the key.

A pair of footmen arrived bearing his trunk. He pointed toward the wardrobe in the corner. "Set it down over there. Thank you."

As they turned to leave, Harrington gestured to the connecting door. "Say, I don't suppose you know where the key to this door might be?"

They exchanged a glance, and no wonder, because what newly married man wanted to bar his new bride from his room? "I'm not sure," one offered, "but I'll ask the butler."

"Great. Thanks."

Harrington tried to distract himself by unpacking his trunks. It wasn't long before a knock sounded at the door. "Come in."

It opened to reveal a grey-haired man with a butlerish look about him, who bowed. "Gavin said you inquired about a key to that door," he said, nodding. "I am sorry, Lieutenant, but we did not receive many keys when His Grace let the house. I am not sure where it might be."

Harrington grimaced. "I understand. Thank you for checking."

The butler bowed again and was gone. Harrington searched the room for some means by which he could secure the door. There were a couple of plush wingchairs in the sitting area, but they weren't the right height to wedge beneath the doorknob. He could tie something around the knob, but there was nothing he could connect it to. He supposed he could push the sofa or the wardrobe in front of the door, but how odd would that look? Besides, he doubted it would be heavy enough to keep Diana out. If he had learned anything about Diana, it was that she was not easily deterred.

That thought made him smile. He quickly wiped the expression from his lips. The last thing he needed to do was moon over her. He had it bad enough as it was.

He threw himself back onto his bed and draped an arm across his face. The next five days were going to be the longest of his life.

CHAPTER 24

At dinner that night, Harrington watched Diana charm Carl Frederick. She conversed with the duke in a mixture of English and French, giving no indication that she understood his native Swedish. It was fairly common knowledge amongst the *ton* that Diana had studied a half-dozen languages courtesy of her Aunt Griselda, who had been born on the Continent. But Carl Frederick's dozen guests consisted mostly of army officers he'd befriended in Hanover and their wives. They did not move in the same circles as Diana and had better things to do with their time than trading petty gossip. Hopefully, no one would know enough to mention the possibility that Diana spoke Swedish to their host.

The meal was a decadent spread of French dishes—ironic, given that Britain and Sweden were sworn enemies of Napoleon. But Harrington had to admit it was delicious. After the *poire à la beaujolaise*—pears stewed in sweetened red wine until they were a brilliant shade of scarlet—were cleared away, the ladies excused themselves to take tea in the drawing room, leaving the men to their port.

After half an hour, Harrington excused himself to use the necessary. He was making his way back to the dining room when someone grabbed him by the arm.

"*What the devil?*" he hissed, rounding on his mystery attacker, fists raised to defend himself.

His hands loosened when he saw it was only Diana. "Don't startle me like that. What if I had struck you?"

"Sorry. I didn't think of that." She peered up and down the corridor, not looking particularly perturbed. "We're clear. Come on."

She tugged him into the room, which proved to be the library, then shut the door behind them. "What's going on?" he hissed. "Why did you drag me in here?"

She gave him a quelling look. "So we can look for the letter. I figure this is as good a place to start as any."

"The letter. Right." He ran a hand over his face. He'd forgotten all about the letter, truth be told. All he'd thought about since that bloody picnic was *not* sleeping with Diana, which effectively meant he was thinking about nothing *but* sleeping with Diana. "Let's have a look around, then."

Diana began rooting through the desk while Harrington inspected the bookshelves. Most of them bore a light layer of dust, making it easy to pick out the handful of books that had been handled recently. Harrington leafed through each one and peered deep into the back of the shelves. Nothing appeared to be out of order.

Diana closed a drawer with a soft click. "Nothing over here. Unless one of the drawers has a false bottom," she amended hastily. "But it looks untouched. There are no papers in the desk, the pens are dried out, and the inkwells are empty. I don't get the impression that anyone has been using this area for their correspondence."

"I didn't find anything suspicious, either." He gestured

toward the door. "Do you think we have time to check one more room?"

"We might as…" She froze as voices filled the corridor. They were accompanied by the muffled thump of footsteps on the carpet.

The voices were growing louder.

Diana's eyes flew to his. He raised a finger to his lips, and she nodded. The drawing room where the ladies had retreated was at the other end of the corridor, but perhaps one of the guests was searching for the chamber pot.

The footsteps paused before the library door. He watched in horror as the door's handle slowly started to twist.

His mind scrambled. They could brazen this out, couldn't they? It wasn't as if they'd been caught red-handed, snooping in the desk. There was nothing inherently suspicious about being in the library. Except Harrington didn't have a reputation for being a great reader. Nobody was going to believe he had decided to forego Carl Frederick's finest port to go looking for a book at eleven o'clock at night.

While he stood there gaping, Diana sprang into action. She placed her hand on top of the desk and vaulted over it with remarkable dexterity, considering she was wearing a silk evening gown. Landing in a seated position, she grabbed him by the front of his jacket, hauled him between her legs, and kissed him right on the mouth.

His thoughts, which had already been fractured, scattered to dust. His hands went to Diana's shoulders of their own volition, pulling her close. He couldn't seem to help himself. He simply had no ability to resist this woman.

Which is why you can't allow her within fifty yards of your bed, a nagging voice inside his head reminded him.

Behind him, he heard the faint sound of the door swinging on its hinges. There was a muffled step as if someone had stopped short, followed by a faint chuckle. Then came the sound of the door clicking shut once more.

And now he understood her strategy. People would expect the newlyweds to steal off together. It was a brilliant cover, although there was probably no reason to keep it up, now that the interloper had moved on.

He could stop kissing her now. And he would.

In one minute.

Maybe two.

At most, three.

Just then, Diana wrapped her arms tightly around him and scooted to the edge of the desk, bringing her core into contact with his straining cock. Groaning into his mouth, she started circling her hips, rubbing herself against him.

Harrington's resolve had just sprouted wings and flown out the window when the door swung open again. There was a startled gasp, followed by a thump, and then a cry of pain.

Biting back a curse, Harrington glanced over his shoulder and saw Mrs. Beasley, a friendly woman of about forty years who was married to a Lieutenant-Colonel. She was crouched down upon the Axminster rug, clutching her toe.

"I'm s-sorry for interrupting," she stammered. "I only meant to return my book and select another. I had no idea that you were, er…"

With a composure Harrington was certain he did not possess, Diana straightened her bodice and slid from the desk. "Please, Mrs. Beasley. I am the one who should be apologizing to you. The fault is entirely ours."

"Oh, no!" Mrs. Beasley cried. "That is… It's been two and twenty years since the Lieutenant-Colonel and my wedding day. But I do remember what it was like, and I would never chastise you for something so natural."

Diana crouched down next to her. "You are too kind." She

picked up Mrs. Beasley's book. "My gracious—*Don Quixote!* Did you drop this on your foot?"

"I did," Mrs. Beasley confessed.

"No wonder you are in pain. Here." Diana draped the woman's arm across her shoulders. "Can you bear a little weight on it?"

"I think so."

As she helped Mrs. Beasley from the room, Diana cast a look back at him. Who would have thought those ice-blue eyes could hold such fire? It was a look that said, *this isn't finished.*

Harrington gulped as the door clicked shut. That was what he was afraid of, all right.

CHAPTER 25

Three hours and eleven interminable hands of whist later, Diana made her way up to her room. It was fortunate that the other ladies only wanted to play for pennies, because Diana had been unable to concentrate on the game. She wasn't sure what had caused Harrington to flee back into his bedchamber that afternoon, but after their interlude in the library, she felt certain that he burned for her with the same white-hot intensity with which she burned for him.

She hurried Veronique through her evening toilette and dismissed her for the evening. It was common for a lady's maid to set up a cot in her mistress's dressing room, but Veronique was not an idiot and had made arrangements to sleep with the household's female servants in the attic.

Diana took a moment to gather herself. She normally slept in a soft, flannel night rail, but tonight she had opted for a lace-trimmed shift made of muslin so fine it was translucent. She had topped this with a dressing gown of pale purple silk. Her blonde hair fell over her shoulder in a single plait.

Nodding at the mirror, satisfied with her appearance, she strode over to the door connecting her room to Harrington's. She knocked twice before pushing it open.

Her husband glanced at her, eyes wary. His coat and neckcloth had been tossed over the back of a chair, and he wore nothing but trousers and a white linen shirt gaping open to his heart. Diana found herself transfixed by the sight of dark hair curling on his chest.

Ignoring the lines creasing his brow, she strode into the room. She walked straight toward Harrington, intending to loop her arms around his neck and pick up precisely where they'd left off in the library, but he gave her his back, turning to face the dresser. "Would you like a drink?" he asked, reaching for the decanter. ·

"I would not." She traced her fingertips across his shoulder. "I want to remember tonight forever."

He spilled the brandy he'd been pouring and muttered a curse.

Diana grabbed a towel from the washstand and moistened it. Crossing the room in three strides, she dabbed at the spilled liquid. "Put that down. You don't need it." She laughed. "Aren't I supposed to be the nervous one?"

He finally looked at her, and his eyes were sorrowful. "This isn't a good idea."

She untied the sash of her dressing gown. His gaze flew to the stripe of whisper-thin muslin that had been bared to his view. She knew he would be able to see the faint curve of her breasts, her belly button, and the blonde curls at the apex of her thighs.

She strolled forward, swinging her hips, and pushed the dressing gown off one shoulder. "I disagree. I think this is the best idea I've had in a long time."

His face was stricken. "I can't."

"Hmm." She cast her eyes toward his groin, confirming

that, once again, he was hard for her. "You can't convince me that you don't want to." She reached for him but stopped when her hand was an inch from the placket of his trousers. She looked up, raising a questioning eyebrow.

Closing his eyes, he leaned forward, pressing himself against her hand. Encouraged, Diana traced his shape through the wool. His face contorted as if he were in agony, and his head lolled back. Having perused Harrington's book of naughty prints with Izzie and Lucy, she had some idea what to expect. But the reality of him, thick and hard and separated from her curious fingers by just a few layers of fabric, excited her unbearably, and a little pulse started to throb between her legs.

He opened his eyes, looking almost drunk. "We should stop."

She responded by shrugging out of her dressing gown, letting it pool on the floor at her feet. Immediately, his eyes were riveted to her body, scarcely veiled from his view by the lace-trimmed shift.

"*Oh, Diana,*" he moaned, his hands coming up to cup her breasts. Now *this* was more like it. His thumbs traced the outline of her nipples, and she shivered, and not from the chill of the room.

As much good work as he was doing with his hands, his expression was the best thing. He looked at her as if she were precious beyond measure. As if he could not *believe* his good fortune, seeing her this way. It was precisely the way a man should look at his bride.

Eager to move things along, she grabbed a fistful of his shirt. Tugging him forward, she stepped back, falling on his bed and pulling him down on top of her.

But instead of kissing her as she had hoped, he scrambled off her, his eyes wild. "We can't do this."

She squinted at him, confused. "Why on earth not? We're *married*."

Eyes fixed on the floor, he gestured to the connecting door. "I need you to go back to your room."

She crossed her arms. "Why?"

Still, he wouldn't look at her. "I… I just do."

Diana narrowed her eyes. As if such a paltry excuse was going to work. She was a *Latimer*. She was so practiced in being intractable as to render it an art form.

And she was not leaving this room without getting some *answers*.

"I will not leave until you tell me what's going on."

At last, he looked at her, guilt written plainly on his face. "Nothing's going on!"

She raised a single eyebrow.

He grunted, scrubbing a hand across his face. "It's unfair. How do you do that thing with your eyebrow?"

She lowered the first eyebrow and raised its companion.

"Fine!" he snapped, but his expression immediately softened. "It's not you, Diana. You're… gorgeous and perfect and, well," he gestured to his groin, "it's patently obvious that I want you."

She strove to infuse her voice with patience rather than annoyance. "What, then, is the difficulty?"

He closed his eyes. "I… I promised your brother."

Her eyes sharpened. "What," she said slowly, her voice full of menace, "did you promise my brother?"

He opened his eyes, and they were full of sorrow. "I promised him I wouldn't make love to you."

In spite of her best efforts, her voice held a note of danger. "Tell me everything."

～

"He made you swear on your brother's *grave?*"

Diana knew that strangling someone was an act usually performed with two hands.

No matter. She was going to strangle Marcus.

Somehow, she would find a way.

She chanced a look at her husband. *Poor Harrington.* She could tell he was genuinely distressed.

He was speaking quickly. "He wants you to have the option to annul the marriage."

Diana rolled her eyes. "Yes, he's been droning on about that to me as well."

Harrington was still speaking, giving no appearance of having heard her. "Should you change your mind. He pointed out that we didn't have a very long courtship, and I couldn't really argue." He looked at her, eyes pleading. "And I do want you to have options, Diana. I would never want you to feel trapped… You know. With me. I know the only reason you even contemplated marriage with me was like you said—for king and country." He made a slashing motion with his hand. "When you change your mind, I want you to come out on the other side unscathed."

She noted his choice of words—*when* she changed her mind. Not if. It was telling that he couldn't even imagine a scenario in which she wanted to be his wife.

She needed to proceed with care.

Taking his hand, she led him to the bed, tugging him down so they were sitting on its edge, facing one another. "I think you are overestimating the chances that I will wish to have our marriage annulled."

"I'm not." He gave a humorless laugh. "Just wait until you get to know me."

She stroked the back of his hand with her thumb. "Your statement that I don't know you as well as I would like is not inaccurate. But I can honestly say that I like you better than any other man I've met."

He looked stunned. "Me?" he asked quietly.

"You," she said firmly. "My brother was wrong to ask that of you. But I would never expect you to break such a vow. I can easily understand why the mere thought is distressing to you."

His shoulders sagged with relief. "Thank you."

She bit her lip. "Tell me the precise wording. Tell me exactly what you promised him."

He frowned in concentration. "I swore that when you returned from this house party, your maidenhead would be intact."

Diana brightened. It wasn't ideal.

But she could work around that.

"Very well, then. We will make absolutely sure that I return to London with my maidenhead firmly in place."

He smiled at her, relieved. "Thank you."

"However," she said firmly.

He stiffened. "However?"

She struggled to find the right words. "I am very innocent in most ways. You were the first man I ever kissed." A soft smile came over his face. Instead of pausing to enjoy it, she soldiered on. "But I am not entirely ignorant of the marital act and what it entails."

He nodded sagely. "I imagine your great-aunt told you what to expect."

Diana scoffed. "Gracious, no. Aunt Griselda doesn't know the first thing about making love." She made a conciliatory gesture with her hand. "Leastwise, not with a man."

For the first time all night, Harrington laughed.

Diana gave him a pointed look. "I trust you will keep that in confidence."

He placed a hand over his heart. "Your Aunt Griselda is

one of my favorite people on the face of this earth. I would never say anything that could cause her grief. Besides, I'm not exactly in a position to cast the first stone."

Diana peered at him, wondering if this curious half-statement was an allusion to the page he had marked in his book of scandalous prints by folding the corner down. The one in which the man was being spanked with a birch—and appeared to be enjoying it.

Part of her wanted to ask. But she was nervous of how he would react to learning that she had snooped through his things. The situation was tenuous enough as it was.

She opted for a half-truth. "I stumbled upon a book of *prints*." She gave the last word extra emphasis, hoping he would catch on.

Understanding flared in his eyes. "Ah. Not ignorant at all, then."

"And I do have married friends." There. That phrasing was vague enough that he could plausibly assume that Ceci had been the one to pull her aside before her wedding and tell her about the birds and the bees. She didn't want to dampen the mood by revealing that everything she knew about the marital act, she had learned from his little sister.

She scooted closer to him on the bed, raising her hand to trace behind his ear. "What I'm trying to say is, we both know there are other things we could do, ways of giving and receiving pleasure, that would not compromise my maidenhead in any way."

Harrington's eyes were wary once again. "But what if I can't stop? What if I lose control?"

"I don't think you will. But we need to trust one another." She took his hand in hers, squeezing it. "We're married. We're partners. When I say that I would never do anything that would cause you to break your vow, I want you to believe me."

"I want to believe you," he said hesitantly. "But as the saying goes, the flesh is weak."

She lifted her chin. "I am not weak." She wanted to add, *and neither are you*. But she held off, because she knew he would argue.

"That's true," he agreed reluctantly.

"Good. Then let me see if I can ease your mind." She took his hand, placing it over her heart, and looked him square in the eye. "I, Diana Latimer... no, Diana *Astley*... solemnly swear on the grave of my mother, Lydia Latimer, that I will return to London at the end of this gathering with my maidenhead intact. That I will not allow my husband, Harrington, to perform any act that would place the vow he made upon the grave of his little brother, John, in jeopardy."

His expression was fraught. "You don't have to do this, Diana."

"I already did." She gave him an arch look. "So, do you believe *I* am strong enough to keep my vow?"

He frowned. "I know you are."

She scooted toward him, climbed into his lap, and looped her arms around his neck. "Then there is no reason we cannot enjoy a few things."

His breath was starting to come fast, and she could feel that he was still hard for her. "Are you sure?"

She pressed a firm kiss to his mouth. "Completely sure." *Sure about you*, she added silently.

"In that case," he said, then claimed her mouth with his.

CHAPTER 26

*H*arrington could not *believe* this was happening.

He was on a bed with the woman of his dreams, and through some strange miracle, she actually wanted him, too.

He couldn't quite shake the conviction that she might change her mind at any second.

Although she showed no hesitation. She yanked his shirt out of the waistband of his trousers with brutal efficiency, her lips never leaving his. While he cradled her face, marveling that she was letting him kiss her, she seemed bent on stripping him bare. Which he *loved*. His deepest sexual fantasies all involved a woman who would boss him around, even *push* him around, tie him to the bed, and spank him, and then force him to pleasure her.

Ever since the day he had first spoken to Diana and had discovered how deliciously strict she could be, he had pictured no one but her.

Not that he would ever tell her as much. It was bad enough that he had these lurid fantasies. He would destroy any sliver of a chance that she would remain his wife beyond the scope of this house party if he let slip what a degenerate he really was.

But the monster inside of him couldn't help but thrill as she yanked his shirt up over his head and tossed it contemptuously to the floor. She swung a leg around to straddle him, and everything inside him purred, loving that she had assumed this commanding position.

He leaned back on his hands, allowing her to explore his chest with eager fingers. It seemed as if she liked what she saw, because she growled like a lioness, fusing her lips to his.

He reached up, framing her face, and kissed her in earnest. Diana might be inexperienced, but she was a natural at this. She had lined her core up with his straining cock, and as they kissed, she started rocking against him. *God*, but she was killing him. He hadn't been with a woman for a duration that didn't bear thinking about, as the only women available on deployment were camp followers from whom the odds of catching an unmentionable disease were alarmingly high. And, considering this was the woman who had been fueling his midnight fantasies for several years, he couldn't take too much of her petting him like this without embarrassing himself.

Then, she went and made it a thousand times worse. With a cry of frustration, she grasped the hem of her chemise and pulled it over her head, hurling it in the same direction as his shirt.

Harrington's brain ceased functioning, completely and utterly, at the sight of Diana in all her perfection. *Sweet Jesus.* He had never imagined anything so beautiful. Her skin was pale with a blue-veined, almost translucent quality. She wasn't what you would call buxom, but Harrington didn't mind in the slightest, as the sight of her delicate, rose-tipped breasts made his mouth go dry. Her limbs were thin. Delicate. Which was ironic, considering he had watched this woman fence her brother into the ground. But these contrasts were part of what made Diana so utterly irresistible.

He managed to gather enough wits to notice that she was reaching for the buttons on his trousers. "No," he said, clamping his hand around her wrist.

She scowled at him. "Will you relax? We already discussed this. We can touch one another without divesting me of my maidenh—"

He silenced her with a ravenous kiss. "That's not what I meant," he said, pleased to note that she was dewy-eyed and stunned speechless. "My God, Diana! Just look at you—you're *gorgeous*! I'll tell you what is going to happen next—you are going to lie back on this bed, and I am going to worship you in the manner you deserve."

The corner of her mouth quirked up. "Hmm." She made a magnanimous gesture. "I suppose I will permit it."

"You're damn right, you will." With a snarl, he tossed her back onto the bed, where she landed with a breathless laugh. He climbed atop her, and she squirmed against him, clearly enjoying the feeling of his skin against hers as much as he was.

He let her enjoy that for a moment, then began kissing his way down her temple, across her jaw, and down her neck. He paused to worship her collarbone—who would have thought that a *collarbone* could be so erotic?—before coming to her breasts.

He couldn't resist. With a groan, he sucked one of her pebbled, rosy nipples into his mouth. She made a sound of pleasure and buried her fingers in his hair, and this was when Harrington discovered that she was exquisitely sensitive there. He experimented with gentle swirls, flicks of his tongue, and deep pulls. Diana seemed to adore them all.

He switched to the other breast. God, but he could do this all day. After all, what man ever got sick of hearing his woman gasp, "Oh, Harrington! Please don't stop—that feels *so good!*"

But all good things must come to an end, and slowly, the sounds Diana was making took on a note of frustration. Finally, she gasped, "Please, Harrington! Please, I need to come!"

He obliged at once, kissing his way down her stomach. "I take it you've touched yourself before?"

"Yes," she panted, looking dazed.

He pressed a kiss against the inside of her thigh. "Was there a picture in that book of what I'm about to do?"

"There was. More than one." Her heavy-lidded, pleasure-infused smile was beautiful to see. "You're the one I liked to imagine doing it. When I was touching myself in my bed at night."

That made two of them. It was gratifying to know that his infatuation hadn't been entirely one-sided. "Let's see if I can live up to your imaginings."

She was so exquisitely aroused after his attentions to her breasts that she immediately knotted her fingers in his hair. He tried to be gentle, but her little rosebud was so eager for him, she was screaming his name and pulsing against his tongue in less than a minute.

He cradled her against his chest while she trembled, but as soon as she recovered, he kissed her cheek. "That was unfair, my darling."

Scowling, she pushed a stray curl back from her damp forehead. "Unfair? Not at all. I fully intend to return the favor."

He silenced her with a kiss. "That's not what I meant. It

was unfair in that it went by too quickly. I wanted to *savor* it. I insist that you allow me to do it again."

He resumed his position between her thighs, pressing them open so he had full access. He knew she would be exquisitely tender, so he stroked gentle patterns with his tongue all around the little bud that was the center of her delight without *quite* touching it.

He kept that up for some time, until her breathing grew harsh, and her skin flushed. He chuckled in delight when she finally knotted her fingers in his hair and guided his tongue precisely where she wanted it, and he was treated to the beautiful sounds of her taking her pleasure once more.

Again, he took her in his arms. And again, he insisted. "Please, Diana. Please. You're so beautiful when you come. Pleasure for me again, darling, that's a good girl." It took longer that time, but Harrington didn't mind. When she reached her third peak, her leg cramped so hard she almost kicked him in the head, which he took as a compliment.

After she recovered, he tried to slide down her body once more, but she swatted him away. "Harrington! Behave. I'll scarcely be able to sit tomorrow as it is."

Damn if that didn't make his chest swell. He secretly liked the idea that the other house party guests might hear her screaming his name tonight and might see her shifting in her seat tomorrow. That they would elbow one another and grin, knowing what the newlyweds had been up to, and that he had done a damn good job of pleasuring his wife.

"Just once more—"

"No!" she snapped, but she was laughing as she pushed him down on the pillows and reached for the buttons of his placket. A wicked gleam came into her eyes. "It's my turn now."

"*Oh, my God,*" was all he could groan. Because how many

times had he imagined this very scene? A naked Diana, opening his trousers and taking out his cock?

At the first press of her soft little hand against his sensitive flesh, he almost unmanned himself. When she slid low, making her intentions clear by planting a trail of kisses across his stomach, he whimpered aloud.

And when she pressed a kiss against the head of his cock, he almost died. It wasn't that she was a practiced seductress. It was apparent that whatever information she had about the act she was attempting to perform had been gleaned from secondhand descriptions and naughty prints.

But Harrington had imagined this moment so many times that the reality of a naked Diana leaning forward to take his cock into her mouth was overwhelming. He was powerless to stop babbling nonsense or to keep his hips from twitching on the bed.

He lasted for less than a minute before the pleasure overpowered him. He would have warned her what was about to happen if he'd had even a sliver of presence of mind, but his climax was so intense, he almost blacked out from it.

When he was next aware of anything, a very smug Diana was smiling down at him. He grabbed her and pulled her down on top of him. She snuggled into his chest, and he wrapped his arms around her, feeling happier than he'd ever felt in his life.

After a few blissful minutes, she tried to slip from his grasp. He tightened his arms mulishly.

She squirmed. "Let me go."

He released her at once. "Sorry. I understand if you want to return to your room."

She rolled her eyes. "I do *not* want to return to my room. But turnabout is fair play. And I believe you are ready for round two."

She wasn't wrong. His cock was already starting to

stiffen, and it swelled even more upon being informed that there would be a *round two*.

But Harrington pulled her close again, burying his face in her hair. "In a minute. Need to hold you."

She yawned. "I suppose that would be acceptable."

It was a damn sight more than acceptable, Harrington thought as he drifted off to sleep.

CHAPTER 27

*D*iana slipped from Harrington's room just as morning light was starting to peek around the edges of the curtains.

They had spent the whole night alternating between spells of pleasuring each other and dozing contentedly together. Thanks to her married friend, Izzie, Diana had had some idea what to expect. But she had formed the impression that some men were unwilling to perform the particular act she had seen depicted in that book of prints, in which the man kissed his lover between her legs.

Harrington, on the other hand, had brought her to four sparkling climaxes that way and had made it clear that he would have been glad to do so again and again, had she not been too tender. This only strengthened Diana's conviction that their hasty marriage had not been a mistake. That Harrington was such a generous lover who genuinely enjoyed bringing her pleasure was an excellent sign.

She couldn't wait to get back to London so they could consummate this marriage in every sense of the word. But there were still a few things from that book of prints that they could do without stripping her of her maidenhead, and there was one in particular that she wanted to try.

After a couple more hours of sleep, Diana rose and allowed Veronique to dress her in a lilac morning dress trimmed with delicate white lace.

Downstairs, she encountered Harrington in the breakfast room filling a plate with eggs and kippers. His eyes sparkled as they met hers, and she fancied she was looking at him in much the same way.

She sidled up next to him at the sideboard, eyeing his plate. "That's a lot of eggs," she whispered.

"I've got to keep my energy up," he countered with a wink. "Someone depleted it last night."

Chuckling, Diana elbowed him in the ribs. Out of the corner of her eye, she caught Mrs. Beasley exchanging an amused look with her husband.

Diana did not mind in the slightest. To be sure, everyone was probably gossiping about the newlyweds, but she expected it was a friendly sort of gossip. Besides, the notion that she and Harrington were prone to stealing away for private interludes would be helpful when searching for the letter from King Gustav.

The morning activity was riding. Diana had to decline. She had grown up riding astride, which was improper, but when had Aunt Griselda ever given a fig for what was proper? More importantly, it allowed her to compensate for her missing hand by controlling the horse with her legs. When riding sidesaddle, a lady used a riding crop to signal her mount on the off side, but managing both the reins and the crop was challenging with one hand, especially when riding in busy places like Hyde Park. She therefore had a specially trained mare that responded to a set of commands Diana could execute with one hand. But, alas, she had left Artemisia back in London.

The handful of ladies who had not cared to ride gathered in the morning room. Noticing a writing desk in the corner, Diana feigned a desire to pen a few letters and was able to covertly search the desk. It did not reveal anything of use, but at least she could cross it off their proverbial list.

The riders returned in good spirits, and, as the weather was fine, the servants laid out a picnic luncheon on the back lawn.

No doubt the other guests thought the newlyweds were whispering sweet nothings to one another on their blanket. In actuality, they were refining their plan.

"I wonder how many other writing desks there are around the house?" Harrington murmured after Diana told him about the one she'd inspected that morning.

"There's no telling," she whispered, making a point to smile as if he'd said something droll. "We've already searched the library, but there could be a study as well."

"We should make a sketch of the general layout of the house," he said, giving her a heated look that made Diana shiver.

They spent the next two days doing just that. They found an additional writing desk in a first-floor parlor and a study that was, ironically, next door to the master suite where Harrington was staying. Neither yielded anything of use.

Time was running out with just one day left of the house party. That night in Harrington's room, after their first round of pleasuring one another, Diana sat up on the bed, wrapping the counterpane around her shoulders for warmth. "I was thinking about our mission."

Harrington, who was lounging against the headboard, opened his eyes, but the contented smile did not disappear from his face. "Our mission?"

She poked him in the ribs. "You know, to find the letter from King Gustav."

He spread his arms wide, stretching. "Right. The mission. What about it?"

"It seems like we've searched every likely location"—she bit her lip, nervous about what she was about to suggest—"other than Carl Frederick's bedroom."

Harrington sat up. "His bedroom." He fell silent, considering the implications. "I think you're right. We've made a good search of most of the house. At this point, I don't see where else it could be."

Diana nodded grimly. "It also makes a certain amount of sense that he wouldn't keep a potentially sensitive letter in one of the public rooms."

"That's true." He winced. "I feel bad, searching the man's bedroom. Carl Frederick has been nothing but kind to me. It seems a rotten way of thanking him."

"There's also the potential that, if we are caught in the act, it could cause a diplomatic incident."

Harrington squeezed his eyes shut. "That would be just my luck."

Diana took his hand, holding it until he looked at her. "It's your mission, and you would be the one to bear the consequences if something were to go awry. You should therefore be the one to decide whether we make the attempt."

His brown eyes were thoughtful. "Yes, but I value your opinion and would like to hear what you think."

Diana's heart tripped. *This* was why she was becoming more convinced with each passing day that marrying Harrington had been a good thing. He respected her. He treated her like a partner, not like a line of credit, or a pretty ornament to wear upon his arm. And that, she was coming to realize, was the quality she wanted in a husband above all others.

"I think," she said slowly, "that there are arguments on

both sides. It is possible that we have been sent on a wild goose chase. That the letter is not even here, or if it is, that it does not contain anything of importance. If we are caught searching Carl Frederick's room, it is likely that your friendship would be ruined, and possible that it could damage relations between Great Britain and Sweden."

Harrington swallowed. In the candlelight, his face had gone pale.

"On the other hand," she continued, "if there is anything of import in the letter, the knowledge of its contents could improve our military strategy. Which is not a small thing, as lives are at stake."

Harrington slumped against the pillows, his brow furrowed. After a moment, he said, "So many of our erstwhile allies switched sides while I was in Hanover, and as you said, lives are at stake. Knowing if our allies can be trusted is not a small thing." His eyes met hers, resolved. "I think I have to try it."

Diana nodded solemnly. "You mean, *I* have to try it."

Harrington frowned. "What do you mean, *you* have to try it? I don't like the idea of you putting yourself at risk."

She shook her head. "It makes far more sense for me to be the one to search the room. I have it all planned out. You see..."

CHAPTER 28

The following morning, Diana was nervous, but she tried to maintain an air of calmness. She and Harrington had stayed up half the night refining their plan to search Carl Frederick's room. Now it was time to put their plan into action.

As breakfast was concluding, Harrington said, "Say, Carl Frederick, as the weather seems to be cooperating, would it be a convenient time for you to show me that game you played growing up?"

Carl Frederick brightened. "You mean varpa! Yes, yes, it is a fine morning for it." He dabbed at his mouth with his napkin, then stood. "Come, I will send a footman to fetch the stones."

Harrington gave Diana a small nod before heading out the door. Diana lingered for five more minutes before excusing herself from the table.

She knew which room was Carl Frederick's. She and Harrington had sketched a rough floor plan of the house and had been systematically checking off rooms as they searched them. The duke was staying in a corner bedroom on the second floor.

When she arrived at Carl Frederick's door, she heard someone moving about inside. She made a show of admiring the paintings lining the corridor.

Five minutes later, a maid emerged. Diana gave her a regal nod before returning her attention to a portrait of a dour woman clutching a little dog.

As soon as the maid rounded the corner, Diana dashed toward Carl Frederick's door and slipped inside. She spied a letter on his bedside table and hurried over, but it was written in English, liberally perfumed, and proved to be from Lady Carmichael, an attractive young widow with a reputation for taking handsome paramours. Diana set it aside at once, unwilling to spare a moment to read the gossip.

She hurried over to a small desk in the corner. Carl Frederick was not overly fastidious in his correspondence. There were letters stuffed haphazardly into the desk's slots and crannies. Three were written in Swedish, but two were from Carl Frederick's mother and one from an old school friend, and she did not find any that bore the crest of the House of Mecklenburg.

It took only five minutes to make a competent search of the desk. Diana scanned the room, finding nothing of obvious interest. Then again, perhaps it was unsurprising that Carl Frederick did not leave highly sensitive correspondence from the king lying in plain sight.

She had just resolved to search his trunk when she heard muffled voices from the hall. "Are those the clean sheets for His Grace's room?" came the voice of Carl Frederick's hired housekeeper.

"Yes, ma'am," a second voice replied.

The conversation continued, but Diana couldn't hear it

over the pounding of her heart. She whipped around to face the bed. Surely enough, it was unmade. Any second now, the maid would open the door and catch Diana red-handed.

She hastily scanned the room. Diana prided herself on being a master when it came to hiding, but of course, this would be the moment that her skills abandoned her. The curtains were too filmy to provide concealment. She tried to slip beneath the bed but was foiled by a trundle tucked underneath it.

She scrambled to her feet, her gaze falling on the window.

The *open* window.

She hurried over, recalling that the house had a cornice rimming its red brick exterior. Which floor was it on?

She leaned her head outside. Surely enough, the cornice loomed a few feet below her. It was wider than she had expected, almost a full foot across.

She heard a soft click from the room behind her. Slowly, the knob began to turn.

Before she could think better of it, she hopped onto the windowsill, swung her legs through, and stepped out onto the ledge.

CHAPTER 29

The good news was that Diana was apparently not afraid of heights. The cornice was wide enough that she was not in imminent danger of falling. In fact, she could shuffle around the exterior of the building without too much trouble.

The bad news was… well. There was so much bad news, she scarcely knew where to begin.

There was the fact that the maid, upon noticing the open window, had promptly closed and locked it.

Diana had checked a couple of nearby windows. They were latched as well. To be sure, she had not checked every window on the second floor, partially because of the next piece of bad news—that she was wearing a primrose yellow dress which stood out like a sore thumb against the house's red brick exterior.

If anyone glanced up at the house, she would be discovered at once. The best option she could come up with was to slip around the side of the building. It didn't offer much in the way of concealment, but it was better than standing against the front façade. The windows were designed in such a way that their frames provided a good grip, so she was safe for the moment. But she was also stuck.

After a few minutes, she decided to see if there was anything of interest going on in the back garden. With careful steps, she edged along the cornice, checking the windows as she went. All locked, unfortunately.

As she neared the corner, she spied a flash of motion in the back garden below. Peering down, she watched as Carl Frederick hurled a flat stone at a short post staked into the ground. Harrington clapped his hands, and his voice drifted up to her. "Good throw!"

So, that was where they had set up to play varpa, the game Harrington had mentioned at breakfast. It looked to be similar to horseshoes, but the objects they were throwing were flat, round stones.

Hope flared in her heart. If she could gain Harrington's attention, he would find a way to rescue her. She knew he would.

Selecting a stone, Carl Frederick whirled around. Diana hugged the side of the house as tightly as she could.

Carl Frederick turned his back to make his throw. She had a clear view of Harrington's profile. She *had* to catch his eye! Now she was leaning out from the wall as far as she dared, waving her arm like a baby bird who had just been shoved out of the nest.

Oblivious to her plight, Harrington bent and selected a stone. Diana pressed herself back into the wall, biding her time.

It took fifteen agonizing minutes before Harrington spotted her. It was not difficult to mark the moment he did. His head jerked around as dramatically as any pantomime actor to grace the stage. His mouth promptly fell open. Even from a distance, she could read the befuddlement on his face.

Carl Frederick murmured a question she couldn't make

out, then started to turn in the direction of Harrington's gaze. Harrington hastily grabbed him by the shoulder, gesturing to the stake.

They continued to play. Diana willed herself to remain calm. Harrington had spotted her. Her rescue was imminent.

Clutching the window frame, she uttered a silent prayer that she could go unnoticed for a few more minutes.

"I say, Lieutenant, what has become of your form?"

Carl Frederick's question was a reasonable one. Harrington was usually a dab hand at this sort of game—not that he'd ever played varpa before, but he had some experience with lawn bowls, pall mall, and the like. He and Carl Frederick had started off neck-and-neck.

But his hands had been shaking ever since he saw his wife standing on that bloody ledge. He needed to contrive an excuse to slip away so he could rescue her.

"Sorry," he said. "I'm not feeling well all of a sudden." It might not have been very creative, but strictly speaking, it was true. He was so racked with anxiety, he feared he might cast his accounts right there on the lawn.

Carl Frederick frowned. "Now that you mention it, your color is not looking so good. Are you able to continue?"

Harrington gave him a tight smile. "I'll be fine. I'm sure it will pass in a minute or two."

He threw another stone, which bounced off the stake and rolled to an inglorious stop five feet away. He normally would have been annoyed at himself for his poor performance. Athletic endeavors were one of a blessed few things he was actually good at, and he did take a bit of pride in his abilities. But right now, he couldn't be bothered to care. All he could think about was how he was going to get

Diana to safety with all possible speed. He was all but certain the cornice wrapped around the base of the second floor. Their bedchambers were on the first floor, so it wouldn't be as simple as helping her back into their own rooms. He wanted to study the house to confirm, but that would only draw Carl Frederick's attention. *Don't look, don't look, don't look.*

When his next throw went sailing into the hedge, Carl Frederick turned to him, his eyes concerned. "Are you quite certain you are all right?"

Bending forward at the waist, Harrington placed a hand on his abdomen. "I'm afraid something from breakfast seems to have disagreed with me. If you'll excuse me…"

Carl Frederick waved a hand. "Yes, yes—please, return to the house. We will finish our game another time."

"Thank you," Harrington called over his shoulder. He tried to make his posture stiff and uncomfortable-looking as he hurried toward the house.

Once inside, he dropped the pretense of being ill and headed upstairs. He went to the second floor, hoping he could find an unlocked room, but as soon as he stepped into the corridor, he encountered a pair of maids.

They jerked apart guiltily, and he suspected he had caught them taking a break from their duties. "Can we help ye, sir?" asked a young woman with light brown hair and freckles.

"Oh!" Harrington made a show of glancing around. "Is this the second floor?"

"It is, sir."

He shook his head, trying to look rueful. "I seem to have gone up one floor too many. Excuse me."

He jogged down to the first floor, trying to gather his thoughts. This was definitely a setback. He supposed he could wait for the maids to leave the corridor. But who knew when that might occur, and there were enough guests staying in the house that it would be difficult to wander the second floor undetected. The excuse he had made, of going to the wrong floor, might seem plausible once, but if he began skulking in the corridor, it was bound to raise suspicion.

One thing he did know was that he couldn't leave Diana out on that ledge for the next hour while he tried to devise a plan.

Once he reached the first floor, he went straight through to the back of the house and entered the servants' stairs. He knew precisely where they were, as he and Diana had spent the past four days mapping out the house. Skipping the second floor, he went all the way to the top level where the servants had their rooms. The corridor was deserted, which made sense, as they were all busy performing their morning duties.

He went to the side of the house where he had last seen Diana and began trying doorknobs. The third one he twisted proved to be unlocked, and he slipped inside.

He didn't bother to look around beyond ascertaining that the room was deserted. Peering out the window, he could see Diana's golden head about six feet away.

He slid the window open, heart in his throat. "Diana!" he hissed. She turned but didn't spot him right away, so he added, "Up here!"

She gave him a brilliant smile; how was it possible that she looked so at ease, standing thirty feet up in the air? His heart was pounding out of his chest as she picked her way along the cornice with small, confident steps, but she looked as cool as a cucumber.

Once she was in position below him, he hissed, "The second floor is crawling with housemaids. I'll come for you as soon as I can."

The wind picked up, tangling her skirts about her legs.

She shook them free as if this were a minor inconvenience. "Can you reach me from there?"

He paused, measuring it up. The attic floor, which contained the servants' quarters, did not have high ceilings like the levels below intended for guests. It just might be possible.

He took a firm grip on the windowsill with his left hand and hooked his left foot around the bedstand for good measure. Then, he leaned out the window from the waist, dangling his right arm down as far as it would go.

Diana reached up, and to his surprise, her fingertips brushed his. He felt vertiginous just watching her standing on that ledge without a grip on anything, but she looked unbothered. "I think I can reach you if I go up on my toes," she said conversationally. "Lean down as far as you can. On three. One... two..."

"Three!" he said in unison with her, stretching down with everything he had. His fingers closed around her wrist, and he felt her return the gesture. "All right?" he asked tightly.

She nodded, and the trust in her eyes, the absolute confidence that he would not let her fall humbled him. And damn if he was going to let any harm come to this wonderful, perfect unicorn of a woman who actually seemed to like *him*, of all people.

He tightened his grip around her wrist and, before he had the chance to consider the consequences if he were to fail, he hauled her up to his level. Once she was sitting on the windowsill, he wrapped her up in a bear hug and pulled her inside, his whole body shaking with relief.

Diana laughed and wrapped her arms around him, and they stood there, holding each other.

After a moment, Harrington chuckled. "Why am I breathing harder than you are?"

She smiled up at him, her eyes sympathetic. "Were you frightened?"

She sounded completely normal, but when he spoke, his voice was unsteady. "Do you mean to tell me that you weren't?"

She shrugged. "The cornice is surprisingly broad. It wasn't ideal, but I wasn't in danger of falling. In better circumstances, I believe I would have found the experience exhilarating."

He laughed, incredulous. "I'm glad one of us enjoyed it. Seeing you standing there probably took twenty years off my life, but you're the perfect heroine, as usual." He tilted his head toward the door. "Come on."

She stayed him with a hand to his forearm. "Don't you want to know what I discovered in Carl Frederick's room?"

He bit back the words, *not really*. That bloody letter was the furthest thing from his mind. But, as Diana clearly cared, he asked, "What did you find?"

"Nothing."

She looked disappointed about it, so he said, "Ah. That's too bad. Well, thank you for looking."

"I was able to search the most obvious areas, but didn't have time to dig through his trunks." She tapped her lip, lost in thought. "Perhaps I can sneak back in this afternoon, once the housemaids have finished making up the rooms."

Oh, hell, no. "That's not necessary. You've already checked the most likely places. There's only so much we can do."

She waved a hand, still not meeting his eyes. "Yes, but if a good opportunity should present itself—"

"Diana." He touched her shoulder, and finally she looked at him. "We're not doing that again."

Her expression softened. "You really were scared."

"I was fucking *frantic*. That was a thousand times worse than having bullets whizzing past my head in Germany. If anything were to happen to you…" His throat constricted, which was probably for the best, as he didn't want to think that particular thought through to its conclusion.

She stepped forward, wrapping her arms around his waist. "I'm all right."

He enfolded her in a hug, burying his face in her hair. He knew it was likely that their marriage would prove to be a temporary arrangement, that she would arrange for an annulment as soon as they got back to London. Seeing her standing on that ledge had brought home how much it was going to hurt to see her walk away.

He rubbed an eye with the heel of his hand. He'd known this was a fake marriage going in. He was probably an idiot for going through with it, regardless. This experience was going to leave his heart in shreds, but he had no one to blame but himself.

"Right," he said gruffly. "Let's make our escape."

He started toward the door. He made it all of two steps before Diana stayed him with an iron hand around his upper arm.

He glanced over his shoulder, his mouth quirking into a smile. She was surprisingly strong for such a little thing. He found her staring intently at a letter lying open on the small table along the wall.

He was about to ask her what was wrong when she looked up at him, her eyes filled with wonder and disbelief. "Harrington, this is it!"

He quirked his head to the side. "What do you mean, this is it?"

"This is the letter!" she hissed, releasing his arm to pick it up. "From the King of Sweden!"

"*What?* In the bedchamber of…" His gaze swept the humble room, trying to ascertain to which servant it might belong.

"The cook," Diana supplied. "Listen to this!"

She read the letter, translating from the Swedish:

Dear Carl Frederick,

I was grieved to hear that you wrote to your Uncle Johann, requesting a copy of <u>his</u> recipe for semla. I thought it was a matter of universal agreement that <u>I</u> have the best recipe for fettisdagsbulle in the family—

"What?" Harrington hissed. None of this made sense. They had been sent to this house party to recover secrets of diplomatic significance. Not for some recipe for… "What the devil is a *fettisdagsbulle?*"

Diana waved her arm, excited. "It is a traditional Swedish dessert, a sweet roll soaked in milk. It's eaten on Shrove Tuesday, which is the literal meaning of *fettisdagsbulle* —'Shrove Tuesday bun.'"

He gaped at her. "Do you mean to tell me that we've been scouring the house for a recipe for Swedish sweet rolls?"

She gave a humorless laugh. "That is precisely what I'm telling you. The king continues…"

Johann's chef uses cream for the filling, which, I am sure you will agree, is inferior in every way to the almond paste I have instructed my chef to employ. I will forgive your negligence on this one occasion, assuming that the only reason you wrote to your uncle was because you did not wish to bother me. But I must insist that you use this recipe for your future Shrove Tuesday observances.

Semla

4 cups flour
2 tsp yeast
½ cup warm milk...

Diana trailed off. "The rest is just the recipe." She pointed to the letter. "As you can see, it's written in a different hand. He probably handed it off to the royal cook."

Harrington ran a hand over his face. "And you're sure this letter is from King Gustav?"

"Reasonably sure. It's signed Gustav IV Adolf." She flipped the letter over, indicating a burgundy wax seal. "And look at this—the bull and the griffin."

"Wonderful," Harrington said in a clipped voice. "So Carl Frederick's comment about 'state secrets' was nothing more than a jest."

Diana cringed in sympathy. "I believe you are correct."

He sighed. "I suppose there's no point in making a copy."

Diana pulled out the chair carefully so as not to make a sound. "Let's do it, just in case. It seems unlikely that there is anything of use here. But it won't take long to copy out, and that way the Foreign Office can satisfy themselves as to whether there's any underlying code."

"Good thinking." Harrington strode back to the door. "I'll keep watch."

Diana pulled the pencil and paper she had brought for that purpose from her pocket and began copying out the letter. Harrington stood guard, his thoughts flying. Their entire mission had been for a fucking pastry recipe. Which meant Diana had married him for *nothing*.

He'd thought he was doing something important for once in his life. He should've known better. When had anything he'd ever tried to do gone right? He should've known it would be a complete fucking waste.

Of course, Diana could annul the marriage. He wouldn't try to stop her. But what if word got around? Her brother would never turn her out, but the world would regard her as ruined. He felt ill, thinking that society might scorn her, and twice as ill at the prospect of her resenting him for her misfortune.

"Done!" Diana whispered from across the room. She rose from the chair and quickly restored the table to its original appearance, positioning the letter as she'd found it.

Shaking himself, Harrington pressed his ear against the door. "It's clear," he whispered. "Let's make a dash for it."

They slipped from the room and scurried down the back stairs, encountering no one on their way to their rooms. Once inside, Diana brushed a quick kiss across Harrington's lips. "I should go and join the other ladies before they remark upon my absence. I'll see you at luncheon."

She hurried out again, leaving Harrington alone with his thoughts.

CHAPTER 30

That night, when Diana entered Harrington's chamber, she found him sipping a brandy in his dressing gown, staring out the window into the night.

She came up behind him and wrapped her arms around his chest. "We did it."

He responded with a humorless laugh.

Diana pursed her lips. The men had gone fishing all afternoon, and she hadn't been seated near him at dinner, so they hadn't had the chance to talk since this morning. She had been expecting to find him in a jubilant mood as they'd managed to find the proverbial needle in the haystack.

Instead, he seemed dour.

Taking him by the shoulder, she turned him to face her. "What's wrong?"

His eyes were rueful. "I was just thinking that, in light of what the letter turned out to be, you must regret it."

Diana did not follow. "Regret what?"

He stepped around her, pacing toward the sideboard. "Marrying me," he said, refilling his glass. "It seemed like an important matter of state when you made the decision. But it turned out to be a recipe for Swedish sweet rolls."

Never had the words *Swedish sweet rolls* been spoken with such derision. But at least she understood the reason for his dark mood.

Truly, he was as thick as the mud in Cornwall. She had been the one to suggest they marry! She came to his room every night, eager for them to touch and pleasure one another. And she had made it clear that, if not for the vow forced out of him by her brother, she would want to consummate the marriage, making their union irrevocable. How was it possible that he had not figured out that she cared for him?

And yet, by all appearances, he had not. She crossed to him again, taking the glass from his hand before he could raise it to his lips and setting it back on the sideboard. "Harrington. Look at me." She waited until he complied with guarded eyes, then took his hand, squeezing it. "I regret nothing."

He blew out a breath, looking away. "You can't mean that."

"And yet, I do." She tugged him toward the bed and forced him to sit. "I did want to discuss our marriage, though. We need to talk about what we're going to do once we get back to London."

He squinted at her. "Do you mean in terms of signing the annulment papers?"

She let out a frustrated huff. "No, I do not mean in terms of signing the annulment papers! I do not want to obtain an annulment, so put that thought out of your head. I mean in terms of where we're going to live."

"I'm staying at Astley House." He cast his eyes toward the ceiling. "Do you see? I don't even have a house! I can't properly support a wife, I—"

Diana cut him off. "I will stay there as well."

He cast her a skeptical look. "You wouldn't want to stay at my parents' house."

She scooted closer to him. "I don't see anything improper about it. Your brother, Edward, and his wife, Elissa, stay at Astley House when they are in Town, do they not?"

He screwed up his face. "That's different. Edward's the heir. It will be his house one day. Besides, they have one of the larger bedrooms on the first floor. I'm crammed into a tiny room on the second floor."

The words, *I would sleep in worse than that, if it meant I could be with you*, were there on her lips. But she sensed he was not yet ready to hear that, so she said, "It will do. At least, until we can arrange to rent a house of our own."

He jerked back as if he'd been stung. "What do you mean, rent a house of our own?"

"Precisely that," she continued calmly. "Or we could buy one, if something we really like should come on the market." She gave him a wry smile. "I can certainly afford it."

His eyes were fixed on the floor. "But Diana, you don't want to buy a townhouse. To live"—he swallowed thickly, then added in a soft voice—"with me."

She took his head between her hand and arm, gently turning him to face her. "Yes, Harrington," she said softly. "I do."

Honestly, she was starting to grow concerned. She was fairly certain that Harrington's reticence stemmed from the feelings of unworthiness Izzie and Lucy had warned her about. But what woman could listen to her husband suggest they live apart, even suggest they get an *annulment*, without it bruising her confidence?

That made what he did next all the sweeter. He grabbed Diana about the waist, hauling her into his lap. She scarcely had time to gasp before his lips came down on hers, hot and eager.

He kissed her until her head spun, then lifted his head. "I can't believe it."

Head spinning, she clung to his shoulders for dear life. "Can't believe what?"

"That you want to go through with it. Our *marriage*," he clarified in response to her dazed look. He laughed, and this time it was full of joy. "I'm the luckiest man in the world!"

"That's more like it," she said, threading her fingers into his hair. "Much better than when you were planning our *annulment!*"

His face turned somber. "That has nothing to do with you. You know that, don't you?" He made an incredulous sound. "I still can't believe that *you* would want to be married to *me.*"

She laughed. "How many climaxes do you have to give me before you realize that there's something in this arrangement for me?"

A devilish grin snaked its way across his lips. "Perhaps a few more. Let's try it and see if I can finally convince myself."

She laughed as he tossed her back on the bed. He rucked her nightgown up as he came to lie beside her. She lifted her hips, eager to help him. In three swift moves, she was completely bare before him while he was fully dressed, but she liked being bare before him.

He kissed her, letting his hands roam everywhere. He soon had her squirming on the bed. She let her thighs fall open as a suggestion, but when he slid down her body, he only made it as far as her breasts. Not that this was a bad thing… at first. He pressed open-mouthed kisses to her soft flesh, and she sighed. He flicked his tongue over her nipples, and she shivered. He suckled her into his mouth, and she moaned.

But he steadfastly ignored her attempts to push him lower, where she was starting to need him rather desperately.

Finally, when she was trembling with pent-up need, she snapped. "Harrington! Why won't you touch me between my legs?"

He grinned, unrepentant. "I want to see if I can make you come just by touching your breasts."

"Not," she said between pants, "before I murder you. Now put your mouth where it belongs!"

If he minded this high-handed treatment, he gave no sign of it. In fact, judging by the moan that escaped his lips, one could be forgiven for assuming that he welcomed it. He slid down, pressing her thighs open and tonguing the little rosebud that was throbbing for him. Diana was so exquisitely aroused, it took her but a minute before she was crying out for him.

He came up and took her in his arms, and Diana thought she might burst with happiness. They were going to make their fake marriage work—she just knew they were.

Buoyed by this sense of optimism, she finally felt courageous enough to try one of the things she'd seen featured in Harrington's book of naughty prints.

She sat up enough to kiss him, undressing him as she did. He helped with eager hands, and she soon had him bare. She straddled him, rubbing her slick pussy against the underside of his swollen cock. "Doesn't that feel good?" she whispered.

"Mmm-hmmm," he moaned, eyes glazed with pleasure.

"Well, you can't have it." She nipped at his ear. "Not yet anyway."

He groaned aloud, and she felt his cock give an eager pulse between her legs. That was… interesting. He seemed to *enjoy* being denied.

Filing that information away for future reference, she kissed him again. "But as soon as we get to Town, it's *yours*."

She slid down his body, pressing kisses as she went. Kneeling between his legs, she took his cock in her mouth, sliding her hand up and down his length the way he'd shown her.

But this time, she let her hand trail lower. She paused to caress his sack, then brought her hand to the place just behind it. Gathering her courage, she started to rub him there.

The book of prints had shown an image of a woman doing this, massaging her lover behind his ball sack while sucking his cock. The caption had said that some men found this exquisitely pleasurable. As she began rubbing him there, Diana felt a little bit nervous, wondering if her husband would enjoy it and how her attempt at pleasuring him would be received.

He responded with a long, low groan. "Diana! Oh, *God*, that feels so good! Rub me even harder, darling. Yes, that's it. Oh, *fuck!*"

She chanced a glance up at him, and his eyes were hazy with pleasure. Encouraged, she rubbed him deeper and deeper as he squirmed helplessly on the bed. As she massaged him, she tightened her lips around his cock, giving him suction, and desperate sounds slipped from his lips. "Diana!" he gasped. "You're going to make me… Oh, *God*… Oh… Oh, *fuck!*"

She tasted the spurt of his seed in her mouth. She had learned over the past few days to keep pleasuring him, at least for a moment. She saw him through his crisis, then gentled her strokes when his body went tense, finally letting his softening cock slide out of her mouth.

He immediately hauled her into his arms, burying his face

in her neck. "Thank you. That was *amazing*. How did you know to do that?"

She smiled. "There was a picture. In that book of naughty prints I told you about."

Harrington laughed. "Your brother must have the same book that I do. There's a similar print in mine."

Diana's smile faded. Fortunately, Harrington's eyes were closed, so he didn't seem to notice her consternation. It made sense that he assumed the book of prints she had stumbled upon belonged to Marcus. She wasn't quite sure how to tell him that it was actually his book she had perused.

She wasn't quite brave enough to broach the subject tonight. So instead, she sighed. "You know, I almost never feel sorry for myself for my missing hand. But while I was doing that, I couldn't help but wish I had two. That way, I would have had one hand to stroke your cock and another to touch you there."

He shook his head. "You're perfect. I promise you, I could not possibly care less. But speaking of naughty prints, you've reminded me of a rather unusual one I once saw. It belonged to one of my fellow students from Oxford. It came from somewhere in the Far East and showed a woman being pleasured by an octopus."

Diana squinted at him, certain she had misheard. "An *octopus*?"

He laughed. "Yes, an octopus! It had a tentacle for each breast, one to hold down each arm, and one for right here." He reached between her legs, stroking her in a way that made her shiver. "There was another pumping inside of her, and another"—he stopped short, clearing his throat. "Well. Suffice it to say, it was touching her in *a lot* of places."

"Gracious." Having been intimate with Harrington for the past five days, Diana thought she had moved past any sense of missish embarrassment. But she found she was blushing just thinking about this image of an octopus, of all things.

He gave her a tender smile. "My point is, I could have a dozen hands, and I still wouldn't have enough to touch you everywhere I'd like. I'm the happiest man alive to have your hand on me. I wouldn't trade you for a thousand octopuses."

She laughed as she snuggled into his chest. "Good."

"And I could help if you like. In fact"—his voice took on an eager note—"you could even *order* me to stroke myself while you're busy doing other things."

She studied him, as yet another puzzle piece fit into place. "And you would like that."

"I would." He looked a little nervous. "If you don't mind."

"I don't mind at all." She yawned. "I have an innate talent for ordering people around."

He murmured something. Diana wasn't sure, but she thought it might have been, "You certainly do."

They lapsed into silence. Diana chuckled. "I still think an octopus is an odd choice for this erotic print. I know they only chose it because it has so many arms. But nothing else about it seems particularly arousing."

He waggled his eyebrows. "I don't know. All of those suckers."

She frowned. "I don't see what's arousing about... Wait. Harrington? What are you doing?"

He had extracted himself from her arms, a wicked grin on his face. Without saying a word, he pressed her thighs open, burying his face between her legs.

"Harrington?" She peered at him, confused. Instead of caressing her with his tongue as he usually did, he had sealed his lips around the little nub between her legs. "Harrington, what are you... Oh. *Oh,* that's... That's very... I... I see what you mean. About the... about the suckers." It was difficult to form words, as her breath was growing ragged. "That's...

that's almost *too* good. I didn't know the pleasure could be... so intense. Oh, *God*, I... Please don't stop! Oh, Harrington! Please keep doing it just like that! You're... You're going to make me—"

It took some time for Diana's thighs to stop trembling. Harrington's smile was smug as he crawled up beside her, took her in his arms, and pulled the coverlet over them.

As she drifted off to sleep, the last thought in Diana's head was that she had a newfound appreciation for octopuses.

CHAPTER 31

They arrived back in London at mid-morning the following day, and Harrington delivered Diana to her brother's home. The plan was for her to pack a few things and join him at Astley House that evening.

He had the coachman take him directly to Horse Guards. William Windham received him immediately. Harrington summarized their search during the house party and presented the transcribed letter. "This is word for word. It looks like a simple recipe to my eyes, but I'll let your office determine if there's anything more to it."

"Good." Windham glanced over the letter. "You picked up Swedish more quickly than I thought."

Harrington hesitated but decided that honesty would be the best approach. "Truth be told, I didn't. I don't know if you heard, but I recently married. It happens that my wife speaks Swedish." He cleared his throat. "I know you said to keep my assignment in the strictest confidentiality, but—"

Windham waved this off. "It seems to have turned out all right. Who is your new bride, if you don't mind my asking?"

Harrington shifted in his seat. "The former Lady Diana Latimer."

The Secretary of State's eyebrows shot halfway to his forehead.

Harrington chuckled. "I take it you've heard of her."

"The richest heiress in all of England? Yes, I'd say I've heard of her." Windham laughed. "And you were the one to land her. Gracious."

"It's not like that," Harrington said hastily. "I don't care about her money. I really don't. She's... well." He swallowed. "She's wonderful."

The corners of Windham's eyes crinkled. "Good for you." He straightened, abruptly somber again. "Excellent work on this assignment, Lieutenant. That's two successful commissions in a row. I will certainly keep that in mind when I find myself in need of assistance in the future."

It was on the tip of Harrington's tongue to say, *Oh please, God, no.* But he managed a tight smile. "Thank you, sir. Should I rejoin my unit in Hampshire, or—"

The Secretary of State cut him off with a sweep of his hand. "Stay in London for the time being. I am sure we will have need of you soon enough."

Harrington rose. "Yes, sir. I'm sure you have a hundred things to do, so I'll take my leave."

Windham, who was already reaching toward a stack of correspondence, waved him out absently.

He headed for the stairs, feeling strangely free. It was the first time in a few years he hadn't been at the army's beck and call. William Windham would probably come up with a new mission for him soon enough, but he might have a few days, or even a few weeks, of relative leisure. The timing could not have been better. He and Diana would be able to enjoy a honeymoon of sorts.

He should probably find out what issues were currently

being debated in Parliament now that he was an MP. The thought still made him shudder, but quickly on its heels came the reminder that he would have Diana not just sharing his bed, but by his side. No more sneaking around, no more struggling to find five minutes to ask her what the hell he should do. The thought settled over him like a warm blanket, followed by the strangest conviction—that with her help, he could do this.

The only other matter of business facing him for the next few days was finding a townhouse to rent. That notion also felt strange. The army was not what you would call a lucrative career, at least, not at the lowly rank of lieutenant. For junior officers, the costs of uniforms and equipment usually exceeded what they received in salary, and it was something of a point of pride for noble families to take on the cost of outfitting their younger sons as an act of service for king and country. Harrington had therefore never given much thought to establishing a household of his own. He'd had no prospect of being able to afford it for at least another decade, if he survived that long.

But he quite liked the thought of setting up house with Diana. Hell, just talking to her was a delight, and if they were living in the same house, he would see her constantly, from breakfast to bedtime. The notion seemed almost too indulgent, like a never-ending dessert course.

And, of course, as they'd made it back to London, the promise her brother had extracted from him had been fulfilled. That meant there was a very real possibility they would make love tonight. The prospect was exciting for obvious reasons, but he also felt trepidation. Because as things stood, they would be staying at Astley House tonight, with his little sister, Lucy, in the room next door.

He didn't want anything to mar their first time making love. Maybe they should get a room at a hotel. Someplace where the sheets weren't infested with fleas—the Pulteney, perhaps? Could he arrange for a room on such short notice?

Harrington was so distracted with thoughts of what he and Diana would be getting up to that evening that he almost ploughed into a man coming up the stairs. He realized with a start that it was General James Gordon, who held the post of Military Secretary.

He snapped to attention. "My apologies, General. I was lost in thought."

"Lieutenant Astley." A smile spread across General Gordon's face. He gestured for Harrington to accompany him. "Come. It happens that you are just the man I was hoping to see."

Harrington complied, because what else could he do? He had a sinking feeling that he had just leapt out of William Windham's frying pan, straight into General Gordon's fire, but he clung to the hope that the general merely had a few questions about the retreat from Hanover.

General Gordon led him to his own office, which was well-appointed for all that it was a fifth the size of the capacious room where William Windham carried out his business.

Harrington declined the general's offer of tea, hoping he could keep this quick. "What did you wish to see me about, sir?"

The general folded his hands in front of him on his desk. "As I'm sure you have heard, there has been a recent surge of interest in light infantry troops, thanks in large part to the efforts of the 95th Rifles during the retreat to Cuxhaven. The army has decided we need more of you. We'd like to start by adding a battalion of skirmishers to the King's German Legion. They'll need training." He leaned forward. "And the army has decided that you're the man to do it."

Harrington replied, "Yes, sir." Because really, there was

nothing else he could say. That was the nature of the army—you received an order, and you followed it.

Although in truth, this didn't sound all that bad. He'd heard whisperings that the 95th Rifles would soon be bound for Argentina, of all places. Harrington couldn't imagine what good they would do halfway across the world. Surely, Napoleon was giving Britain enough trouble to deal with in this hemisphere.

But training troops was something he thought he would be good at. Regular infantry soldiers carried muskets, which were so inaccurate that there was little need to aim beyond pointing them in the general direction of the enemy. The idea was that if an entire line of men fired in unison, a few bullets were bound to find a target.

But light infantry troops, or skirmishers, as they were often called, carried Baker rifles. They did not partake in the traditional tactics of forming lines and squares. The job of skirmishers was to fan out in front of an advancing line, taking cover where they could find it behind walls or trees, and to demoralize the enemy by picking off his troops one by one. A skirmisher had to be a good shot, and that was where Harrington could help them.

It occurred to him that training troops would take place on domestic soil. It was as safe a mission as he was likely to get. And that meant Diana could come with him!

She had made noises about heading out that afternoon to start looking at townhouses. He should send her a note. It seemed they wouldn't be renting in London after all, but in…

"Where will the training take place, sir?" Harrington asked.

"Ireland. Bandon, to be specific. It's a little town in County Cork."

"Bandon. Very good." A quiet Irish town was quite the departure from the busy whirl of London. He wondered if

Diana would be willing to make the change. "When do I depart?"

Gordon laughed. "That's why I'm so glad I ran into you on the stairs. I'd heard Windham had sent you on some errand or the other. I was worried you wouldn't make it back in time, but here you are."

Harrington tilted his head. "Will I be leaving soon, then?"

"At high tide." The general stood. "Go and pack your trunk, Lieutenant. You'll be sailing for Ireland tonight."

$\mathcal{H}$arrington's first stop was Latimer House.

The long-time family butler, Ellery, greeted him warmly but informed him that Diana was out.

"Do you know where she went?" Harrington asked.

"She said something about going to look at townhouses." Ellery frowned, noticing Harrington's drawn expression. "Is anything the matter, Lieutenant?"

"Yes. No." He cleared his throat. "It's nothing bad, but I do need to speak with her with some urgency."

"Of course. She did not mention any specifics to me, but I will ask Lady Griselda and—"

"Astley." The sound of crisp footfalls echoed on the marble tiles as Marcus Latimer strode into the entry hall. "Good. You're here."

Harrington gave a nervous laugh. "I'm fairly certain those words have never before crossed your lips."

The duke placed a hand on his shoulder, steering him toward the grand staircase. "Come. You can sign the annulment papers."

Harrington jerked out of his grasp. He should have

fucking known. "Now see here, Trevissick. I spoke with Diana last night—"

"Last night?" The duke's eyes narrowed. "What were you two doing *last night?*"

Harrington dropped his voice to a hiss. "I kept my vow. A vow you should never have asked me to make. I won't have you impugning my honor."

Trevissick raised a haughty brow. "Then there should be no impediment to having the marriage annulled."

"We don't want to have the marriage annulled. Neither of us do. We want to make a proper go of it."

The duke's nostrils curled as if he had smelled something particularly foul. "No doubt you did not read the papers you signed prior to the ceremony. Diana's fortune will remain in her own name. You cannot touch it."

"Of course, I read them," Harrington snapped. He was hardly going to make the mistake of signing something without reading it again. "I don't care about her fortune. I *want* it to stay in her name. I would never want her to think, even for a second, that I married her for her money. And, in my line of work, I could get shot next month. I want her to be provided for!"

"Well," the duke said tightly, "it happens that Diana has not signed the papers yet. If you're so confident that she wants to remain married to you, why should you hesitate?"

Harrington rolled his eyes. "I don't have time for this. I just received word that I'm being sent to Ireland—"

"Ireland?" Lady Griselda asked, entering the room.

"That's correct," Harrington confirmed. "A town called Bandon, in County Cork. I'm going to be performing some training with the King's German Legion."

Lady Griselda smiled broadly. "Diana will love Ireland. She is so sick of London." She held up a finger. "Wait right there. I have something for you."

Trevissick grabbed him by the sleeve of his jacket and tried to drag him toward the stairs. "Come. This will only take a moment."

"Will you stop that?" Harrington snapped, jerking his arm free. "I'm not going to sign your bloody papers."

Trevissick glowered at him. "What if Diana does not wish to go to Ireland with you?"

The possibility sank like a cannonball into the bottom of his gut, but Harrington forcefully set it aside. "Then we will cross that bridge when we come to it. But I'm going to ask her what she wants to do. We're going to have a conversation about it. And when I say *we*, I mean she and I. *You* will not be involved. Until then, you can sod off!"

"Ah, good. You are still here." Lady Griselda had returned. Harrington saw that she had one of her dogs with her.

She handed Harrington the lead. "Please consider her to be a wedding present." She bent down and scratched the dog under the chin. "*Braver Hund.* Oh, how I will miss you, my Inge! But you must be good for Lieutenant Astley, *ja?*"

"This is *Inge?*" Harrington couldn't believe his ears. Inge was the best tracker Lady Griselda had ever trained. A few years ago, when his sister, Izzie, had been kidnapped, Inge had been the one to track her scent through the streets of London.

He dropped his voice low. "Lady Griselda, I couldn't possibly take Inge. I know how special she is to you."

"First of all, you must call me Aunt Griselda. You are family now." She bent down and rubbed Inge behind her ears. "Secondly, I want you to take Inge. I am not so spry as I used to be, but Inge? She is young and lively. London is no place for her. She wants to run through the woods, over the fields!" She met Harrington's gaze, and he was surprised to see that the fierce woman's eyes were bright with unshed tears. "She is my most precious treasure, but the time has come for me to let her go. She needs to be happy, to be free, to live a life of her own making." She pointed at him with a bony finger. "That I am entrusting her to you is a great honor. You are not to let me down!"

Harrington blinked. "Are we still talking about the dog?"

Aunt Griselda laughed. "You always were more clever than you let on."

Harrington bowed his head. "Well, thank you. I will take care of your precious treasures. Both of them." A clock chimed somewhere down the hall, and he groaned. "I've got to go. The ship sails at high tide, and I need to see if I can secure a cabin for myself and Diana."

Trevissick's voice was snide. "Assuming she wants to go with you."

Harrington gritted his teeth. "Yes. Assuming she wants to come with me."

Aunt Griselda pressed the leash into his hands. "Here, take Inge with you. She will enjoy the sights and smells of the dock. Yes! *Braver Hund!* Be good for Lieutenant Astley. I know you will be. You are the best of dogs."

Harrington climbed back into his carriage and instructed the coachman to take him to the Royal Dockyard at Deptford. Traffic was heavy and the journey took three-quarters of an hour. He found that Inge made a pleasant companion. He angled the windowpanes open for her, and she spent the journey sitting up on the seat, eagerly taking in the sights and scents of London as they flew by. He found it soothed his strained nerves to stroke her silky fur. She would occasionally turn and lick his face, and after his encounter with Diana's brother, it was nice to be in the presence of someone who actually liked him.

He located the ship he was to sail on, the *Mercury*, without too much trouble. Captain Bannister had a bit of good news for him, in that it would be no trouble for him to bring Inge on board. But the news was mostly bad. All the cabins were spoken for. There would be no possibility of bringing Diana along. She would have to find her own passage to Ireland in the coming days. Worse, the ship would be making sail earlier than Harrington had realized.

"You need to be back here with your things no later than six o'clock," Captain Bannister informed him. "We make sail at seven."

"Six o'clock?" Harrington checked his pocket watch. "But that's in just four hours!"

The captain clasped his shoulder. "The tide waits for no man. Best hurry home and pack, Lieutenant."

Harrington did just that. He lost almost an hour on the carriage ride back to Astley House. There, he learned that Lucy, Izzie, and Harrington's mother had accompanied Diana on her townhouse hunting expedition.

Harrington explained his situation to the family butler, Yarwood. "When she comes by to return Lucy and Mother, make sure to detain her. It's very important that I speak to her before I'm forced to sail."

Yarwood bowed. "I will watch the door personally."

Edward wandered into the foyer to see what the commotion was. Harrington explained about his hasty deployment. "Come," Edward said, "I'll have my valet assist with the packing of your trunks."

"That would be appreciated," Harrington said. "Actually, could you oversee the process?"

Edward frowned. "You're going out?"

Harrington dropped his voice low. "I have to find Diana. Can you imagine how furious she'll be if I board a ship bound for Ireland without even informing her?"

Edward's eyes flared with understanding. "Furious." He clapped Harrington on the shoulder. "Go. Find your bride. I'll take care of your trunks."

Harrington's eyes were sincere. "Thank you."

He ordered a saddle horse so he could weave in and out of traffic, making better time. He checked Izzie and Thorpe's house on the north side of Mayfair, but she hadn't been there in hours.

Mayfair, which would certainly be Diana's first choice for their new residence, wasn't all that large, so he rode around, hoping he might be able to spot the carriage Yarwood had informed him the ladies had taken—a glossy burgundy coach picked out in gold, bearing the crest of her brother the duke on the door. But he didn't have any luck.

After an hour of riding around at loose ends, he stopped by Latimer House again. Ellery was apologetic. "Her ladyship has not returned, Lieutenant."

"Do you have any idea where she might have gone?"

Ellery shook his head. "Apparently your mother had compiled a list of potential houses while the two of you were away at the house party. I believe Lady Diana put herself entirely at the countess's disposal."

Harrington nodded grimly. At least his mother had thought the marriage would stick. A comforting notion, but one he didn't have time to contemplate at present.

Lady Griselda—no, *Aunt* Griselda—strode into the foyer. "Ah, you're back! How is Inge?"

Harrington leaned down and patted the pointer's neck. "Inge makes an admirable companion. Not that I am the least bit surprised."

Aunt Griselda bent forward and rubbed the dog's ears. "Good. Good!"

"Listen," Harrington said, his gaze encompassing both Ellery and Aunt Griselda, "it turns out I have even less time than I thought. I have to be on that ship by six o'clock, and we make sail at seven. If I don't find Diana in time—" His voice cracked, and he had to take a moment to compose himself. "She's going to hate me," he concluded quietly.

"She won't," Ellery insisted.

"Do not worry," Aunt Griselda said. "I have her trunk packed and ready to go, in case she returns in time. And in case she does not, we will tell her how desperate you were. How distraught. How pathetic—"

"Thank you, Aunt Griselda," Harrington cut her off, not caring to see what adjectives she would come up with next. He shot Ellery a grateful look. "Tell her how sorry I am. How hard I tried to find her. That I…"

He trailed off. It was on the tip of his tongue to add, *tell her that I love her.* But he wasn't yet confident enough to speak those words aloud, not two and a half weeks after he'd stumbled back into her life, even if he knew they were true. Besides, it wasn't the sort of message you sent by proxy.

"Tell her," he finally said, "that I will be miserable without her. And that if she will consent to join me in Ireland, that I will be the happiest man in all of Christendom."

Ellery placed his hand over his heart. "We will."

"Of course, we will," Aunt Griselda added brightly.

"Thank you," Harrington said simply. Down the hall, the clock struck half five. He had to hurry if he was going to catch his ship. "I'd best be—"

"Astley," a supercilious voice called. Harrington discerned the sharp click of footsteps on the marble tiles. "Good, you're back. Now you can sign the—"

"Fuck off," Harrington called. "I haven't got time for your nonsense."

Ignoring the duke's outraged sputtering, Harrington turned on his heel and walked out the door.

CHAPTER 33

Harrington left it as late as he possibly could.

But eventually, he could delay no longer. He gave Edward a hasty hug, pounding his brother on the back, then climbed into the carriage with Inge.

He was quiet during the drive to the Royal Dockyard. Not that there was anyone to talk to. Edward had offered to accompany him, but Harrington had asked him to stay behind and convey his regrets to Diana whenever she turned up. Which, knowing his luck, would be two bloody minutes after he left.

He blew out a petulant breath. Inge, seeming to sense his mood, left her perch before the window to lay her head in his lap. He stroked her head, grateful that he had her for company.

On board the *Mercury*, Captain Bannister showed him his quarters. He had a bunk in a room with a handful of junior officers. Which was fine, as the voyage shouldn't take more than a few days. He had certainly slept in worse conditions during the retreat from Hanover, when he got to sleep at all. He opened his trunk to see what Edward had packed for him.

Right on top of a stack of clean shirts was a thick book. He peered at its spine. *The Complete Works of Plutarch.* Harrington groaned. This was what came of asking his bookish brother to pack for him. But, upon a cursory inspection, Plutarch aside, Edward and his valet had done an admirable job. There was plenty of clean linen, all his officer's accoutrements—sword, pistols, canteen, that sort of thing—and a box of his favorite tea. There was even a miniature portrait of Diana that belonged to Lucy. It was a thoughtful thing to include, but seeing her cool gaze felt like a punch to the gut, and he closed the lid of his trunk with a snap.

He knew he should probably introduce himself to the officers of the King's German Legion. This was usually a part of his job that he was actually good at—gladhanding with his fellow soldiers, making a friend of every man he met, whether he was a foot soldier or a field commander. But Harrington found himself in an uncharacteristically foul temper and thought it better that he keep to himself. If he spoke to anyone right now, he was going to put the wrong foot forward, and he bloody well knew it.

He wandered the ship until he found a relatively uncrowded spot at the bow, just behind the figurehead of a curly-haired god in a winged hat.

He sat cross-legged on the deck, rubbing Inge's neck and feeling sorry for himself. As the sun sank low, the sailors untied the mooring lines and the ship drifted into the Thames. He hung his head. There was a certain finality about slipping away from the shore, an irrevocability.

An *irrevocability*? What a bunch of tripe. When had he become so fucking overwrought? At this rate, he might as well go back to his bunk and read the Plutarch.

He should probably go and join the other officers. At least it would distract him from his melancholy. But he couldn't seem to muster the will to move from his solitary perch, where the same set of miserable thoughts circled round and round inside his head. Diana was going to be furious with him, and who could blame her? He was abandoning her without a word just one week after their wedding! It was a despicable thing to do, no matter how you looked at it. And, now that he couldn't do anything about it, he was starting to second-guess every bloody decision he'd made today. It wasn't as if he could disobey an order from his commanding officers. But he might have asked for more time. Given his status as a newly married man, surely such a request was reasonable. God, he should have at least asked. The worst they could have said was no.

Then there was his decision not to sign those annulment papers. At the time, he had felt that signing them would be an insult, signaling that he had no wish to continue their marriage. But the papers wouldn't be legal unless Diana signed them, too. What if she *wanted* to end their marriage, in light of his desertion? Considered another way, signing those papers would have given her options. Isn't that what he had said he wanted to do?

Splendid. Now she had another reason to despise him…

They were sailing past the East India Docks when Inge lifted her head. She held perfectly still for a moment, scenting the air, then scrambled to her feet and went bounding across the deck.

Perfect. Even his dog had deserted him.

That was when he heard it—a feminine laugh. "Inge! *Braver Hund.* I've been looking all over for you!"

Harrington watched in disbelief as Inge returned, trailed by… his wife?

"Diana?" He scrambled to his feet. "What…? How…?"

She smiled up at him, which seemed odd. Didn't she hate him? "I returned Lucy and your mother to Astley House a quarter of an hour after you departed. Your brother told me what happened. I had to make a quick dash back to Latimer House to collect my trunk, and then I came straight here." She laughed. "It was a near thing—they were pulling up the gangway when I arrived. I had to shout at them to put it back down."

He shook himself. "But… the captain said there was no room. That the cabins were all spoken for."

She lifted her chin, her face falling into a characteristically insouciant expression. "What is the point of being the richest heiress in all of England if I can't even bribe my way onto a ship?"

"Bribe?" Harrington said dumbly. His poor brain was still having trouble processing the fact that she was here.

She shrugged a negligent shoulder. "I paid the first mate a handsome fee for surrendering his cabin. But I suspect Captain Bannister would have found a place for me regardless." A smug smile twisted her lips. "I have my ways."

Diana was nothing if not diabolical. "Dare I ask what you mean by that?"

She clutched his sleeve, making her eyes large and tremulous. "Oh, please, sir! I can't bear to be parted from my husband!" Her shoulders drooped, and she gave a great sniff. "We've scarcely been married a week!"

Harrington took an involuntary step back. "Good God. Don't do that!" He held his palms out as if to ward her off. "It's more than a man can take!"

Diana perked up, dropping her pathetic façade as easily as she had donned it. "True. But you must admit, it was effective. Now, have you gone and made my brother any more imprudent promises?"

"I—no." Harrington blinked. "That is, he asked me to sign some papers annulling the marriage. But I told him, er…"

Diana's eyes were keen. "What, exactly, did you tell him?"

"I told him to fuck off," Harrington admitted.

She laughed, a bright, sparkling sound. "That would explain his temper."

He squinted at her. "Aren't you mad at me?"

"No. Why would I be?" she asked, bending down to stroke Inge's back.

He shook himself, sure he must have heard wrong. "Because I abandoned you without a single word."

There was sympathy in her eyes. "Yes. But, from what I heard, you didn't have any choice in the matter. And everyone I spoke to emphasized the fact that you spent all afternoon riding around Mayfair searching for me."

He rubbed the back of his head. "Did they use the word *pathetic* to describe me?"

She wrinkled her nose. "Only once or twice."

He ran a hand across his face. "Perfect."

"Harrington!" She laughed, tugging down his arm. "You're forgetting the most important thing."

He struggled to think. "What's that?"

She stepped forward, jabbing him in the chest with a finger. "You are finally free of the vow you made to my brother. Which means that we are going to consummate this marriage."

Oh, God. His thoughts had been consumed by his complete and utter failure and how Diana was going to hate him.

Sex had been the furthest thought from his mind. But she was here. She was here, and that stupid vow he'd made to her brother no longer impeded him, and—

"Did you say we have a cabin?" he blurted, his cock already stiffening.

Her gaze traveled downward, and a satisfied smile cropped up on her perfectly pert pink lips. She swung her eyes up to meet his. "Yes. Yes, I did." She seized his hand in hers, tugging him after her. "Come, husband. I have need of you."

As she led him down the length of the ship, he heard snickers all around him. No doubt word had spread like wildfire that his new wife was aboard. It didn't take a genius to guess what they were heading off to do, and they were surrounded by *sailors*, for God's sake.

If Diana minded these lewd murmurs, she gave no indication of it. Harrington, on the other hand, secretly loved it. Oh, the fellows would rib him about it later, the way his bride had dragged him across the ship with his cock already starting to thicken in his trousers. It wasn't *that* embarrassing. They were newlyweds, after all, and every man aboard would have been in a similar state had they been fortunate enough to be in his position.

But Harrington specifically loved the fact that it was *slightly* humiliating. He loved this high-handed version of Diana. He loved her ordering him about, treating him like her war prize. God, but he was eager to serve her. He'd spend the rest of this voyage with his head between her thighs and not utter a word of complaint.

Captain Bannister's smile as they approached was amused. "Ah, good. I see that you found your husband." He turned to face a boy of about twelve years with straw-colored hair. "Benjamin! Take charge of Lieutenant Astley's dog for the duration of the voyage."

Young Benjamin surged forward, looking delighted by this assignment. He dropped to his knees and began petting Inge, who responded by licking his face. "Yes, sir!"

Harrington leaned toward the captain, dropping his voice low. "Diana told me that your first mate gave up his cabin. I didn't mean to indispose anyone."

Captain Bannister's expression was kind. "I can assure you, Kirkpatrick was happy with the arrangement. Besides, the voyage is short, and we all remember what it was like, being a newly married man." He straightened, adopting a commanding voice. "Lieutenant Astley!"

Harrington snapped to attention. "Yes, sir!"

"You are relieved of duty for the duration of the voyage."

Harrington's cheeks burned. "Thank you, sir!"

Beside him, Diana was fluttering about, batting her eyelashes in a distinctly un-Diana-like manner. "Oh, thank you, Captain!" She took Harrington's hand, smiling at him fondly. "I don't know what I would have done without your assistance."

Captain Bannister bowed. "That's quite all right, my lady. I've given orders for your husband's trunk to be moved to your cabin. Do you remember the way?"

Diana seized upon this excuse to leave. "I believe so." She was already towing Harrington toward the central hatch. "Thank you again!"

As he followed his wife, Harrington heard a mixture of sniggering, cheering, and lewd whistles. He ducked his head, but Diana kept hers up the whole time, smirking like the cat who got the cream.

The cabin Diana led him to was not what you would call spacious. The bunk along the wall was designed to sleep one. Harrington's trunk had been tucked beneath it. You had to squeeze past a small square table to reach the bed. And in the corner, there was a cannon, a twelve-pounder, by the look of it. But the silver lining was that the presence of a cannon meant they had a window, so at least there was a bit of light.

Harrington chuckled nervously. "Well, isn't this romantic? Did you ever imagine you'd spend your wedding night next to a cannon?"

She grabbed him by the front of his coat and shoved him down on the bed. Harrington was so startled that he offered no resistance. Hiking up her skirts, she crawled on top of him, straddling him, then proceeded to kiss him with such ferocity he forgot where he was entirely.

"I don't give a fig about the cannon," she said when she finally lifted her head. "Take off your clothes. Now!"

"*Oh, my God.*" Harrington's cock pulsed in his trousers. Diana shoving him down on the bed and ravishing him was his every sexual fantasy come true.

But it wasn't just the fact that she was making his cock bear more than a passing resemblance to the ship's mast. Her following him onto this ship, refusing to let him go, dragging him off to a cabin and climbing on top of him… it made him feel *wanted*.

He'd honestly never thought that anyone would want him. Not for more than a quick roll in the hay.

The thought that this brilliant, perfect woman wanted him had his throat seizing up and him blinking rapidly to hold back the sudden moisture in his eyes.

Fortunately, Diana chose that moment to distract him by reaching her hand down and teasing him through the placket of his trousers.

He groaned as his head lolled to the side. She seemed to know how much he liked what she was doing, if the smug grin she was giving him was any indication. "You like this, don't you?"

"Yes," he panted. "Possibly a little too much."

She arched an inquisitive eyebrow. "How could you like it too much?"

"If you keep bossing me around, this is going to be very, very short." He straightened, giving her a quick kiss, then scooped her up, depositing her next to him on the narrow bed. "Although it's probably going to be short regardless."

For once, his preternaturally confident wife looked unsure. "Is that a good thing, or a bad thing?"

"Difficult to say." He peeled his coat off, tossed it on the floor, and yanked at the stock around his neck. "It depends on what you like. I suppose we're about to find out."

Her eyes were fierce as she grabbed his shirt and pulled him down on top of her. *"Let's."*

They rolled around, kissing and groping, until Diana was naked before him and he was down to his trousers. He lay her back onto the narrow bunk—he still couldn't believe he was sharing his wedding night with the daughter of a fucking duke in a plain wooden sailor's bunk!—and pressed her thighs open.

She frowned when he started to slide down. "Harrington! We've done that part before. I want to experience the rest of it."

"You will." He pressed a kiss to the inside of her thigh. "Believe me, you will. But you'll have an easier time of it if you're sopping wet."

She held her pout. "I think I'm already… already quite…" She trailed off on a gasp as he delved between her folds with his tongue. After a couple of panting breaths, she waved a hand magnanimously. "F-fine. I suppose we can try… your idea."

He couldn't help but grin. Lord knew his new wife loved to be licked and fondled on the little button between her legs. And he was damn glad he was the man who got to do it.

He wondered if she would like the rest of it as well. Because of the vow he'd made to her brother, he hadn't dared to slip so much as a finger inside of her while they'd been at the house party. He was far from a blushing virgin, and he knew from experience that some only derived pleasure from the spot he was currently fondling.

Continuing to tongue her, he slipped a finger inside of her, palm facing up. She was as wet as Cumberland. It went in easily, but he noticed that she stiffened and then started to squirm.

He lifted his head. "Does that hurt?"

"N-no!" she sputtered.

Harrington frowned. Diana's expression was difficult to read. She looked vaguely… startled? Maybe she was hesitant to admit that what he was doing was less than pleasant. "Maybe it would be more accurate to say uncomfortable?"

He trailed off. Diana did not seem to be attending. She squirmed on the bed, pressing her hips down against the mattress, then gave an experimental wiggle.

Harrington frowned. "Is everything all right?"

She sighed, moving her hips again. An expression came over her face, and this time, he recognized it.

It was bliss. Pure, unadulterated bliss.

He started circling his finger inside her, rubbing her front wall. She gasped in response. "Does that feel good, then?"

Her eyes rolled back in her head. "*So* good!"

He slipped in a second finger. She squealed, but this time, he was certain it was a good squeal.

He tried to lower his head again, but strong fingers knotted in his hair. "Oh, no, you don't!" She yanked him upward. "Get up here, you silly man. And take off those bloody trousers!"

Harrington had never been so happy to obey an order in his life.

CHAPTER 34

*A*s Harrington settled on top of her, Diana mused that this was the best day of her life, even better than her wedding day.

Just this morning, she had thought she would be stuck in London for the foreseeable future, attending boring balls and insipid dinners, listening to the same vapid gossip over and over until she wanted to scream into her pillow.

Instead, here she was, on this ship with Harrington. She was going somewhere. *Doing* something.

She was on an adventure!

And, if that thing he had just done with his finger was any indication, married life was going to suit her *splendidly*.

Harrington seemed to be more nervous than she was. His Adam's apple bobbed as he swallowed thickly. "Are you sure about—"

"*Yes.*"

"Because we don't have to—"

"We're going to," she said firmly, then paused. "Unless you don't want to?"

He gave her a look that said, *are you daft?* Which, given the circumstances, was actually reassuring.

But then, he said, "Shit. I don't have a sheath."

"We don't need one." It was an odd thing to say to one's wife, not that Diana wanted to pause the proceedings so they could discuss his comment. There were more pressing matters at hand.

Although... now that she considered the matter, it wasn't a bad thought. If she wanted to follow the drum and accompany Harrington on his future deployments, it would be significantly easier if she didn't have a babe on her hip. Although she did want to have children someday, it was probably best to postpone that happy event for a few years, to the extent that it was possible. As for today, Izzie had explained how to count the days between her cycles so she knew when she was most likely to conceive. She should be all right for the next few days.

She reached down, aligning his cock with her opening, and squirmed with anticipation. He made a strangled sound in response. She wrapped her arms around him, pulling him close and urging him to slide forward. He complied with a muttered curse.

Diana had always been led to believe that this portion of the act would involve pain and blood. But much to her surprise, Harrington slid inside her with relative ease.

He stiffened atop her. "I'm sorry. I didn't mean to go so fast. Did that hurt?"

She gave an experimental wiggle. "You know, it didn't."

He lifted his head. "Really?"

He looked so adorable with that confused-yet-hopeful expression on his face, Diana couldn't help but smile. She ran her fingers through his hair. "Really. In fact..."

Suddenly, his eyes were intent. "In fact?" he asked, slowly pulling back and pressing forward again.

She exhaled shakily. "Do that again!"

He grinned his scoundrel's grin and proceeded to do just that.

Diana bit her lip, squeezing her eyes shut. It hadn't been her imagination—that felt *good*. And it would feel especially good if he would brush her in that particular spot he had been rubbing earlier. Diana shifted her hips around, trying to find the right angle…

His voice in her ear was smug. "You like that."

She opened her eyes, dazed. "What? Yes, I do."

This time, at the peak of his thrust, he ground his hips against her. She gasped as he rubbed against the little nubbin he'd been licking earlier. "And how about that?"

"H-Harrington!" she gasped. "I didn't realize it would feel so… so…" He did it again, and she lost her train of thought mid-sentence.

He grinned. "Let's see how you like this, then."

He sat up, sliding out of her. Diana snarled in protest. He merely laughed, scooping her up and bringing her with him. He flipped her around as easily as if she were a doll, positioning her on her knees, and came up behind her.

He slid inside her again, and it felt so good that she had to grab one of the rafters overhead to keep from swooning onto the bed. He made an approving sound, wrapping his arms around her midsection, and began thrusting in and out. Diana arched her back against him, trying to get him to rub that spot inside of her.

Harrington seemed to know what she wanted, because he slid one hand low, over the thatch of golden hair at the juncture of her thighs. He pressed down with the heel of his hand, and she gasped. Now, he was hitting that spot with every stroke.

"Ha!" he said in her ear, triumphant. "Like that, do you?"

She had lost the ability to form coherent sentences. "I... I..."

His voice was full of mischief as he said, "Let's see how you like this."

He brought his other hand to the first spot he had shown her, the one on the outside, and began rubbing her with rapid strokes. The effect was almost instantaneous. She could hear herself babbling nonsense. Her thighs started to quake, and the pleasure grew so intense it was almost unbearable.

Just when it became too much, the tension broke. Her body bucked against his as she cried out her pleasure. He was pounding into her fast now, gripping her hips, and she felt his body turn to stone behind her. Then, it was his turn to shout her name.

He surprised her by pulling out of her at the last second, and she felt the pulse of his seed splattering onto her backside and dribbling down her thigh.

His breathing was harsh. "Jesus Christ," he muttered. He leaned down to fish his handkerchief out of the pile of clothing strewn across the floor. He tenderly wiped her clean, then tossed it toward the washbasin in the corner.

Pulling her into his chest, he lay down on the narrow bunk. Diana smiled as she settled against his shoulder. "And here I thought my first time was supposed to be a miserable experience. That was *incredible*."

He gave her a squeeze. "It was incredible for me, too."

"Good." She bit her lip, because the question she wanted to ask him was a bit awkward. "I noticed that you withdrew before your peak." He said nothing, but his body remained relaxed beneath her head. She added, "You also mentioned not having a sheath—an odd concern with your wife, surely."

He shrugged. "Part of that is force of habit. I've never lain with a woman without one before."

Good. Not that she was an expert on such things, but she

knew there were diseases one could get through sexual intercourse. She knew Harrington did not have the reputation of a choirboy, but it was reassuring to know that he had taken precautions. "And the other part?"

His expression was thoughtful. "I suppose I still can't believe it. That *you*"—he made a gesture that swept the length of her nude body—"would want to be married to the likes of *me*. I think a part of me is still trying to keep the door open for you, in case you decide you want an annulment after all."

She squeezed him tight. "We're not getting an annulment. I defied my brother to marry you. I came to your room every night during that house party. I bribed my way onto this ship, then shoved you down on the bed and ravaged you. What more do I have to do to convince you that I want to be your wife?"

He smiled. "I *love* the fact that you came after me. I'm not too proud to admit that I was in something of a state before you showed up. I was so certain you would be furious with me for leaving without a word."

"Have you learned nothing about us Latimers? Beneath the elegant façade, we're mulishly stubborn." She stroked a fingertip across his chest. "And we do not hesitate to take what we want."

"And what you want is me?" He shook his head, and his voice held a note of incredulity. "I guess there's no accounting for taste."

She tickled his side. He tried to squirm away, but there was nowhere to go in the narrow bunk.

She took pity on him, sitting up. He settled on his back, smiling up at her.

She swung a leg across him, straddling his hips, and feigned a put-upon expression. "I can see that you will require a little more convincing."

"I certainly wouldn't object," he said, his voice husky.

She leaned forward, kissing his jaw and trailing a fingertip down his taut stomach. Her body hummed with satisfaction as she felt his cock harden and rise between her spread thighs, eager to make her acquaintance once more. "I believe I can guarantee that you won't have any objections."

As usual, Diana was correct.

CHAPTER 35

$\mathscr{I}$t was the best week of Harrington's life.

He and Diana didn't leave their cabin for two days. They made love so many times, he lost count. It was *glorious*.

When they weren't busy giving one another an ever-increasing number of orgasms, they talked. And—he couldn't believe he was even thinking this—that was just as good! He adored her acerbic wit, which was a perfect complement to his own.

At one point, she mentioned that perhaps he should obtain some French letters once they reached Ireland. Her cheeks—and other areas that were delightfully exposed to his view—had flushed a becoming shade of pink as she added, "I do hope we'll have children one day. But it will be easier for me to follow you on your deployments if we can delay that happy event for a few years."

Harrington had readily agreed. He was still gobsmacked by his good fortune at having Diana as his wife, and if there was anything he wouldn't do to make this woman happy, he certainly couldn't think of it.

He didn't have the heart to tell her that safe assignments like this one would be few and far between. The Rifles were prized as fighting men. There was little possibility that his superior officers would send them to languish in some sleepy outpost with comfortable lodgings. He would surely be back on the march by this time next year. Although officers' wives did sometimes accompany their husbands, those women typically came from military families and had grown up following their own fathers' battalions. They weren't the sisters of a bloody duke.

But he didn't want to spoil their little idyll, so he merely nodded and smiled.

When they finally gave in to the need to stretch their legs, they dressed. Harrington offered to assume the role of Diana's lady's maid, but she surprised him by pulling out a pair of front-lacing stays and a simple wrap gown of plain grey wool. The fact that she had a single hand was no impediment; she was into her gown by the time he finished buttoning his coat.

"What's this?" he asked, looking her up and down. "I didn't realize you owned anything that wasn't dripping in lace and seed pearls."

"Ha-ha. I was raised by *Aunt Griselda,*" she said, twisting her hair into a knot, holding it in place with her right arm, and deftly pinning it into place. "And she was the one to pack my trunks for me while I was gallivanting across London, blissfully unaware that I would be sailing for Ireland that night."

Harrington grinned. "Edward oversaw my packing while I was out looking for you. He sent me off with *The Complete Works of Plutarch.*" He gave a mock shudder. "But I shouldn't complain. Otherwise, he did a bang-up job."

Diana laughed, the happy sound making their spartan

cabin seem bright. "Aunt Griselda could not have done better." She stroked the plain fabric of her skirts appreciatively, as if it were the finest cashmere. "She had the good sense to pack some practical dresses. Honestly, I've missed wearing things like this. Wearing all of that lace and seed pearls is not as enjoyable as you might think."

Harrington regarded her. He didn't give a damn what she wore.

The only thing he cared about was that she continued to sport the brilliant smile currently gracing her lips. "I think it suits you tremendously."

Her face brightened, as if this were the best compliment she'd ever received. "Thank you." She looped her arm through his. "Shall we go and see how Inge is getting on?"

Inge was, indeed, glad to see them, although it was clear that Benjamin had been spoiling her rotten. She spun in happy circles as they stood at the railing, enjoying the blue sky overhead and the crisp sea air.

It happened that they were sailing past the section of Cornwall where Diana had been born. They borrowed a spyglass from one of the lieutenants, and Diana pointed out various villages and landmarks, although the ducal mansion where she had spent her early years was too far inland to be visible.

The soldiers of the King's German Legion were also enjoying the sights on deck. One of them thought he could get away with making a ribald remark about the newlyweds in his native tongue, but Diana promptly responded in German. Whatever she said earned her a round of laughter, and the soldiers seemed delighted by the officer's wife, who spoke their language with such fluency.

They dined with Captain Bannister and his officers that night, and if Diana felt superior to this unexalted company, she gave no sign of it. One young lieutenant, in particular, with a face full of spots, blushed and stammered upon finding himself in the presence of such a beautiful young lady. Diana treated him with quiet dignity, asking him about his home in Northumberland and showing no signs of impatience with his halting answers. It struck Harrington that these officers, who were meeting her for the first time, would no doubt be astounded to learn that this agreeable woman had the reputation for being something of an ice queen amongst the *ton*.

They passed another day in this pleasant fashion, staying in their cabin or strolling the deck as it suited them. The ship made port briefly in the Welsh town of Pembroke to resupply and take on a few more passengers. From there, they would make the crossing to Cork.

Things went wrong shortly after their departure. A violent gale sprang up out of nowhere, tossing the ship about. Unable to go up top without getting soaked, they whiled away the hours in their cabin. This was not entirely bad. Harrington had no objections to staying abed and making love to his wife all day, even as it became a tricky proposition due to the roiling seas. Let it not be said that Harrington Astley wasn't up for a challenge.

But even between their bouts of lovemaking, being with Diana was simply, for lack of a better term, *fun*. They told each other stories—he, of his exploits at school; she, of her adventures with Aunt Griselda. He laughed until he cried at Diana's recounting of Aunt Griselda shooting her horrible father in the arse with a blunderbuss when he tried to kidnap his daughter from her remote home on the Yorkshire moors. They played cards, wagering an array of sexual favors. Harrington was just as happy when he lost as when he won. And Diana helped him with his German. He was surprised by how much progress he was able to make. Based on his performance in school, he'd always figured that he was the dim one in the family. But German was much easier to pick up than Greek.

When the storm stretched into its fourth day, they even cracked open the Plutarch. Harrington had to admit, it was better than he'd thought. It was an English translation, thank God, and included biographies of Julius Caesar, Alexander the Great, and other notable military figures. At least he now understood why Edward had included it—he had probably figured that, as a soldier, Harrington would find the bits about military strategy and leadership useful.

On the sixth day, there was a marked decline in the quality of the food. There was no tea at breakfast that day. The tray young Benjamin brought to their room contained bread without butter and salt pork. This type of fare was fairly standard military rations and was more or less what Harrington had eaten on the retreat from Hanover. But it had to look very poor indeed to the sister of a duke.

For dinner that night, they each received one bowl of plain pea soup. Diana smiled and ate it without a word of complaint. But Harrington felt a knot growing in his stomach that wasn't only due to hunger. Diana was only here because of him. She had probably assumed that whenever she married, she would take her bridal trip to Paris or Rome. Which wasn't possible, of course, due to the war. But she deserved a damn sight better than to spend it in a cramped cabin on a storm-tossed ship, eating salt pork and pea soup!

But apparently, that was all Harrington was capable of giving her.

The seas calmed overnight, but the following day at breakfast, they received only a small loaf of bread to split between them. Harrington handed the loaf to Diana, insisting that he wasn't hungry. He was, of course, but he would be damned before his wife went hungry on her bloody bridal trip. He ducked out of their cabin to see what was going on.

Captain Bannister was apologetic. "The journey to Cork should take two days, three at the most. Unfortunately, we were blown off course by that blasted gale. We're heading in the right direction again, but we didn't supply for a long journey, and we're running out of food." He dropped his voice low. "We'll have to put in at the first place we make landfall."

Nodding grimly, Harrington returned to their cabin. Diana had dressed and was in good spirits. She had also saved him half of the bread, which she insisted he eat.

At least with the seas calm again, they were able to stroll the deck once more. There was nothing for luncheon, but the green shoreline he'd had to squint to see that morning was growing ever closer. Diana accosted the spotty-faced young lieutenant and asked where they were.

"We're coming into Bantry Bay, my lady."

"Bantry Bay!" She gave a startled laugh. "Is that not on the wrong side of Ireland?"

"It is," he agreed with a grin. "We're making for the port of Bearhaven. We'll be able to put in there for a few days and resupply."

Unfortunately, the winds, which had been excessive for the past few days, now abandoned them entirely, and their progress ground to a halt. At midafternoon, Captain Bannister gave the order for them to drop anchor off a stretch of barren coastline.

The captain attempted to put on a brave face. "This is Bere Island. The army has some Martello Towers here and a storehouse. We'll be able to secure some food."

The sailors began ferrying everyone to shore. Harrington offered Diana a hand as they disembarked from the rowboat, but she gamely scrambled up the slippery rocks to the stretch of grass above. Once she was settled, he went to speak with the captain about their current situation.

Once again, the winds had done them no favors. The island wasn't large, only about six miles in length and a third of that in width. But the storehouse was on the opposite end. There were no houses nearby, but there was a Martello Tower about a mile away. Harrington set off to see what kind of accommodations it might be able to offer his gently born wife for the night.

The tower housed twenty British soldiers, who were alarmed to learn that three hundred hungry members of the King's German Legion had just come ashore. Such a number would deplete their stores in a matter of days.

The soldiers were more than willing to offer Diana a bed for the night, but the prospect was not appealing. It was apparent at a glance that the men occupying the tower were suffering from an infestation of lice. Harrington forced a smile, thanked them for their kind offer, and said he would let them know.

He remonstrated himself all the way back to the place where the ship was anchored. It was his job to take care of Diana, to provide for her. And he was a fucking failure! Here they were, stuck on this muddy island without food or shelter.

It had seemed like a dream, these past few days with her. Well, harsh reality had decided to rear its ugly head. He should have known that it eventually would. Diana was no doubt regretting their marriage, trying to determine the fastest way to get back to London and the hell away from him. Not that he could blame her one bit. But his life as a soldier would taste that much more bitter now that he'd had a tantalizing glimpse of how wonderful each day could be with Diana by his side.

He came over a rise and the fledgling camp came into

view. Someone had made a fire, and soldiers were milling about in clusters. Diana, who was standing a short distance from the group, wasn't hard to spot in her dark green gown.

He squinted down the beach. What he saw… didn't make sense.

He broke into a run. "Diana!" he screamed.

CHAPTER 36

*D*iana beamed at Inge as she came bounding up the shore. She rubbed her dog's neck as she removed a seagull from her mouth. *"Sehr gut, Inge. Braver Hund!"* She pointed back toward the beach. *"Hol!"*

Inge took off, tail wagging, as glad to have some useful employment as Diana herself.

Taking in the vista—the blue sky overhead, the sparkling sea below, the verdant stretch of grass—she couldn't help but laugh aloud. It was ironic that she felt happier here than in her brother's gilded ballroom. But feel happier she did.

She was *free*!

She turned to young Benjamin. "Now, watch how I do it again. I know you'll master the trick of it."

She positioned the seagull on its back on the ground, wings outspread. Placing one foot on each of its wings, she seized its legs in a firm grip. She began to pull upward. "Move slowly. It's important to use steady pressure. If you jerk too hard, it won't come away cleanly. And... *voila!*" she exclaimed as the feet separated from the bird's body, taking most of the feathers with them and exposing the breast meat.

"Cor!" Benjamin exclaimed. "I can't get over how quick it goes. How'd you learn to do that, m'lady?"

She bent down to collect her handiwork. "My great-aunt taught me. There are a few ways to field dress a game bird, but that one is the easiest for me, given my arm." She handed the top half of the bird to a German soldier, who nodded his thanks and began cutting the breast meat away from the head. Another man picked up the legs and began peeling the skin back from the bird's thighs.

An hour ago, it had occurred to Diana that the seabirds roosting on the nearby rocks were their most promising source of supper. She pulled her fowling piece from her trunk and started picking them off, and a handful of soldiers promptly joined her. Between them and Inge, they had settled into a smooth system, with a few men doing the shooting, a few helping to clean the birds, and others roasting the meat over the fire.

She smiled as Inge came trotting up the bluff, another seagull clutched in her mouth. "You try this one, Benja—"

"Diana!" someone shouted.

She turned, surprised, to see Harrington sprinting toward her, his eyes wild. Alarmed, she looked around, searching for whatever danger he had apparently spotted.

She frowned. The sky was blue, and the sun was shining. She couldn't see any armed assassins waiting at the top of the rise. Everything seemed… fine?

"Harrington?" she asked as he skidded to a stop. "What's wrong?"

"What on earth are you doing?" he gasped.

She glanced around. Surely it was apparent? There were two dozen birds roasting over the fire, after all.

She was saved from having to answer by Benjamin. "She's teaching me to field dress a seagull! You should have seen her

—she pulled a shotgun right out of her trunk and took down a half dozen birds with her first shot!"

"They weren't expecting it," Diana demurred. "And they do roost closely together."

"Inge's been fetching the birds," Benjamin continued. "We've all got jobs—Lieutenants Schneider and Bauer are doing the shooting. Gassner and Kleinendorst here are roasting the meat. And the rest of us are cleaning the birds!"

Harrington gaped at her. "You had a *shotgun* in your *trunk?*"

"Well, of course." She laughed. "I did mention that Aunt Griselda packed for me. Surely you did not imagine that she would send me off into the great world without a proper fowling piece." She turned to Benjamin, holding out the gull Inge had just collected. "Go on. Give it another try."

She watched him attempt to get into the proper position. "You must place your feet closer to the body of the bird," she advised. "Closer… Yes, as close as you can get them. Good. Now pull up on the feet, slowly… That's it, slow and steady now…"

Benjamin gave a cry of delight as the skin slipped away, revealing the breast meat beneath.

"Excellent!" Diana leaned down, peeling a few stray entrails off the bird and tossing them aside.

She smiled up at her husband, only to find him gawking at her. "What?" she asked, confused.

"How did you learn to do that?" he hissed.

She sighed. Really, this was starting to become tiresome. "Harrington. I need you to forget all that nonsense about the silk gowns and the seed pearls. None of that is me. I am going to explain this as clearly as I can." She looked him steadily in the eyes. "I was raised by *Aunt Griselda.*"

She watched as comprehension flared in his eyes. His mouth fell open, and he took a staggering step back. "*Oh, my*

God," he said, pressing a hand to his heart. "You're the perfect army wife!"

"Yes! I am!" She shook her head. "It's about time that somebody noticed."

His face was still full of consternation. "Look, Diana. This is wonderful, what you've done here—"

She laughed, wrinkling her nose. "I'm not sure you'll feel that way once dinner is served. The meat certainly doesn't smell very good." She raised a finger. "But it is plentiful!"

He dropped his voice low. "I need to speak with you."

She studied him a beat. She wasn't sure why he was so upset, but clearly he was. "All right." She gestured to her hand, which was dirty from cleaning the game. "Give me a moment to—"

"Lieutenant Astley, there you are." Captain Bannister came striding up to the group. "Your wife has created a very efficient operation."

Harrington straightened. "Yes, sir. Not that I am the least bit surprised."

The captain's eyes gleamed. "It appears you've chosen well for yourself. How did you find the Martello Tower?"

"There are about twenty men stationed there. No significant store of supplies. They're nervous that we'll eat them out of house and home."

Captain Bannister nodded. "Apparently there's a larger storehouse across the island. We'll resupply from there tomorrow. But tonight"—he cast Diana an amused smile—"it looks like we'll be dining on seagull. Which is where you come in, Lieutenant."

Harrington's brow furrowed. "Sir?"

"I'm given to understand that you're one of the best shots in all of England," the captain said. "I presume you brought a fowling piece with you?"

"I... Of course."

Captain Bannister nodded toward a pile of luggage. "I had your trunk brought over. Get out there and shoot us some supper. We'll need a good supply of birds, as we've over three hundred mouths to feed."

Harrington inclined his head. "Yes, sir."

He moved off toward the stack of trunks, but not before shooting Diana a pregnant look.

As her husband walked away, she wondered what he had wanted to discuss with her so urgently.

She had no idea. But she meant to find out. Tonight.

CHAPTER 37

$\mathscr{H}$arrington had to admit, Diana had been right—
the seagulls did not taste very good. The meat
was tough and had a distinctly fishy flavor.

But the soldiers and sailors were all so hungry after two
days of limited rations that everyone ate the humble meal
with good humor.

Diana sat next to him on a rock, gnawing on a spitted
breast without complaint. They were gathered around a
campfire with the other officers, who were debating the
merits of sending men overland to obtain food supplies from
the storehouse on the island versus sailing for the fishing
town of Bearhaven. The distance to Bearhaven was trifling,
but given how unreliable the winds had been of late, there
was some disagreement.

Harrington heard little of their chatter. He was dreading
his impending conversation with Diana when he had to
inform her that there was no bed to be had. He had churned
the question of her sleeping arrangements over in his mind
during the hours he'd spent stalking seagulls. The Martello
Tower was out, and they hadn't brought any tents, as there

were barracks for the troops in Bandon. But he could ask Captain Bannister to have some of his men row the two of them back to the ship. He hated to create extra work, but he didn't see what choice he had. It wasn't as if he could ask his lady wife to sleep on the bare ground.

It was fully dark when Harrington finally found a chance to pull Diana aside. "About our sleeping arrangements tonight. I paid a visit to the tower, and although they offered to put us up, I would not recommend it." He dropped his voice low. "They seem to have an infestation of lice."

Diana's eyes widened. "Indeed, that is not a good option."

Harrington nodded. "I'll ask Captain Bannister to prepare one of the small boats to ferry us back to the ship."

"Oh!" Before he could turn to go, she grabbed his arm. She gestured to the men, who were starting to bed down in the soft grass. "That won't be necessary. Benjamin prepared us a pallet." She glanced over her shoulder. "I believe he said he was going to arrange it a short distance from the main group, so we'll have a bit of privacy."

Harrington shook his head. "It's out of the question. I would never expect you to sleep on the muddy ground."

He wasn't sure what response he had expected from Diana.

But it wasn't for her to laugh.

"Is that what this is all about?" she asked.

He frowned. "What *what* is all about?"

"This," she said, reaching up to stroke his creased brow. "You've had that expression on your face for the past three days."

Something inside of him snapped. "Well, let's see—in the past three days, you've been tossed about in a cramped cabin, been served such illustrious fare as salt pork and pea soup, had to hunt for your own dinner, eaten *seagull*, and now, you're going to be forced to bed down on the bare ground!

And, in case it wasn't abundantly clear, this is the closest thing to a bridal trip I am capable of giving you." He huffed. "I can't imagine what there is to frown about."

Her smile was strangely tender. She looped her arm through his. "Come with me."

She led him away from the group to what he presumed were their blankets. They were positioned at the edge of the meadow, just above the rocks leading down to the sea. She sat, cross-legged, and pulled him down beside her.

She gestured to the sky overhead. "It's been years since I've slept out under the stars."

Harrington paused, peering up at the sky. He had to admit, it was a nice night. There wasn't a trace of clouds, and without any residual light from houses or streetlamps, thousands of stars twinkled overhead.

Diana squeezed his arm. "You never see a sky like that in London. Not that they were common in cloudy Yorkshire. But Aunt Griselda used to take me stalking on the moors all the time. For grouse and pheasant, mostly. And sometimes, when the weather was fair, we would sleep beneath the stars." Diana chuckled. "Of course, in Yorkshire, the weather has a way of turning, so it didn't always stay fair. And yet, I survived."

She nudged him with her elbow, and when he glanced down, she was smiling. "I'm not the delicate hothouse flower you seem to think me."

He shifted uncomfortably. "I know you're not. I'm not implying that you're not capable of roughing it for a night. Merely that you deserve better."

"But what if I prefer roughing it?" She shook her head. "I was miserable in London."

He turned to her, surprised. "Were you truly?"

She nodded sadly. "I know it seems strange. At first glance, you could be forgiven for assuming I had everything a young lady could possibly desire. All the pretty dresses I wanted. Life in a glittering mansion with servants to wait on me hand and foot. A dowry that ensured that handsome young men danced attendance on me wherever I went." She looked back up at the stars. "I know how fortunate I am. And I must admit, it was diverting at first."

She shivered, and he wrapped an arm around her. She immediately scooted closer to him, which made him feel good. "Only at first?" he asked softly.

She shrugged. "It didn't take long for a few things to become apparent. One, the vast majority of my so-called suitors didn't care a whit for *me*. They only had eyes for my dowry. Two, although it is diverting to dress up in a pretty gown every once in a while, it is much less enjoyable when you're expected to be turned out to perfection at all times and for all occasions. I shudder to think how many hours I have spent over the past three years changing clothes." A shudder passed through her, proving her point, and Harrington chuckled.

"Three," she continued, "the vast majority of my new acquaintances were neither witty nor clever." She cast him a sly look. "Especially after a certain lieutenant left Town to join his regiment."

He ducked his chin. "That's me, a veritable court jester. Always good for a laugh."

Her eyes flashed in the starlight. "That is not what I meant. Don't think I haven't noticed this habit you have of disparaging yourself."

"I'm in good company," he countered. "Everyone else thinks I'm a wastrel."

She drew herself up. "Well, I don't. Consider this, husband—I could have married anyone, anyone in the world. And who did I choose to marry?" She jabbed him in the chest with a pointed finger. "*You*."

Harrington didn't know what to say to that. Not that it mattered, as he didn't think he could get any words around the lump that had sprung up in his throat.

Diana continued, unrelenting. "It's as you said to Joseph Cumberworth and Berkeley Blachford when you caught them disparaging me back in London—I do not suffer fools. So, if I suffer you, what is the obvious conclusion?"

He was only able to clear his throat by way of an answer. Why was it so much easier to make a jest, to refer to himself as *cannon fodder*—which, when he thought about it, was pretty awful—than to even consider the possibility that he was a decent sort of chap?

He always told himself he didn't care what other people thought of him. Except that was all wrong. Clearly, he did care because the thought of Diana regarding him as worthy made him feel *things*. Things like joy—just a sliver of it, but it was definitely there. A hearty portion of longing.

But mostly what he felt was dread. Because she had no idea that she'd married a crackpot who dreamed of her *spanking* him.

She thought they were building their marriage on a solid foundation. But it was really just a house of cards, and he knew with a horrible certainty that the whole thing would come crashing down if she were ever to find out what a degenerate he really was.

Her face softened, and she slipped her arms around his waist and squeezed. "I won't belabor the point. I can see you're struggling with this. But the important thing for you to understand is that I am not *tolerating* being here with you, eating seagull for dinner, and sleeping on the bare ground. I *prefer* it." She laughed. "I would a thousand times rather be here, with you, than be back in London, trapped inside my gilded cage."

Ah. It made more sense now, why she had wanted to

marry him. It wasn't so much *him*, per se, as the opportunity to escape the life she had hated. He had been a means to an end, nothing more. He didn't mind. Really, he didn't. He understood.

Although perhaps a tiny part of him was… disappointed.

There was no use thinking like that. Had he known before the wedding, would he have done anything differently? Hell, no. He would have seized upon any chance to be with Diana. And he refused to tarnish his time with her by feeling sorry for himself.

Diana was still speaking. "The other thing you need to understand is that I'm coming with you."

He gave her a wry look. "I'd noticed that. I mean, here you are."

"Not just on this assignment, but wherever you get deployed," she clarified. "I intend to follow the drum."

Now that got his attention. Never once had he imagined that Diana would want such a thing. "It's too dangerous."

A mulish set came over her jaw. "And yet, other women do it."

It was true. It wasn't uncommon for officers to bring their wives along on deployments, even in times of active warfare. Sometimes, this meant renting lodgings in the nearest town, which might be two miles from where their husbands were encamped, or two hundred.

But some women insisted on staying much closer to their husbands' sides, sharing their billet, when housing was available, or sleeping with them in their tent when it was not.

A handful went even further, sleeping next to their husbands on the bare ground, and searching for their fallen partners on the battlefield, sometimes while fighting was still going on around them. It was far too easy to picture the dauntless Diana doing just that, an image that made his heart tighten and his vision go fuzzy around the edges.

He hit upon a convenient excuse. "Your brother won't like it."

That earned him a glower. "My brother is not my keeper."

He snorted. "We can carve that on my tombstone after he murders me."

She waved this off. "Don't be absurd. He's not going to murder you."

He rolled his eyes. "I wouldn't be so sure. I've faced the French, and I am far more frightened of your brother."

"Harrington." She squeezed him again. "I'm not going to be rash. I've no intention of riding into the battle with bullets whizzing past my head like Susannah Dalbiac."

"That's exactly what I'm afraid you'll do," he muttered.

A slight narrowing of her eyes was the only sign she gave that she had heard him. "But I believe it is possible for us to find some middle ground. Every moment of a deployment is not spent locked in combat. I have formed the impression that you spend most of your time sitting around, waiting for something to happen."

Damned if he could argue with that. To be sure, there were long marches and the occasional battle. But soldiers spent upwards of ninety percent of their time waiting to receive orders.

He tried to choose his words carefully. "The problem is, the handful of moments when you aren't waiting can be very, very dangerous. And the situation can shift quickly."

She nodded. "And that is why it will be important for us to discuss the particulars of each situation. If danger is imminent, I will fall back to a safe distance." She caught his gaze and held it. "But you must acknowledge that there will be times when you're billeted in a town a hundred miles from the enemy, awaiting orders, and there is no reason I could not be there with you."

He frowned. "I'm not sure if it's a good idea."

She did that thing with her eyebrow. "Are you suggesting that I have bad judgment?"

That brought him up short. "No. I know you have the best judgment."

Her eyes flashed, and he knew this had been the right thing to say. "Then we must trust one another. We will discuss the particulars of each situation and make a rational decision. *Together.*"

He sighed. "I still don't know."

She crawled into his lap, and he knew enough about military strategy to recognize her shift in tactics. Her voice was husky as she said, "You must admit, there are some advantages to having me along."

His breath had gone ragged. "Are there?"

"Mm-hmm." She stroked his chest. "I've demonstrated my competence with a shotgun. I'm sure at times there will be better game than seagulls." Her hand drifted lower, lingering on his stomach as she leaned forward and whispered, "Imagine returning to your tent after a hard day of drilling your troops to find a pair of pheasants roasting over the fire."

As appealing as the image was, he wasn't thinking with his stomach at the moment.

"I could arrange to have your laundry done. I could rub your back at the end of a long day. I could polish your rifle for you."

Her hand lingered at the waistband of his trousers. His back and his rifle weren't the things he was imagining her rubbing and polishing, as he imagined she knew.

Her voice was husky as she said, "There are so many things I could take care of for you."

He gasped as she let her hand drift over his cock where it tented his trousers, and she began to stroke and tease him.

"Diana," he gasped. "S-soldiers. Just over the rise.

Someone will"—he made a strangled sound as she started flipping open the buttons of his falls—"h-h-hear."

She gave him an arch look. "And what do other officers and their wives do during a deployment? When conditions force them to bed down on the ground together, or when only a thin layer of canvas separates them from their men's listening ears? You can't tell me their husbands don't have... *needs.*"

Harrington shuddered as she slipped her soft little hand inside his trousers and wrapped it around his straining cock. "They do. Everyone can hear them coupling, of course. It's unavoidable. But people tactfully pretend not to hear anything."

He could hear the smile in her voice. "Fascinating." She peeled the topmost blanket back and crawled inside. He watched as if in a dream as she undid the wrapped tie on her gown, then pushed it off. Her stays and petticoats immediately followed until she wore nothing but her shift. God, but she looked beautiful in the moonlight.

She lay back on the blankets and lifted the hem of her shift, exposing the intimate flesh between her thighs to the starlight. "Take off your coat," she encouraged. "And your boots. I want to make you *comfortable.*"

God help him. He was probably damning himself to hell. But he wanted her about as much as he wanted oxygen, and in spite of his good intentions, he removed his clothing with trembling hands.

"Good," she whispered as he settled between her spread thighs. "That's so good." She arched her hips, eager for him. "Give me what I need."

He shuddered. It was as if she somehow knew every one of his secret desires. How he loved to be praised in bed, how he longed for it.

Of course, the ultimate catharsis was to be told that he'd

been good after he'd received a spanking, then been forced by his partner to "atone" for his misbehavior. Preferably by placing his head between her thighs and giving her an absurd number of climaxes. It was difficult to explain, but after a good spanking, he felt as if he had been absolved of his sins. That was when he most craved praise and adoration from his partner, because for the briefest of moments, he could bring himself to believe all the wonderful things they said were true.

But hearing Diana tell him he was good made his heart glow, and even if the feeling wasn't as intense as it would have been after a proper spanking, it was as much as he was ever going to get. He would never ask her to spank him. It was important that she never find out what a degenerate he really was.

She reached down, taking his cock in her hand, and guided it to her entrance. He groaned as he found her already wet.

"That's it," she sighed as she helped him slip inside. "That's so good. This is what it will be like. After a long day drilling your men, you won't be alone. You'll have me by your side, and in your bed."

He moaned because that was everything he'd ever wanted.

This was all too much. Diana was overwhelming him with the tantalizing promise of comfort and caring and even love. Suddenly he was on the brink of his own climax, before he'd had the chance to bring her to pleasure.

He might not have access to his full array of tricks with half the King's German Legion bedded down a few yards away. But he would be damned if he didn't make sure his wife found her pleasure. Slipping a hand between their bodies, he found that special spot between her legs where she loved to be petted and gently circled his finger. Diana gave a breathy gasp and spread her legs wider, giving him access.

Somehow, he managed to hold off until her thighs started to quiver and her fingers dug into his back. "Harrington!" she gasped in his ear. For a second, it made him feel like a king in a palace, instead of a humble soldier lying on the muddy ground, to know that he had brought her to pleasure.

Then it was his turn to groan and shake and tremble in her arms as white-hot pleasure burst behind his eyes.

Afterward, she pressed kisses against his jaw as she snuggled against him. "I'm going to make you see. I truly am happy being here with you. And our marriage is going to be an unequivocal success."

Harrington felt peace wash over him as he drifted off to sleep beneath the stars.

CHAPTER 38

It took them a full week to reach their final destination of Bandon. At the rate they'd been going, Harrington supposed he should be pleased they'd made it there at all.

They spent another day on the island, then two days in the small port town of Bearhaven, where they were able to resupply sufficiently to resume their journey. This time, the voyage went smoothly, and they anchored in Cove Harbor outside of Cork the following day. From there, they made their way overland to Bandon.

Bandon was a pretty town that was unusual in that it had been founded by English settlers sent to Ireland by Queen Elizabeth some two hundred years earlier. For a time, the town was exclusively Protestant, and Protestants remained the overwhelming majority of the population. Although just last year, the first Catholic-owned business had opened on Main Street—a pie shop run by a man named Paddy Gaffney who was so good-natured, people were willing to set aside their religious differences. Because of this history, Bandon had a reputation for giving British troops stationed there a warm welcome.

The soldiers were quartered in four-story barracks buildings made from plain grey stone. But, as Harrington was a married man and Diana had the means, they were permitted to rent accommodations of their own choosing. Diana found them a cottage on the outskirts of town, and they hired a local woman named Maeve to come over each day to cook and clean.

On their third night there, the officers and their wives were invited to dine at Castle Bernard by the Earl and Countess of Bandon. In spite of its name, other than an old medieval tower, the castle was newly built and boasted every modern convenience. The earl and countess were particularly delighted to discover that a duke's sister would be taking up residence in town, a significant addition to the local society.

By day, Harrington drilled the troops of the King's German Legion and instructed its officers in a new set of tactics. It wasn't easy to convince the men, much less the officers, to give up the rigid lines and squares that were the bread and butter of infantry troops. And when he informed them that the individual soldiers would determine when to fire their weapons, rather than waiting for an order from their commanding officer, their first thought was that he was joking. Slowly, very slowly, he brought them around to this new strategy for waging war.

Harrington had been an officer of the 95th Rifles for three years, so he had a solid understanding of light infantry tactics. Additionally, he was a marksman of some repute, so he felt that instructing the soldiers in shooting—especially now that they were armed with rifles and actually expected to aim—was a good use of his abilities.

Once everyone wrapped their heads around the

fundamentals of skirmishing, the most peculiar thing happened—he gained the respect of his fellow officers. Not that he hadn't been well-liked amongst the officers of the 95th Rifles. But there, his knowledge of light infantry tactics had merely made him fit in, rather than stand out.

But here, he was looked on as an expert, both in terms of strategy and marksmanship. Both officers and rank-and-file soldiers appreciated the fact that he was there, sharing his knowledge. He, Harrington Astley, the family scapegrace, the black sheep who had been on the brink of being sent down from school every single year for his abominable misbehavior, was now regarded as a key factor in the success of an entire regiment! It was heady stuff for a fellow such as him.

While he was busy drilling with the King's German Legion, Diana was forging friendships amongst the officers' wives. Nine such ladies resided in Bandon. Diana was the youngest by almost a decade. But they were all hale and hearty women who had been following their husbands on campaign for years, and Diana confessed to Harrington that in spite of their differences in age and station, she had more in common with them than with the vast majority of the ladies of the *ton*.

Each night, she would regale him with stories of how she had spent her morning with her new friends, usually riding or going for long walks with Inge trotting happily at Diana's heels. When Diana mentioned that she would feel safer riding astride, as she'd had to leave her specially trained mare, Artemesia, back at home, her new friends did not appear the least bit scandalized. Mrs. Phipps, the wife of a captain, remarked that it was the logical thing to do. Everyone murmured in agreement, and that was that.

In the afternoons, Diana informed him, the ladies might gather to sew, which Diana could do using a tabletop embroidery stand. But because that made for slow going, she would often volunteer to read aloud to the group. And a few times a week, she would call on Lady Bandon at the castle.

Many evenings, the officers and their wives would gather together for dinner. These occasions were sometimes grand, such as when the Earl and Countess of Bandon were hosting at Castle Bernard. But they were often simple. One night, Harrington and Diana even hosted their new friends at their humble cottage. They had to crowd around the table, and the fare, which was a combination of pies purchased in town and simple side dishes prepared by Maeve, was far from gourmet. But no one cared a whit, and by all appearances, everyone had a marvelous time.

Other nights, Harrington and Diana were on their own, which he found even more enjoyable. They never seemed to run out of things to talk about. After dinner, they would curl up in front of the fire, and Diana would help Harrington with his German. But they never managed to study for too long. They always seemed to wind up making love on the sofa, not that Harrington had any complaints.

The most astounding thing of all was how happy Diana looked. Really, what were the odds—*Diana Latimer*. Happy. With *him*! But as improbable as it seemed, the woman known as an ice queen in London greeted him every evening with a glowing smile and a kiss, eager to tell him about the adventures she'd had that day.

He was doing important work, work he was good at. He had earned the respect of his colleagues. He was married to the woman of his dreams, and she seemed to delight in his company.

He should have been happy, and he supposed he was. But beneath the happiness was an uneasy feeling deep in his gut. It was the conviction that a great oaf like him could not possibly attain this level of success and happiness. That something was going to go wrong.

And, indeed, it did.

Diana noticed the stranger three weeks after their arrival in Bandon.

He wore a wide-brimmed hat, floppy and plain, the same kind worn by the farmers who came to town on market day. His coat was shapeless and brown, and his boots were scuffed. But he didn't *look* like a farmer. He lacked the round-shouldered posture and bulky strength of a working man.

Diana felt at once that something was off about him, but when she turned to study him, he ducked down a side street and was gone.

She shrugged it off. Who knew what the man was doing in town? It was probably nothing.

Except she saw him again the following day while she was collecting their post from the local inn. She had arranged to have *The Times* sent to her each day. The news was two weeks out of date, but she enjoyed reading it, and on that day, she'd had a letter from Aunt Griselda and another from Lucy, so she'd been eager to return to the cottage.

She almost missed him when she stepped out of the inn. He was standing across the street, leaning against the wall of the bootmaker's shop, hat pulled low over his face. Diana stopped so short she almost stumbled. She had just resolved to get a closer look when a cart laden with cabbages rumbled down the street.

By the time it had passed, the man was gone.

She went on her way. But she saw him the following day, lingering at the edge of the churchyard after Sunday services. Harrington, who had already befriended half the town, was busy chatting with their laundress, Mrs. Mulroney, and by the time Diana gained his attention, the stranger had once again disappeared.

She told herself she was being silly. What act could be less suspicious than attending church, after all?

Still, she couldn't shake the uneasy feeling in the pit of her stomach.

On Monday, she spotted him as she passed through town on her way to call on Lady Bandon. On Tuesday, she saw him across the street as she went to the home of Mrs. Hayes, the wife of a colonel who was hosting an afternoon gathering for the officers' wives.

It was on Wednesday, when she spotted him while out on a morning walk with Mrs. Monroe and Mrs. Phipps, that she truly grew concerned.

She gestured across the field. "Do you see the man standing next to that hazel tree?"

Mrs. Phipps paused, turning her head. "What about him?"

Diana dropped her voice low even though the man was fifty yards away. "Does his appearance strike you as… unusual?"

Mrs. Monroe stared across the field for a beat. "He looks like a farmhand."

"Then why isn't he working?" Diana asked.

Mrs. Monroe shrugged. "He's probably taking a short rest."

Diana swallowed. "I keep seeing him around town. I'm starting to feel like he's following me."

Mrs. Phipps studied her with kind eyes. "I know that must seem unnerving. But surely it is not unusual to run into the same man a few times in a town so small as Bandon. After all, what reason would he have for following you?"

Diana bit her lip. She had not been entirely forthcoming with her new friends about the details of her life back in

London. They knew she was the sister of a duke, but they didn't know that she had a dowry of a hundred thousand pounds, or that she would one day inherit Aunt Griselda's fortune, which was easily worth twice that.

Mrs. Phipps wrapped an arm around Diana's shoulders. "Come. I'm sure it's nothing. Let's not let it spoil our walk on such a fine morning!"

They had all chuckled, because it was what the Irish called a soft day with a steady sort of drizzle. But Diana couldn't help but glance over her shoulder as they departed.

The strange man was gone. But Diana's sense of unease refused to budge.

That was when she decided to mention it to Harrington.

CHAPTER 39

*H*aving spent the last hour trying to figure out what she wanted to say to Harrington, Diana was pacing the floor when he got home. Part of her was afraid that he would dismiss her concerns, as Mrs. Monroe and Mrs. Phipps had done.

But part of her was also concerned that he would respond the way Marcus typically did—by locking her in a gilded cage in response to the slightest risk.

She could not decide which reaction she feared more.

She whipped around as the door swung open. There was Harrington, brown eyes crinkling into a smile as he scraped his boots against the mat. "Good evening, darling. How was your..." He trailed off, and she could mark the moment he noticed her drawn expression.

He was across the room in four strides. "Diana. What's wrong?"

She took him by the hand and led him to the sofa. There, she explained about the man she kept seeing again and again. About how he did not seem to have any obvious occupation or reason for being where he was. And about how he promptly disappeared each time she spotted him. Harrington listened quietly, eyes intent on hers, not saying a word until she had finished.

He rose and paced over to the mantelpiece. "In light of this, I think we need to make some changes."

Diana's spine stiffened. That didn't sound promising, but she reminded herself that she should hear him out rather than rushing to judgment. "What kind of changes?"

He turned to face her, raking a hand through his hair. "To your daily routine."

No, no, no! She had been so happy here, happier than she'd ever been in her life. She had thought that in Harrington, she had found not just a husband but a partner. Someone who respected her, someone who would let her have a say in her own life.

Had she instead exchanged one tyrant for another?

She could not keep the sharpness from her voice as she asked, "And what, precisely, would you have me change about my daily routine?"

"For starters, these walks you go on." He waved a hand dismissively, and Diana bristled. It was as bad as she'd feared. He was going to forbid her to leave the cottage!

But when he looked at her, his brown eyes were full of concern. "Do you bring your sword with you?"

She blinked. "My sword?"

As he had resumed pacing the room, Harrington did not seem to notice her discomfiture. "Because I would feel much better knowing that you had your sword at hand." He stroked his chin. "I know you bring Inge on your rambles. But perhaps it would be a good idea to take her with you everywhere, even just to the other side of the village." He paused, meeting her eyes. "What do you think?"

She found herself discomfited. She had not realized that

What do you think? were the most romantic words in the English language.

But, given the way her heart had started to trip over itself, they were clearly as good as anything to emerge from Shakespeare's pen. "I think... those are both good suggestions."

He sat back down on the sofa, propping his elbows on his knees. "Don't take this the wrong way. I don't mean to imply that you're not capable of defending yourself if it should come to blades." He chuckled. "Indeed, I can't imagine the man who would best you. But I wonder if you should also carry a firearm."

She could not quite wrap her head around the direction the conversation had taken. "A firearm?"

"Mmm. You know my sister, Anne, of course. She has occasion to visit some of the worst neighborhoods in London."

Anne ran a charitable organization, The Ladies' Society for the Relief of the Destitute, and the nature of her work occasionally brought her into rough areas of Town. "Oh?"

"I set her up with a little Queen Anne pistol." He held his hands about eight inches apart. "They're remarkably compact. Not nearly as cumbersome as carrying a rifle or even a dueling pistol. They're still heavy, of course, but I'll wager Mr. Kincannon could make you a holster."

Mr. Kincannon was the village's cobbler. She blinked at him. "Let me make sure I understand—your plan is to buy me a gun and holster."

Harrington brightened. "We could have one custom-made to hold both your sword and the pistol." He turned to face her on the couch, taking her hand and stroking its back with his thumb. "I know it will be an annoyance, having to lug a pair of heavy weapons around with you everywhere you go. But I wouldn't risk you for the world. What do you think, darling?"

Diana did the only thing she could possibly do under the circumstances.

She wrapped her arms around his neck, crawled into his lap, and kissed him.

Harrington's eyes went wide with something that might have been confusion. But then he groaned, placing his hands on the small of her back and pressing her against him.

When she lifted her head, they were both breathing hard. "What's this?" he asked, swiping his thumb across her cheek, sweeping aside a stray tear.

"It's not what you think," she said quickly, dabbing at her other eye with her sleeve. "They're happy tears. I was afraid your solution to my problem would involve telling me I couldn't leave the house."

He drew back in surprise. "Couldn't leave the house? But that would make you miserable!"

"It would," she agreed.

He rubbed her back with a warm hand. "But Diana, surely you know I couldn't bear such a thing."

She shrugged. "Marcus would tell you the same thing. And in his next breath, he would lock me in my room without a second's hesitation. A paradox, my brother."

Harrington shook his head. "You have good judgment. Probably better than mine, if you want to know the truth. I can't imagine the situation in which I would have to force you to do anything."

"Thank you," she said softly. "And you don't give yourself enough credit. I think your suggestions are excellent, and I mean to adopt them all."

He brushed a stray curl back from her temple, smiling softly. "Do you want me to procure you a Queen Anne pistol, then?"

She slipped from his lap, sinking to the floor. "I already have one."

His eyes flew wide as her fingers went to the buttons on the placket of his trousers. "You… you do?"

She smiled wryly as she flipped one open. "As I've mentioned, Aunt Griselda packed my trunk. I'm probably better armed than the King's German Legion."

He gave a breathless laugh. "I don't doubt it." He frowned as she popped two more buttons loose. "Say, Diana, you don't have to, err…"

The final button gave way, and his cock, which was already fully erect, sprang free of his trousers. "Are you sure? You seem rather interested."

"No, I mean"—he gasped as she wrapped her hand around him—"I am."

She smiled, loving the way his voice had turned husky. "I feel a sudden, irrepressible urge to pleasure you with my mouth."

He really was adorable when he was confused. "But… why?"

Because you're not trying to lock me in a gilded cage. Because you asked me what I thought. Because you respect me.

Because I love you.

She wasn't quite brave enough to say all of that aloud. So instead, she said, "Because you are the best husband in the whole entire world, and you deserve a reward."

As she uttered the compliment, he groaned, and his cock pulsed within her hand. "Say… say that again."

Diana was not surprised by this request. She had noticed that Harrington seemed to grow excited—and by excited, she meant, sexually excited—whenever she gave him a compliment.

She decided an experiment was in order.

"You've been so good to me," she purred, pulling his cock

out of his trousers. "So thoughtful. So caring." She pressed a kiss against his tip. "You deserve some appreciation."

He was breathing hard, head tipped back, eyes closed. "I do?"

"Mmm." She ran her tongue up the length of the underside of his cock, pausing to swirl it at the base of his head. "You're such a wonderful husband. So very, very good to me. And so, I'm going to make things very, very good for you."

He made a strangled sound, and his hips shifted desperately on the sofa. She decided to put him out of his misery, closing her lips around him and sliding down. She stroked him with her hand at the same time, and the bead of moisture that had formed at his tip made his length slippery.

"Diana!" he gasped, threading his fingers into her hair. "I... I'm not going to last long. That feels *so good*, what you're doing, I—"

She responded by wrapping her lips around his tip and sucking, and he broke off with a cry. She gave him no quarter, sliding her hand down to the place behind his sack and massaging him deeply there, the way she knew he liked so well.

"*Jesus fuck!*" he shouted, squirming on the sofa. "Diana, I... I... You're going to make me..."

He cried out in pleasure as his hips bucked against the sofa. She sucked down every drop of his release, rubbing him firmly with her hand, then gentling her touch when he started to squirm.

He was boneless afterward, collapsed against the sofa with his head lolling to the side. After a moment, he stirred himself enough to scoop her up and place her on his lap. He wrapped his arms around her and buried his face in her hair. She smiled against his neck as she listened to his breathing gradually slow.

He pressed a kiss against her temple. "Thank you."

She turned her head to kiss him back. "Thank *you*. I meant what I said, you know. If you're going to insist on being so wonderful, you'd best be prepared, because I won't be able to stop myself from shoving you down on the sofa and having my wicked way with you."

He laughed. "You're providing me with a powerful incentive to behave."

She twined her fingers in his curly hair. "Upon further consideration, I should not like for you to behave *all* the time. I'm also quite fond of your rakish side."

His eyes were closed, and a soft smile graced his lips. "And if I misbehave, you could always…"

He trailed off, and she felt him stiffen beneath her. Was it Diana's imagination, or did a faint flush rise to his cheeks?

"I could always?" she prompted.

It wasn't her imagination. He was blushing. "Nothing."

She could not help but think of the page he had marked in his book of naughty prints. The print that showed the gentleman bent forward while his lover paddled him with a birch. Had the words he had stopped himself from uttering been, *you could always punish me?*

Diana thought of the print again, of the pure, unadulterated bliss on the man's face as he received a spanking. Which Diana had to admit, she did not understand.

But if it was something Harrington would like, something that would bring him pleasure, then she wasn't opposed to trying it.

She summoned her courage. "Because if there is something you would like to try—"

"There's not," he said at once. "What you just did for me was wonderful."

She tried to catch his eye, but his gaze was fixed on the

empty grate in the fireplace. "I'm glad. But if there is something that could make it even better—"

"Better than that?" He laughed. "Impossible." She started to speak, but he silenced her with a deep kiss.

He rose from the sofa, lifting her high in his arms, and strode toward their bedroom. "Now, quit distracting me, minx. I have plans for you."

She decided to let it go, as Harrington clearly didn't want to discuss it. "Plans, you say? What sort of plans?"

He tossed her onto their bed and lay on top of her. "The kind you're going to enjoy."

She raised a haughty eyebrow because she knew he secretly liked it. "You think so, do you?"

His grin was a mixture of wickedness and delight as he reached down and started rucking up her skirts. "I *know* so."

In the end, Diana was not too proud to admit that her husband had been right.

CHAPTER 40

*D*iana took Harrington's advice and started arming herself and taking Inge with her whenever she left the cottage.

She continued to see the man in the wide-brimmed hat around the village. As before, he managed to melt into the forest or disappear behind a corner each time she spotted him.

But the following Sunday, things finally came to a head.

The morning service at Christ Church had just concluded. As she and Harrington stepped outside, she spotted the familiar floppy hat across the churchyard.

Harrington was bent over, busy unknotting Inge's leash from the small tree to which they had secured it.

Diana crept up behind him. "Don't look. But he's here."

He stiffened, then slowly straightened, keeping his eyes locked on hers. "The man who's been following you?"

Diana gave a tiny nod. "He's standing just behind the steeple. *Don't look,*" she emphasized as Harrington started to do just that.

He swallowed. "What would you suggest?"

Frankly, Diana was sick of this nonsense. She wanted to feel safe when she left her home, wanted the feelings of lightness and ease she had experienced in her first days in Bandon.

She wanted this to be over. Which meant catching whoever this man was in the act.

"Round up a dozen or so soldiers," she said. "I want to set a trap."

She and Harrington made a great show of lingering in the churchyard, chatting with their friends, never glancing toward the steeple.

At last, Harrington bent his head to her ear. "Everything's ready. We're going to walk toward the market and see if we can get him to follow. A half-dozen men will be waiting for us there. Another half-dozen will follow at a discreet distance. Let's see if we can get him to take the bait."

Diana took Inge's leash in her left hand and looped her right arm through Harrington's. She was careful not to look toward the steeple as they exited the churchyard. "I appreciate you arranging this."

He patted her arm. "Of course. Hopefully, we'll end this today."

As they walked through the village, Harrington kept up a flow of chatter, insisting that it would look more natural than walking in tense silence. Diana knew he was right but struggled to attend to the conversation with the confrontation looming ahead. What if this man was violent? Just because they would have him outnumbered twenty to one didn't mean he couldn't cause significant damage. What if he had a gun? What if he shot someone?

What if the person he shot was Harrington?

The thought was too terrible to even contemplate, like a black pit of despair gaping before her. It was a strange thing, but the thought of losing him was worse than the possibility of being shot herself…

"Diana? Diana, are you ready?"

She blinked. They were crossing the bridge over the River Bandon. "I'm sorry. You were saying?"

He inclined his head toward the market stalls just ahead. "This is where we'll lay our trap. The soldiers will be waiting to box him in. Let's see if he'll take the bait."

Diana nodded, and Harrington turned, leading her down a narrow alley between the empty market stalls. Her heart was pounding, and the smile she forced to her lips felt tight, and—

Just then, Inge stopped short, yanking the leash from Diana's hand and running back the way they'd come. "Inge!" she cried. "*Hier!*" But the usually obedient dog ignored her.

That was when she saw the stranger, or at least his floppy hat, lurking between two market stalls. Diana's heart seized. Was her usually unflappable dog going to lunge for the man's throat?

Instead, Inge padded up to him, her demeanor strangely cheerful. Diana narrowed her eyes as she watched the pointer lick the man's hand.

She froze. The man's hand was immaculately manicured and bore a gold signet ring.

A *familiar* gold signet ring.

Scowling, she stormed down the row of stalls.

"Diana!" Harrington shouted. "Stay behind me. He could be dangerous!" He gave chase, but she was already upon the stranger.

She ripped the floppy hat off his head, revealing a glossy head of pale blond hair. "Marcus!" she snapped. "What the devil are you doing here?"

CHAPTER 41

*D*iana adored her brother. He was one of her favorite people on the face of this earth.

That did not change the fact that right now, she wanted to kill him.

"What is *wrong* with you?" she snapped. "You followed me all the way to Ireland! Why can you never leave me alone?"

The duke lifted his chin, unrepentant. "I had to satisfy myself as to your well-being."

"And you thought stalking me was the logical solution?" Diana shot back. "I was *frightened*, Marcus! I thought someone was trying to kidnap me!"

A trace of regret stole into his eyes. "I am sorry for that. I did not realize you had spotted me."

Diana was not prepared to offer him absolution. "You should have known better. Subtlety has never been your forte. But here we all are. Have you satisfied yourself sufficiently that you can now leave us alone?"

"Satisfied myself?" Marcus wrinkled his nose as he flicked his hand toward the weather-beaten market stalls. "Name one thing about your present living situation that is *satisfactory.*"

Diana cast her eyes heavenward. "We're staying in a perfectly nice cottage."

"I have seen it. A *cottage.*" He spat the last word, as if it were a vile curse. "For the sister of a duke!"

Diana nudged Harrington and offered him a commiserating smile. "Just wait until he hears about the seagulls."

She had expected her husband to grin.

Instead, his face fell. He looked… crestfallen.

"Harrington?" Diana pressed his arm. "What's wrong?"

She would be lucky if he could even hear her over Marcus's outraged shouting. "Seagulls? What do you mean, seagulls?" He rounded on Harrington. "I should like to know how you can possibly justify this foul mistreatment of my sister!"

Harrington held his hands up, palms out. "I know it's not what she deserves."

Diana would not have thought it possible to feel more annoyed than she already was. She would have been wrong. What was wrong with Harrington? She had explained multiple times that she much preferred her life with him to her gilded cage in London.

What was it about her brother that made Harrington fold so easily?

She glowered at Marcus. "I *deserve* to be happy. And I am. Here." She looped her arm through Harrington's. "With Harrington."

Harrington shot her a look of desperate gratitude.

Marcus looked baldly skeptical. "You cannot convince me that you are happier here than you would be in London, with servants to wait on you and every luxury at your disposal."

"Isn't it amazing how that works?" Diana shot back. "You

refuse to listen to a word I say, and then you have no understanding of what I actually want!"

"I was surprised, too." Harrington's voice came out gruff, and he looked somewhat startled to find that he had spoken. "But she assured me again and again that she prefers adventure to comfort." He rubbed the back of his head, not meeting Marcus's eyes. "I mean, she did grow up with Aunt Griselda. When you consider that, it's not surprising that she isn't some wilting flower."

Diana squeezed his arm encouragingly. That was more like it.

Marcus's blue eyes narrowed to two frosty slits as they fixed themselves on Harrington. "Even if that is the case, the fact remains that *you* are unworthy of my sister. And you know it!"

Harrington's gaze was fixed upon the ground. "I... I..."

Diana glared at her brother. "Marcus! Stop!"

Ignoring her, Marcus took a step forward, and Harrington shrank back. It fell to Diana to pull on his arm so he did not retreat into the wall of a nearby booth. "Why do you not do the decent thing for once in your life and leave my sister alone?"

Harrington swallowed, and his eyes were defeated as he said, "Because I love her."

Marcus frowned. "Because you... you *what?*"

Harrington spoke to Marcus, but his eyes, which were full of sorrow, were fixed on Diana. "I love her. I know I shouldn't have done, but..." He waved a hand. "How could I help myself? I don't know if you've noticed, but your sister is incredible. She's perfect. She's"—he ran a hand over his face—"everything I've ever wanted."

Diana stepped closer to him, pressing his arm. "I love you, too, Harrington," she said softly.

She wasn't sure if he heard, for he continued, "There's

nothing I wouldn't do for her. I'd crawl through the mud. I'd step in front of a bullet. I'd dress in motley and perform jests if she asked it of me." Blinking, he shifted his gaze to Marcus. "What I'm trying to say is, I don't have the strength to leave her. Frankly, I don't understand why she wants me around, either. But as long as she does, I'm going to be right here. With her."

Diana had heard enough. Harrington's speech had left her feeling elated and frustrated in equal measures. Elated because his feelings for her were everything she could have hoped, a perfect echo of what she felt for him. But frustrated because, in spite of her reassurances to the contrary, he persisted in believing that he was unworthy of her.

Something was going on. She suspected it went deeper than all those childhood pranks he had played on her brother.

She meant to get to the bottom of it. *Today.*

Tightening her arm around Harrington's, she pulled him toward the main street. "Come, husband. We have things to discuss."

Marcus started to follow them, but Diana rounded on him, jabbing a finger in his chest. "I cannot stand the sight of you right now! Go back to... wherever it is you've been staying."

"With Lord Bandon," Marcus supplied.

Diana sighed. How like Marcus, to show up on the local lord's doorstep, expecting to be accommodated, and for the local lord to be delighted. "*If* I am able to set aside my ire, I will summon you tomorrow."

"Diana!"

She could hear Marcus shouting behind her. She ignored him.

She meant to resolve whatever it was that was troubling Harrington, once and for all.

CHAPTER 42

*H*arrington was silent as Diana marched him back to their cottage as efficiently as any general in the British Army.

He was dreading the conversation to come. They had *things to discuss*, according to his wife. Damned if those were words any man wanted to hear. Still, he didn't see how he could avoid the conversation other than making a run for it and hiding behind a tree, which seemed unbecoming for an officer and a gentleman, to say nothing of a man of nine and twenty.

So instead, he allowed his petite wife to drag him down the lane and propel him through the cottage door to face his doom.

Sunday was Maeve's day off, so they had the cottage to themselves. Diana let Inge out into the back garden, then whirled to face him.

Harrington cleared his throat. Maybe if he ignored the problem, it would magically go away. "Are you hungry? Would you like me to—"

"Harrington." It was just his name, but she said it with a

sharpness that he secretly liked, one that let him know she wasn't here for any of his nonsense. She regarded him cooly with crossed arms and still blue eyes. "Would you care to explain what *that* was about?"

No, thank you. It was God's honest truth, not that it mattered a whit. It was the wrong answer, and well did he know it.

This called for a diversion. "You mean the part where I said I loved you?" He swallowed, because this was only a mite less nerve-wracking. "I do. I've been trying to work up the courage to tell you. I'm sorry I did it in front of your—"

"And I love you, too," she said in that voice that brooked no argument.

He would have thought hearing those words fall from her lips would fill him with elation. But he would have been wrong, although perhaps there was a sliver of joy mixed in with the queasiness.

"But," Diana continued, and he suppressed a groan. He'd known there was a *but.* "We will discuss that after we have resolved the issue at hand."

"Right." He was rapidly running out of options. "What, exactly, is that, again?"

She seized his hand in a surprisingly strong grip for a girl who looked like she could be the model for one of those frilly porcelain figurines ladies liked to put on the mantelpiece and dragged him to the sofa.

She boxed him into the corner by the fireplace so there was no possibility of escape, then turned to him, her eyes solemn. "When we were marooned on Bere Island, we had a good talk. At least, I thought we did. I thought we had resolved your concerns that life as an officer's wife was somehow beneath me. I thought you finally understood that this is what I want." She brushed her thumb across the back of his hand. "That *you* are who I want."

"You did," he reassured her. "It's like I told your brother—you prefer adventure to comfort. I received your message, loud and clear."

She looked at him steadily, and he could tell she wasn't fooled. "I noticed that you were able to muster a defense of my desire for a life outside of the gilded cage where my brother would prefer to keep me. But I also noticed that you presented no argument whatsoever when my brother—my idiotic, wrongheaded brother, might I add—suggested that *you* were not good enough for me."

Well, shit. He usually loved the fact that Diana was so clever. Came in bloody handy when he was trying to untangle some political mess.

It was a damn sight less appealing when she was turning all that perspicacity on him.

"I…" He cleared his throat, then attempted to smile. "I mean, isn't a fellow supposed to feel dumbfounded that his beautiful wife would even glance at a poor sod like him?"

Diana's gaze did not waver. "No."

He gave an awkward laugh. "There's a compliment in there somewhere."

She crossed her legs, scooting closer to him. "Except there isn't. I would have no problem with you waxing rhapsodically about how wonderful I am." She waved her hand airily. "In fact, I look forward to hearing you expound upon that subject later this evening. But there is a world of difference between praising your wife and castigating yourself." She peered at him. "Do you see?"

Deciding another diversion was in order, he pulled her in for a hug. "There, there, Diana. You know I don't mean anything I say." He patted her back once… twice… three times. "Off you go."

She pulled back, narrowing her eyes. "What is *wrong* with

you? Did you truly believe I could be placated with such an asinine statement?"

"A man can hope," he muttered.

She tossed her head, a gesture that would have looked patently ridiculous on ninety-nine people out of a hundred. Naturally, Diana pulled it off with aplomb. "The issue is not that I do not wish to hear those remarks. It is that I do not wish for you to think them."

He forced a chuckle. "That's going a bit far, don't you think? I'm sure you wouldn't like it if I gave you a list of things you weren't allowed to think."

She dismissed this with a flick of her fingers. "I believe we have stumbled upon a rare exception to that general rule."

Shit. Why did she have to be so bloody clever?

He sat there struggling to come up with a response. After a moment, Diana continued, "What I would like to know is why you persist in thinking that you are not good enough for me. This is the only way we can resolve this—to identify the cause and pluck it out at the root."

Because I'm a degenerate and a freak. Not that he could say as much, even if it was true. "Um..."

When he did not elaborate, Diana took matters into her own hands. "Is it because of the pranks you pulled on my brother?"

He answered honestly. "No."

She was studying him in a way he didn't much care for. "Is it because you were not academically inclined during your school days, and perhaps you compare yourself to your brother?"

As far as excuses went, this was a good one. Of course, the fact that he was the village idiot while Edward had been the bloody Senior Wrangler, the top student in mathematics in all of Cambridge, had done a number on his confidence over the years. He could have said, *yes, that's it*, and let Diana go chasing down the wrong rabbit hole.

But to his surprise, although he couldn't muster the courage to tell her the truth, he also couldn't seem to form the lie with his lips. Diana deserved better than that. So, he whispered, "No."

Her eyes softened, as if she realized that even this much honesty was hard for him. "Then what is it?" she asked gently.

Harrington shifted in his seat. Perhaps he could tell her something that wasn't an outright lie. Hint at the truth without telling her everything. "As I'm sure you're aware, I wasn't exactly a choirboy prior to our marriage."

She stiffened. "Are you trying to tell me you contracted a disease?"

"No!" He jerked back, shocked. "God, no. I was always very careful."

She blew out a breath. "That's a relief." She threaded her fingers through his. "Then what is it that you think is so bad?"

He made a jerky motion with one shoulder. "It wouldn't be inaccurate to call me… you know. A degenerate."

She looked unimpressed. "I'm sure the same thing could be said about my own brother."

This was unequivocally true. During his time at university, Trevissick had kept not one mistress, but two—a pair of buxom blondes who reportedly liked to do *everything* together. Trevissick had been at Cambridge, but the rumors had reached Harrington and his friends at Oxford, where the duke had been the envy of every student, most of whom couldn't afford more than a half-hearted tug job from their bedmaker once a fortnight. If there was anyone who could rival Harrington in terms of depravity, it was Marcus Latimer.

When he didn't respond, Diana added, "I'm sure the same thing could also be said about your friend, Henry, who is now married to your sister. And yet, you seemed pleased about that match. Why are you so willing to overlook his past transgressions, yet so severe upon yourself?"

"Because I'm worse than Henry," he blurted.

"How so?" Diana asked softly.

His neck felt hot and itchy because they had veered alarmingly close to the truth. How had Diana maneuvered him so adroitly? "I just... am."

Her eyes sharpened to diamonds. "You're going to have to be more specific."

"I can't." His voice came out gruff, and he found that he was blinking rapidly. Was this it? The moment his marriage fell apart? And not even an hour after Diana told him she loved him. That was just his fucking luck...

Diana's voice was surprisingly gentle as she said, "You can. In fact, you need to." He tried to look away, but she ducked her head, scooting into his field of vision. "Because we need to trust one another, Harrington. What kind of marriage would we have if we can't do that?"

He tried, and failed, to make his voice light. "One like the vast majority of the *ton*?"

She shook her head. "That's not the kind of marriage I want."

He could feel sweat dripping down his collarbone. This was it, then. There was no getting out of it now. He was going to have to tell Diana the truth, going to have to see the disdain in her eyes, the derision. His happy little idyll was coming to an end. How the fuck could he even explain it?

That was when he recalled that Diana's brother had the same book of pornographic prints as him, and that she had perused it. If she had seen the particular print he liked best... at least it would be a starting point in trying to explain.

"You know that book of prints of your brother's?" he said in a clipped voice. "The one that shows couples in different poses?"

Her eyes were steady on his. "Yes."

"Some of them are… pretty bad." This seemed to be as much as he could muster.

Diana's eyes flared with comprehension. "And you are trying to tell me that one of those prints shows something you like."

"Yes," he said, his voice as gruff as scouring paper.

Her eyes were stern. "Which one?"

Panic rose in his throat. "I… I can't tell you that."

She pressed his hand so hard it hurt. "Which. One?"

Fuck. As if he could deny her anything when she was giving him that look.

He squeezed his eyes shut. "There's one that shows a man on all fours. And his lover is"—his mouth had gone dry, but he somehow forced the words out—"spanking him. With a birch." He hung his head. "That's it. That's what I like. I'm… depraved. Disgusting. Horrible," he added weakly.

"Harrington Astley!" Diana released his hand, and he felt the sofa cushions shift beside him as she stood.

It was as bad as he'd thought. She couldn't even bear to be near him. He ran a hand across his face and realized it was trembling.

Her voice was sharp. "Look at me. Now!"

Terrified, he opened his eyes to find her glowering at him, her hand on her hip.

Her eyes were furious as she said, "Is that all?"

CHAPTER 43

*H*arrington blinked at his wife, certain he had misheard.

"Is… that all?" he repeated, waiting for her to correct him.

Instead, she rubbed her brow. "I'm sorry. Clearly, you regard this as a distressing revelation. But Harrington!" She made a frustrated gesture. "You tried to leave me! *Multiple times*! You intentionally tried to push me away." She was shouting—shocking for the woman who never raised her voice because she could command a room with a raised eyebrow and an icy glare.

But now, she was raving. "What if I had taken you at your word? We could have very easily spent the rest of our lives without one another! Were I not the most stubborn woman in all of Christendom, we probably would have!"

He shook his head, hoping to clear it. The words she was saying made sense… and yet, they made no sense at all. "But… I knew you wouldn't want me once you found out. Really, I was just doing the decent thing. Saving you the trouble of having to throw me over."

Diana's eyes blazed. She crossed to the sofa in three

strides and placed one knee on the cushions, looming inches from his face.

"Well, I *do* want you! I don't give a fig if you like being spanked." She jabbed him in the chest with a finger. "Don't you dare try to push me away again! I will not tolerate it!"

He tried to answer her, but the only sound he seemed capable of forming was a sad sort of blubber. That was around the same time she, and the rest of the room, went blurry around the edges.

Wait. Were those… tears? Was he *crying*? Surely not. He was a Rifleman. Soldiers didn't *cry*!

"Harrington." Her voice still held a note of frustration, but the fight had gone out of her. She climbed onto his lap and wrapped her arms around his neck. He immediately hugged her to him and buried his face in her hair.

When he recovered the ability to speak, he murmured, "I can't believe it."

She sat back enough to look him in the eyes. "Perhaps you should. I was raised by Aunt Griselda, and…"

Harrington had no idea what this had to do with Aunt Griselda. Was it possible that she, too, liked being spanked? And Diana somehow knew about it?

He gave her a moment. When she did not elaborate, he gave her a gentle squeeze. "And?"

Her eyes were guarded. "I mentioned it once before. She had a friend. Miss Amelia Marsden. I never met her, as she died before I was born. But I can tell by the way Aunt Griselda speaks of her that they weren't merely *friends*. She felt about Miss Marsden the same way I feel about you. But society would not permit them to be together in that way, openly, before the world."

Harrington said nothing but rubbed her back. After a moment, Diana continued, "I know many people would say it was a sin. But I can't see anything wrong with it. Who was hurt by their love? No one." She straightened her spine, eyes blazing. "And no one is harmed by what you like, either."

He couldn't assail her logic. Yet… it didn't feel right. Not the bit about Aunt Griselda. He didn't give a damn what she had felt for, or what she had done with, this Miss Marsden. Aunt Griselda was one of the good ones, and he couldn't imagine much that would convince him otherwise.

But him? He was a degenerate. A wretch! He wasn't loveable.

Was he?

Diana was studying him with a sharp gaze. "What are you thinking?"

"N-nothing," he sputtered.

She narrowed her eyes. "I'll warrant I know exactly what you're thinking. You're thinking that it's fine for Aunt Griselda to like what she likes. But it's somehow different for you."

He slumped against the couch cushions. "Sometimes I wish you were less astute."

"Too bad." She said it cheerfully, but then, her expression turned somber. "Although, you're probably giving me more credit than I deserve. There's something I've been meaning to tell you. A confession, of sorts."

She looked guilty, and Harrington had to suppress a snort. Whatever she had to say, it couldn't possibly hold a candle to his sins. "Oh? What's that?"

Her cheeks had turned rosy. "When I first told you that I had perused a book of risqué prints, you assumed it was a book belonging to my brother." She swallowed and closed her eyes. "It wasn't my brother's book. It was yours. Izzie found it hidden beneath your mattress, and she took it to show Lucy and me."

It was a bit embarrassing, but Harrington couldn't say he

was surprised. That certainly sounded like something Izzie would do. "Oh?"

Diana opened her eyes a slit, cringing. "There was a certain page that you had… er, marked. By folding down the corner."

His heart rate kicked up a beat because he knew exactly which page that would be—the one he had just described. Which meant that Diana knew.

Of course… he'd already known that she knew. They'd been discussing it for the last ten minutes. To be more precise, this meant that she'd always known.

There was a roaring in his ears. The room went blurry around the edges.

She'd… always known.

About him. And what he liked.

And she'd married him anyway.

From her perch in his lap, words tumbled from Diana's lips. "I'm sorry. I should have told you from the start. It's just that I was embarrassed, and… In retrospect, perhaps I shouldn't have looked at it at all. But after my father died, I suddenly found myself on the Marriage Mart, facing the prospect of an imminent wedding, and I had so little information! I merely wanted to learn about the acts I might soon be expected to perform. And I thought it was just a book. I didn't realize it would be personally revealing in any way." Her eyes were beseeching. "Truly, Harrington. I'm sorry."

"It's all right." He gave her a quick kiss on the forehead. "It's natural that you were curious. I can't say I'm pleased about my little sisters knowing that I, er…" He cleared his throat. "But it occurred to me… you saw that page. The one where I'd turned down the corner. So… you already knew."

"About your proclivities?" At his nod, she continued, "I certainly suspected."

He could hear the disbelief in his own voice. "And you still wanted to marry me."

"I did," she said fiercely. "I meant it when I said I don't care about that."

"I'm so glad, I just…" He ran a hand across his face. "I suppose, if I'm being honest, I'm having a hard time believing it."

Diana studied him with that all-knowing gaze of hers. "I can see that. I think there's only one thing to do." She rose from his lap and walked toward the front door.

"What's that?" Harrington asked.

She was rummaging around in the umbrella stand. "I'm going to prove it to you."

"Prove it to me? How are you going to…"

The words died on his lips as Diana turned, the object she'd been searching for in her hand.

It was a riding crop.

"Well?" she said, offering him a wicked smile.

With each passing second, Diana felt more ridiculous. Harrington was gaping at her. His mouth was hanging open, and if he didn't shut it soon, she was fairly certain the drop of saliva forming in the corner of his mouth was going to fall.

She thought that, perhaps, it was an interested kind of gaping. Although it was difficult to be sure.

Something occurred to her, and she dropped her gaze to the falls of his trousers and—

Ahem. There was no *perhaps* about it.

It was *definitely* an interested kind of gaping.

Her confidence buoyed, she took a seductive step toward him. "Well? How about it?" When she reached the sofa, she reached out with the crop, stroking the side of his neck.

"Diana," he said in a choked voice, "let me make sure I understand. Are you offering to… to spank me?"

She gave him what she hoped was a seductive smile. "That's precisely what I'm offering."

His breath was coming fast. "You… you don't have to do that."

She tucked the crop beneath her arm and swung a leg over him to kneel straddling his lap. She reached straight for the bulge tenting his trousers, stroking him through the woolen fabric, and his head fell back with a groan. "It seems that you would like it if I did."

He was gasping for air. "I've only been dreaming about you standing over me with a crop for the last three years."

"Hmm." She leaned in, kissing his ear. "What else have you been dreaming about?"

He drew back, his eyes unfocused with pleasure. "You're sure about this?"

She gave his cock another stroke. "Yes."

She relished his gasp. "Absolutely sure?"

"Absolutely sure. Only…" She swallowed. "I'm not sure how to go about it. Do I just swat you a few times with the crop, or…?"

He shook his head. "There's a lot more to it than that. But if you're truly willing—"

"I am," she said fiercely.

He studied her for a moment, then nodded. "All right. The first thing you're going to do is catch me misbehaving…"

CHAPTER 44

$\mathcal{D}$iana paced the front room nervously. When she'd taken up the riding crop, she hadn't realized she would need to do more than swat Harrington a few times on the bottom.

Little had she realized how complicated his desires were, and how deeply rooted they were to his inner psyche.

Still, although there were a surprising number of steps, he had given her detailed directions, and she thought she just might be able to pull this off…

She cleared her throat. He had said he would need but a minute to get into position.

Gathering her courage, she opened the bedroom door.

Harrington lay naked atop the counterpane, eyes closed, stroking his erect cock.

Her instinct was to climb on the bed and join him, but she suppressed it. One thing he had emphasized was that the sterner she was with him, the more he would like it.

He had also said that the interlude should commence with her catching him "misbehaving." It was important that he earn his spanking. She therefore assumed that was how he wanted her to interpret his masturbation.

She narrowed her eyes and made her voice sharp. "Harrington Astley! I specifically told you that I wanted your cock tonight. And yet, here I find you, about to spend without me!"

An expression of purest pleasure washed over his face. "Diana. Oh, my *God*!"

She ignored him, striding up to the bed. "You leave me no choice but to punish you." She felt completely ridiculous saying the words, but this was what he had assured her he wanted, so she forced them out. It helped that he groaned, his face a portrait of ecstasy, as she uttered them.

She swatted the outside of his thigh with the crop. "On your hands and knees."

He complied but gasped, "Not yet. Don't spank me quite yet. So good, Diana. Draw it out. Please!"

On the one hand, this was reassuring. On the other... draw it out? How on earth was she supposed to do that?

Well, he had been "misbehaving" by touching himself.

Perhaps that was something she could use...

Dropping the crop on the bed, she knelt beside him. Reaching beneath him, she took his cock in her own hand and began stroking up and down. "Is this what you like?"

He groaned in response, head lolling to the side.

An idea occurred to her. "I've told you, you're only allowed to spend inside of me. You're not allowed to spill on the counterpane." His cock pulsed in her hand. She stroked him faster. "Don't come. Don't come. You're not allowed to come."

A dreamy smile washed over his face, as if this ridiculous demand were the nicest thing she could have said to him. "You're going to make me come."

"Don't you dare," she said, careful to keep her voice strict.

"You're not to spend. You'll be in *so* much trouble if you spend."

"Diana!" He made a strangled sound but didn't move to stop her from stroking him. "It's too good! You're going to bring me off!"

"No. No, no, no." She timed her strokes to match her words. "Don't come. You mustn't come. I will have no choice but to punish you if you—"

He cut her off with a cry as his body stiffened and his cock pulsed in her hand. Helpless, Harrington shuddered as his seed spilled onto the counterpane. After a moment, his cock, and his body, went limp.

Inspiration struck again. "Oh, dear. Look what a mess you've made."

He turned his head, smiling as if she'd said something wonderful. "You're not going to punish me for it. Are you?"

She picked up on his cue. "I most certainly am," she said, climbing off the bed and taking up the riding crop. "Don't even think of protesting. You know you deserve it."

He groaned, angling his backside toward her for easy access. She gave him a light swat across the buttocks. "Harder," he said at once. "You can hit me harder than that."

She swallowed and tried again. The crop made a sharp snap as it contacted his skin. Harrington moaned, but not in pain.

Encouraged, she swatted him again, and again. The crop left light red marks on his pale skin.

Harrington squirmed in what appeared to be a mixture of pleasure and pain. "Talk to me," he gasped. "It makes it better when you tell me how naughty I've been."

She spanked him again. "You certainly have been naughty," she improvised, trying to think of something to say. She noticed that his staff had thickened again between his thighs. "And what is this?" She leaned forward and ran the tip of the crop gently up and down his length. "Why, if I didn't know better, I would think you were enjoying your spanking!"

He dropped his head. "God, you're so good at this!" He glanced at her over his shoulder, his eyes filled with affection. "I knew you would be."

Relief washed through her. She felt ridiculous, but she was doing this for him, not for her. As long as Harrington seemed to be enjoying it, that was the main thing.

She started to reach for his cock again, but then hesitated, because doing so would require her to put down the whip, and she wasn't sure that he was ready for his spanking to end.

"What is it?" he asked, sensing her unease.

"I was thinking I should stroke your cock again," she admitted. "But I also feel like I should spank you some more."

"Order me to do it," he suggested eagerly.

Ah. That would work. She made her voice haughty. "Take your cock in your hand, if you like it so much." She snapped the crop against his bottom. "That's an order!"

He groaned as he complied. She spanked him twice more. "Look how naughty you're being, touching yourself when I've specifically told you not to!"

This was a patently ridiculous statement, as she had been the one to order him to touch himself. But, judging by the delighted smile Harrington cast her over his shoulder, it had been the right thing to say. "So naughty!" she cried, swatting him again with the crop. "So very, very naughty! Don't spend. You mustn't spend. You *know* you're not allowed to spend…"

She was starting to feel like she was getting the hang of it. Harrington certainly seemed to be enjoying her attempts, clumsy as they felt. She carried on spanking him, telling him all the while what a very naughty boy he was being, until he gasped, "I can be good! Really, I can. Let me make it up to you."

This was the next phase that he had told her about. When he was ready for the spanking to end, he would offer to make it up to her.

She had a feeling she knew what his method of choice was going to be and felt a damp pulse between her legs at the prospect. But she lifted her chin and tried to sound aloof. "I should like to know how you think you can make up for your abominable misbehavior."

A soft smile graced his face. He sat up, wincing slightly as his bottom touched the soft surface of the bed. He was already drawing up her skirts. "Let me show you."

He knelt at her feet, crawling beneath her skirts as he pushed her thighs apart. She must have enjoyed tormenting him more than she'd realized, because when his tongue found her little pearl, she was ready for him.

She knotted her fingers in his hair, not troubling to be gentle as her breath came hard.

"That's it, Diana," he breathed against her thigh. "You taste so good. Let me give you some tongue."

He proceeded to do just that, driving her over the edge in a matter of minutes.

He scooped her into his arms, laying her out on the bed and stripping her naked. "If you think you're forgiven," she began.

"Not yet," he said, smiling as he stroked his hands up and down her arms. "But there's more I can do for you. Let me show you how good I can be."

He proceeded to stroke every inch of her body. He kneaded her shoulders. He caressed the length of each finger. He rubbed her feet with firm strokes.

It was relaxing and arousing in equal measures, and when he came to her breasts, he made no pretense of "massaging" her there, instead suckling a nipple into his mouth and titillating her until she was squirming on the bed.

"Harrington!" she gasped, spreading her thighs wide and trying to push his head down where she needed it most.

He grinned. "Oh, do you need a more... *intimate* massage?"

She tossed her head against the pillow. "You know I do!"

"As my lady commands," he said in a husky voice, lowering his head between her trembling thighs.

He suckled her until she came again, then insisted on doing it once more. She was, by then, exquisitely sensitive, and it was almost too good, but he went slowly and managed to tease her into a third peak.

Dizzy and disoriented with pleasure, she remembered the final thing he had told her to do. He had said this was the most important step of all—to praise him lavishly after he had "atoned" for his misbehavior. "Good. So very good."

His head popped up. His brown eyes were bright. "Could you possibly be referring to me?"

"Yes. You've more than made up for your previous transgressions. In fact..." She reached for him, opening her thighs suggestively, and made her voice husky. "I would say that you've earned a reward for being so very, very good."

He made a sound of delight as he climbed on top of her. She kissed his neck as he aligned himself with her entrance. "Good," she murmured between kisses. "So very good to me. Go ahead. Take your pleasure."

She continued to utter words of praise as he pumped into her, a look of bliss on his face. As it had when he'd first told her about this part, her heart squeezed at the thought that this was the thing he longed for most of all—to be told that he was good, that he deserved to feel this pleasure, that he was *worthy*.

He was all those things, even if he couldn't quite bring himself to believe it.

But she was going to convince him. Someday soon.

She would make it her personal mission.

And so, she stroked his back, whispering all the while how wonderful he was, how good he had made her feel, and how much she loved him. It didn't take long for his motions to become frantic.

"That's it, Harrington." She pressed a kiss against his ear. "Come inside me. I want you to feel as much pleasure as you gave me."

He was pounding against her then. "Diana," he gasped. "I'm… I'm almost…"

She wrapped her arms around his shoulders, holding him tightly. "Come inside me. That's an order."

He cried out as he came, his body first going stiff and then being wracked by shudders. Diana clung to him, whispering soothing words as his crisis passed.

She stroked his back as his breathing grew less ragged. When he lifted his head, his expression was content. "Thank you," he said, kissing her on the lips.

He climbed off her, rolling them both onto their sides and pulling her against him.

"There's no need to thank me," she replied, snuggling into his chest. "I enjoyed making you feel good."

He shook his head. "I can't believe—"

Quick as a snake, she brought her hand up and covered his mouth. "None of that."

Comprehension flared in his eyes, and she removed her hand. "I'm sorry. You're right, of course. It's probably going to take me a while. But I am going to do my darndest to get it through my thick skull that you do, in fact, want me." His voice turned gruff. "And I promise, Diana, I will never turn away from you again." He laughed. "You've done it now. You're stuck with me for the duration."

She hugged him tight. "Good."

They fell into a companionable silence. After a moment, Diana yawned. "Now, we just have to figure out what to do about my brother."

Harrington didn't respond right away, and she wondered if he had fallen asleep. But when she glanced up, she found his eyes fixed upon the ceiling. "I have a few thoughts on that." He looked at her, and his brown eyes contained a burgeoning resolve. "I think it's time I faced my demons."

CHAPTER 45

The following morning, Harrington sent a note over to Castle Bernard asking if he might call upon the Duke of Trevissick that afternoon. He received a response not from Trevissick but from Lord Bandon, indicating that the duke was willing to speak with him.

And so, after he finished his daily drill with the King's German Legion, Harrington headed over to the castle. Lord Bandon received him warmly and ushered him into the library, where Trevissick was waiting. The earl was extremely gracious, settling them both in leather wingchairs before the fire and pouring them each a glass of his best whiskey before clasping his hands. "I'll leave you to it, then." He exited the room, shutting the door behind him with a click.

Harrington had tossed and turned for most of the night, rehearsing what he was going to say. "Well."

"Well," the duke replied, his voice cold.

Harrington ignored his tone. This was Diana's brother, the most important man in her life, excepting him. He doubted they would ever be friends. But he was determined to be cordial for Diana's sake.

He took a sip of his drink and set it on the side table. "I want to start by offering you an apology. My conduct toward you when we were at school was inexcusable."

The duke rolled his eyes. "And now that you're married to my sister, you expect me to let bygones be bygones. All you need do is speak two little words, and we'll be the best of chums."

"No," Harrington said quickly. "I don't expect you to forgive me. I'm not sure that I would, if I were in your shoes, and frankly, I can't argue that I deserve it. But I do think we should reach some sort of understanding, for Diana's sake."

The duke arched a haughty eyebrow. "What sort of understanding?"

"A détente, if you will. It will only cause her distress if we're at one another's throats. And causing her distress is the last thing I would ever want to do."

Trevissick regarded him with a wrinkled nose, as if he found it distasteful that Harrington had made a good point. "Fine," he muttered, turning to glower at the fire.

Harrington listened to the crackle of peat burning in the grate. After a moment, he said, "So. Going forward, how would you like me to—"

"Why did you do it?" The duke stiffened, looking surprised that the words had slipped from his lips.

It would be an awkward conversation, but Harrington wasn't going to avoid it. "I was jealous."

Trevissick cast him a withering look. "Because I was rich, and the heir to a dukedom, and it never occurred to you that I might have problems of my own?"

"No," Harrington said quickly. "I suppose the last part was true. You were bloody good at hiding the fact that anything was wrong at home. Not that I gave it any thought. I was twelve years old. I wasn't what you would call introspective."

The duke narrowed his eyes. "Then why?"

Harrington forced himself to look at Trevissick steadily as he said, "Because you were friends with Edward."

The duke blinked. It occurred to Harrington that this was the first time he had just looked at him, not sneered, or glared, or glowered. "You remained close to your brother. It's not as if I displaced you."

"That's true," Harrington acknowledged. "But you were the one he chose. I'm just the idiot he was stuck with through some accident of birth."

The duke was back to scowling. "You will not convince me that Fauconbridge ever said as much."

"Of course not. Edward would never do something like that." He sipped from his drink, then set it aside. "But some of the other boys did, and it bothered me more than I could admit at the time. It was only years after the fact that I came to understand the real reason I mocked you so relentlessly. Because I was jealous and searching for a way to take you down a peg. To demonstrate that you weren't better than me, in spite of what everybody said."

He paused to see if Trevissick would say something. He merely sat, studying Harrington through narrowed eyes.

Harrington cleared his throat. "I apologize. Unreservedly. It was poorly done of me all around, and I deeply regret it. However…"

The duke arched a supercilious eyebrow. "However?"

"I want to make it clear that I will never absent myself from Diana's life for the sake of sparing you discomfort." He leaned forward, looking the duke square in the eyes. "So long as she wants me around, that's where I'm going to be."

The duke's only response was a grunt.

Placing his hands on his knees, Harrington stood. The

conversation had not been a roaring success, but it had probably gone about as well as could be expected. "Diana and I would like to invite you to dinner tonight." This was part of the plan they had discussed. Although the cottage wasn't what you would call fancy, hopefully showing the duke that it was clean and respectable would help him resign himself to his sister's new life.

Trevissick sighed heavily. "Fine."

Harrington inclined his head. "I'll see you in an hour, then."

CHAPTER 46

*D*iana was not unreservedly happy to see her brother darkening their doorstep that evening. But if Harrington could manage to be civil in the face of Marcus's provocations, so could she.

Marcus was not particularly subtle in his inspection of the cottage. He poked disdainfully at the shabby fabric of the sofa and ran a finger across the mantelpiece, checking for dust. He wrinkled his nose in disappointment when it came away clean but found something new to sneer at when he turned around and saw that the dining table was housed in the main room.

But even a duke could not find fault with the housekeeping, and when Maeve came bustling in with a delicious-smelling pork roast, he visibly relaxed. Had Marcus truly believed that Harrington had her scouring pots and pans? Perhaps he had. Goodness knew her brother had always assumed the worst where Harrington was concerned.

As the meal wore on and Marcus presumably saw that she was well-fed and well cared-for, his brow visibly unknotted and his shoulders lowered. Harrington made an effort to be solicitous, asking about Marcus's sea crossing and inquiring about friends back in London.

Diana made sure that she was the one to tell the story of their ill-fated sojourn on Bere Island. She was careful to frame it as a lark and emphasize how much she had enjoyed having a bit of an adventure. Every time Marcus started to protest, she cut him off by pointing out how similar it had been to the many excursions they had taken with Aunt Griselda over the years. Marcus could be spectacularly muleheaded, but she was a Latimer, too, and matched him glower for glower.

After dinner, they repaired to the sitting area before the fireplace. Harrington brought over a bottle of wine. "One of the fellows in the King's German Legion gave me this," he said, presenting the bottle to Marcus for inspection. "It's a sparkling white wine, made in the Rhine valley—"

"A Riesling," Marcus supplied.

"Precisely." Harrington rocked back on his heels. "It's probably not the quality you're used to, but—"

Marcus waved a hand. "Let's try it."

Harrington fetched three glasses, then opened the bottle. "Would you like some, darling?" he asked Diana.

She took one of the glasses and held it up. "Yes, please."

As Harrington poured, she caught Marcus watching them through narrowed eyes.

It turned out to be a very good wine, and they chatted for another hour while they shared the bottle. Finally, Marcus rose to take his leave. As he donned his hat and greatcoat, Diana invited him to join her for her morning walk tomorrow, an offer he stiffly accepted.

The morning was cool and misty. Diana noted with amusement that, now that his identity had been discovered,

Marcus had returned to dressing as himself, wearing a silk-lined greatcoat of the softest wool instead of the shapeless brown sack he'd procured from goodness knew where, and Hoby boots polished to a high sheen in defiance of the impressive Irish mud.

Diana took him on her favorite walk, dutifully pointing out notable sights. "This is the Mulrooney farm." She waved at a figure on the far side of the field, who waved back. "As you can see, Mr. Mulrooney is tending his herd. He is renowned for his fine cheddar cheese and his—"

"Is he always like that?" Marcus asked abruptly.

Diana gave her brother a strange look. "Mr. Mulrooney is usually hard at work, from what I have observed. Why do you ask?"

Marcus scowled. "I meant your husband."

"Oh." Diana considered, taken aback. "Largely, yes. He was perhaps a bit nervous last night."

Marcus waved a hand. "He seemed… solicitous. Of you," he clarified at Diana's puzzled expression. "I observed that he gave you the most tender slice of the pork roast, taking the slightly charred end piece for himself. He also insisted that you have the last almond biscuit, correctly noting that they are your favorites, and went to let Inge into the back garden himself so you would not have to get up."

Diana bit back a smile. It was on the tip of her tongue to say, *if you believe that to be solicitous, you should see him in bed.* But she had the feeling this was not the sort of thing her brother would wish to hear. "I can assure you, this behavior is characteristic. I could not ask for a kinder, more considerate husband."

Marcus gave her a hard look. "Truly? You are not just saying that to placate me?"

"I swear, I am not. I wish you could have seen his distress

when we became marooned on Bere Island and it became clear that we would have to sleep beneath the stars. I know you will not countenance it, but you would not have been half as severe on him as he was on himself."

Marcus frowned. "I know you think I am an overbearing arse—"

"However would one form such a preposterous impression?" Diana asked dryly.

Marcus acknowledged her riposte with a smirk. "But I hope you understand that my intentions are sincere. It is a sad truth that a woman surrenders a great many rights the second she signs a marriage contract. In the blink of an eye, she surrenders power over both her finances and her person. Should her husband choose to mistreat her, in all but the most severe cases, the law turns a blind eye. Including..." He paused, clearing his throat. When he spoke again, his voice was uneven. "Including the same sort of mistreatment our mother was subjected to at the hands of our father."

She seized his hand. "Harrington is nothing like our father."

His expression remained guarded. "Is he not?"

"I swear, he is not. You will find it difficult to believe, but he is exceptionally kind." Diana paused, scouring her memory. "I cannot recall a single cross word he has said to me. Ever."

In an instant, the cold reserve Marcus wore like a cloak was gone. His eyes were urgent. "Truly? He is treating you well?"

"He is." Diana inclined her head back toward town. "Let's return to the cottage so we can talk."

They settled on the sofa before the crackling fire. Maeve, seeming to sense the tension in the air, announced that she was heading to the market, leaving them alone.

Diana explained everything. Well, perhaps not quite *everything*. She left out the sort of intimate revelations a brother would not wish to hear. But she told him how Harrington had sought her advice, again and again, as he found himself in over his head with regards to his new position in Parliament. And that this was the main reason she had wanted to marry him—that he appreciated her not for her dowry, but for her intelligence. That he respected her and valued her opinion.

When she finished, it was the rare occasion that Marcus looked sheepish. "Cecilia tried to tell me he was no longer the boy he'd been at Eton. Fauconbridge, too. But I could not stop fixating on the possibility that he might be mistreating you. He acted contemptuously toward me for so long, it is difficult for me to picture him any other way. But if you swear that he is treating you kindly—"

"He is," Diana said swiftly. "As severe as you are on him, had you seen him for the last few weeks, I think even you could find no fault in his conduct."

Marcus nodded. "I am sorry, especially that I frightened you by following you around town. I know you think me ridiculous. The truth is, although I might harp on the size of your cottage, or"—he glanced down, giving a visible shudder —"this *hideously* ugly sofa, I don't care about those things. The *only* thing I care about is that you are happy and that you are being treated well."

She scooted closer to him and laid her head on his shoulder. "I do know that, Marcus." It was a funny thing, considering that Diana had been the one to suffer at the hands of their father before Marcus contrived to remove her to Aunt Griselda's house, while their father had never struck his only son and heir. But paradoxically, the scars Marcus bore as a result of the old duke's abuse were at least as deep as Diana's. He had been older, for one, his memories clearer. He had witnessed far more violence, directed toward their mother, than Diana had experienced, as the servants had helped her to hide, and Marcus had acted quickly to remove her from that situation. He had even been there the day their mother died, and although he had not witnessed her death, he had been close enough to hear her scream.

Additionally, Marcus had always held himself responsible for their mother's death. He had forgotten his sword that morning, and although he had been all of eleven years old, he had it in his head that it had been his duty to protect her from their father. At least that had been one burden Diana had never had to shoulder. She regarded their father's abuse, both toward her and her mother, as his failing alone. But Marcus sincerely believed he also bore a share of the blame.

The truth was that both of them bore scars from their childhood. They were neither of them quite whole, and perhaps they never would be. But Aunt Griselda had taken the task of mending Diana's broken places quite seriously. She could remember feeling powerless and terrified as she hid behind curtains and beneath sofas as she listened to her father's footsteps while he searched for her.

But she was powerless no more. Aunt Griselda had made sure of that. Poor Marcus, meanwhile, had been alone at Eton during the darkest period of his life, too afraid to confide even in his closest friends about the wreck that was his family. He had therefore not made as much progress as Diana.

But he would. Just look at how fondly he doted on Alaric. He had managed to take the right lessons from their terrible childhood and had understood that their father was a model of what *not* to do. And, although she didn't much appreciate his meddling, she knew that his intentions were pure. That, and the fact that he had come by his neuroses honestly, made it easier for her to make allowances for his misguided behavior.

"I forgive you," she said. "But you have to try. Give Harrington a chance. And try to get it through your thick skull that I'm no longer a helpless two-year-old."

He wrinkled his nose in distaste. "I will try."

EPILOGUE

$\mathcal{M}$arcus stayed in Ireland for another week. Lord and Lady Bandon hosted a number of dinners, to which Harrington, Diana, and his fellow officers and their wives were invited. This enabled the duke to see that the society in which his sister found herself was better than he had supposed.

He and Harrington remained stilted in one another's presence. It was strange seeing two men known for their sardonic wit behaving with such stiff formality. But, Diana mused, it was better than being at one another's throats.

Harrington's deployment lasted another nine months, after which the army recalled him to London. Their return voyage was far less eventful than their initial crossing had been.

And so it was on a crisp evening in March that Diana found herself disembarking at the Royal Dockyard at Deptford, with Harrington by her side and Inge trotting at their heels.

Part of her wanted to go straight to Latimer House. She longed to wrap Aunt Griselda in a tight hug and press kisses to Alaric's perfect, blond head. But she knew that if they went there, Marcus would insist they stay as his guests. And Diana was determined to establish their independence.

She and Harrington therefore took a room at the Pulteney Hotel and sent messages to their respective families informing them of their return, and that they hoped to see them on the morrow.

They slept well in the plush bed. Having grown accustomed to keeping military hours, they were dressed and finishing breakfast at eight o'clock when a footman wearing the Latimer family's familiar pale blue and gold livery presented himself at the door.

"James," Diana said, rising from her chair and crossing the room to press his hand. "How wonderful to see you."

James's eyes were warm as he bowed over her hand. "My lady. I apologize for the early hour, but they said downstairs that you were already up and about."

"You were informed correctly. I assume you come bearing a message from my brother?"

"Yes, indeed." James presented a crisp white envelope with a flourish.

Diana cracked open the seal and found an elegantly calligraphed card:

To Lieutenant Harrington Astley and Lady Diana Astley,
Their Graces the Duke and Duchess of Trevissick
request the honor of your presence
at Latimer House
on Tuesday, the 24th of March
at two o'clock in the afternoon.

"So formal," Diana observed, showing Harrington. "And gracious—this is today's date." She turned to James. "What is the occasion?"

"Forgive me, my lady. I am not at liberty to say."

Diana arched an eyebrow. "So mysterious. Well, you may tell my brother that I will be able to attend."

"I'll try to make it over as well," Harrington said, "but I've been summoned to Horse Guards to discuss my next assignment. Hopefully, my meeting will have concluded by then."

James blanched. "His Grace instructed me that I was not to leave until I had extracted a promise that you would both be present."

Diana exchanged a curious glance with Harrington. "Well, Marcus will have to manage his disappointment. My husband's career must come before... whatever this mysterious summons might be."

James turned to Harrington. "With whom will you be meeting?"

"With General James Gordon," Harrington supplied.

"General Gordon," James muttered, pulling a small notebook and pencil from his breast pocket. "His Grace can send the general a note, advising him of the need for your meeting to conclude prior to two." He nodded to himself as he tucked the notebook away. "The duke will take care of it. I am sure that he will."

"James," Diana said, unable to conceal her exasperation, "please tell my brother that he is not to meddle in army business. It's unbecoming. This is Harrington's career!"

James bowed deeply. "Never fear, my lady. His Grace will know precisely how to handle it. I daresay he can smooth everything over by extending General Gordon an invitation to the..." He trailed off, clearing his throat. "Never mind!" He reached behind him for the doorknob. "It was wonderful seeing you, my lady! Lieutenant!"

"James!" Diana protested. "I insist that you tell me what is—"

"Until this afternoon!" James cried, and then the door clicked shut behind him.

Diana rubbed her brow, exasperated. "My brother is a plague."

Harrington laughed, coming up behind her and rubbing her shoulders. "Your brother is a duke, which I suppose is its own form of pestilence. Are you truly surprised?"

She sighed. "No. Well, you are wanted at Horse Guards. I take it I am not to visit Latimer House before two, but perhaps I will drop in on Izzie and Lucy."

But much to Diana's annoyance, none of the Astleys were at home when she called at their townhouse on Cavendish Square.

Their longtime butler, Yarwood, clucked sympathetically when she asked where they had gone, and at such an early hour. "I am terribly sorry, my lady. But I have been sworn to silence."

Diana bit back her irritation. She knew that none of this was Yarwood's fault, and Marcus was the one who deserved her ire. "Never mind," she said brightly. "I shall head to the Nettlethorpe-Ogilvy manse and see what Izzie is up to."

Yarwood cleared his throat. "My apologies, Lady Diana. But I fear you will find that Lady Isabella is similarly occupied. Unless you wish to spend the morning with Mr. Nettlethorpe-Ogilvy's parents, I would advise you to give their household a wide berth."

Diana smiled tightly. "Thank you for the warning, Yarwood."

Lacking any other way to pass the time, she sent one of the Pulteney's footmen over to her brother's stables to fetch her mare, Artemisia, and spent the morning riding in Hyde Park. That it was not the fashionable hour was an enticement rather than a shortcoming, as the park was empty and this was the only time of day when one was permitted to gallop.

She returned to the hotel to find that Marcus had sent over her lady's maid, Veronique, along with a few of her old dresses. She allowed Veronique to dress her in a silk gown and poke and prod her with the curling tongs for what felt like an inordinately long period of time until she looked like her old self, the sister of the duke, the richest heiress in all of England, rather than a humble officer's wife.

Harrington gave a low whistle when he returned from Horse Guards. Diana smiled as he met her eyes in the mirror. "Do you prefer me in silk and seed pearls, then?" she teased.

He pressed a kiss into her palm. "I prefer you with that smile on your face. Shall we go see what your brother is up to?"

She rose from the padded stool. "Let's."

Diana felt her throat constrict as the carriage Marcus had sent for them drove between the familiar pair of lion statues flanking the drive of Latimer House. It only grew worse as the door was opened by their long-time family butler, Ellery. When little Alaric ran into the room, arms extended overhead for "Aunt Diynah" to pick him up, she began sniffling, and by the time Aunt Griselda came down the stairs and enveloped her in a hug, tears were streaming down her cheeks.

Lucy and Izzie broke the tension by flying into the foyer, crowing with delight and almost bowling her over in their enthusiasm. And by the time Marcus strolled into the room, Diana was laughing through her tears.

He scowled. "Why are you crying?"

She gave him a baleful look. "Happy tears, Marcus. I am merely overwhelmed at seeing everyone again."

He leaned close to whisper in her ear. "And you are still happy in your marriage?"

She swiped her thumb beneath her eyes. "Extremely happy."

He rocked back on his heels. "Good. In that case." He offered his arm to Diana, and much to her astonishment, slung an arm around Harrington's shoulders.

Marcus led them toward the turquoise parlor. Diana could hear a hum of conversation behind the gold-and-white gilded doors. She drew their party to a halt. "Marcus, what's all this?"

He smirked, then nodded for James to open the door. "Your wedding breakfast."

Round tables draped in pristine white cloths had been scattered throughout the high-ceilinged room. Crystal glinted before each place setting, and Diana saw that Marcus had pulled out the family's best china, a set of Sèvres porcelain rimmed in blue and gold and adorned with hand-painted roses.

Diana did not have long to admire the décor, because they were immediately mobbed by Harrington's entire family. Even Freddie, whom Diana had only met on a handful of occasions, as he was still in his final year at Eton, had come down to London for the occasion. It was startling to see that little Freddie was now as tall as his brothers.

While Fauconbridge enveloped Harrington in a bear hug, Marcus's wife, Cecilia, strolled up to Diana with a baby in her arms.

Diana leaned forward. "This must be little Griselda!"

"We've been calling her Zelda," Ceci explained. "Here, take her. She is the most agreeable creature."

Diana made a sound of pleasure as Ceci handed little Zelda over. Beneath the three yards of lace she wore, Diana saw she had a mop of honey-colored curls and the same fine, dark eyes as Ceci. She thought Zelda might protest being taken away from her mother, but the baby immediately returned Diana's smile, reaching a tiny hand up to touch her aunt's cheek.

Diana leaned in close to nuzzle her perfect head. "Your Aunt Diana is going to teach you to fence. We shall practice until you are every bit as ferocious as your namesake."

Marcus strolled over, holding Alaric in his arms. "Isn't she marvelous?" He smiled at his wife. "I know you will think me conceited, but truly, Cecilia and I produce the most outstanding children."

Diana gave him a wry look. "Conceited? You?"

After a few minutes, Ellery began ushering the guests toward their seats. Zelda and Alaric were taken off for their own luncheon, and Diana and Harrington took their places at a table in the front of the room, flanked by Marcus and Ceci on one side and Lord and Lady Cheltenham on the other.

Marcus stood, a glass of champagne in his hand, and directed a pointed look at Aunt Griselda. "Someone brought it to my attention—several times, might I add—that I ought to have given my sister a wedding breakfast on the day of her nuptials."

Aunt Griselda raised a shoulder, her expression unapologetic. "So what if I did? It is true."

Chuckles swept across the room. Once they had subsided, Marcus inclined his head. "As usual, my aunt is correct. I am glad now to have the opportunity to correct my oversight." He raised his glass. "Please join me in offering my heartfelt congratulations to my sister, Lady Diana Astley. I also wish to formally welcome my new brother-by-marriage, Lieutenant Harrington Astley, to the family!"

Glasses were raised and cries of *hear, hear* filled the room. Diana slanted her eyes toward her husband. His smile was bashful, and when he looked up, his brown eyes were shiny. She reached beneath the table, caught his hand, and squeezed, and then she thought that she would never, not if she lived to be a hundred, forget the way he looked at her in that moment.

The meal was everything that extreme wealth and exquisitely good taste could provide. The food was French, the wines cost more than most men made in a year, and the desserts were decadence itself.

After the meal, Harrington approached her brother and shook his hand. "Thank you, Trevissick. Truly. That was the nicest wedding breakfast I've ever attended. It really means a lot to me."

Diana's breath caught. Marcus hosting this wedding breakfast seemed like an olive branch. She hoped it meant that he was finally accepting her marriage to Harrington.

Still, it seemed too much to hope that Marcus would truly give him a chance.

Marcus rolled his eyes. "I'm trying to decide which is more insufferable—all the pranks you used to pull on me at Eton, or this obsequious drivel."

Diana's heart sank. Harrington blinked but held his composure. "You don't wish for me to be… polite?"

"I would much prefer for you to be amusing." Marcus beckoned a footman bearing a bottle of brandy. Much to Diana's surprise, he poured a glass and handed it to Harrington before pouring another for himself. "My wife informs me that, all evidence to the contrary, you have a rather fine wit. If we're to be stuck together for the next fifty years for every conceivable holiday and social occasion, then I must insist that you make use of it."

A grin stole across Harrington's face—his real grin, Diana noted. He took a sip from his cup. "So, I was thinking—now that we're brothers, I suppose I ought to call you Marcus."

Marcus said, "Absolutely not." But Diana recognized that smirk. He was enjoying himself.

Hope flared in her heart.

Harrington shook his head. "Don't be that way, Marcus. This is a happy day for you."

Marcus narrowed his eyes. "Is it really?"

Harrington slung an arm around his shoulders. "You always wanted your sister to marry one of the Astley brothers."

Marcus gave him a baleful look, but the corner of his mouth was twitching. "Fauconbridge. I wanted her to marry Fauconbridge."

Harrington shrugged. "I'm the next-best thing."

Marcus huffed. "You honestly think I wanted my sister to marry the man who once informed the Unitarians that I was eager to learn more about their religion?" He shuddered. "They hounded me for *months*."

Harrington took a sip of his brandy. "Sorry about that, mate. I'm also sorry for the time I wrote that letter to the editor of the *Reading Mercury* in your name, complaining how unsightly the local 'peasants' were."

Marcus groaned. "I had forgotten about that one. But not about the rumor you started that I sent my laundry all the way to France because I insisted upon it being dried in fields of lavender."

Harrington laughed. "I was amazed anyone believed that one! I mean, you used the same laundress as the rest of us. But it spread like wildfire."

Marcus rolled his eyes. "Then there was the time you informed a traveling menagerie that I wished to purchase a tiger cub, which they delivered to Long Chamber, along with a bill for a hundred and fifty pounds."

Harrington's expression turned abruptly serious. "Now

see here—I won't apologize for that one. You loved Rajendra. Admit it."

Marcus sighed, a faraway look coming into his eyes. "I did. He was a magnificent creature, and so lively. Although he shredded my favorite coat to ribbons, it was worth it for the few days I was able to spend with him."

"Ha!" Harrington gave Marcus a squeeze. "I knew you secretly enjoyed my pranks."

"*Enjoyed* might be overstating things."

Harrington ignored him. "School would have been deadly dull without me."

Marcus drained his glass. "I suddenly find myself craving a dull moment."

Harrington grinned. "Too bad."

Alaric came toddling into the room, and Harrington knelt before him. "Good afternoon, Alaric. I'm your new Uncle Harrington."

Alaric regarded him with huge eyes. "Mummy said you'd teach me to shoot."

"I will. When you're just a bit older." He leaned forward, his eyes twinkling. "I'm going to teach you everything I know."

Marcus ran a hand over his face. "God save me."

Alaric toddled away, and Harrington stood. "Don't be that way, Marcus. I'm the boy's favorite uncle!"

Marcus groaned, but Diana could tell he was secretly enjoying his new sparring partner. "You're his *only* uncle."

Someone slipped their arm through Diana's. She turned to see Lucy smiling at her. "May I steal you away?"

Diana glanced at Harrington. He shot her a wink. Marcus was busy refilling Harrington's glass, his lips twisted into a smirk.

She turned to Lucy. "You may. I don't believe I'm needed here."

She could hear Harrington chuckling as Lucy led her away.

~

Two hours later, as the party was winding down, Diana stole up behind Harrington and slipped her hand into his. "Come with me," she whispered.

Harrington glanced about, curious, as she led him up two flights of stairs and down a long corridor toward the back of the mansion. "Where are you taking me? Please tell me it's your bedroom."

"It's not."

He ignored her. "I can debauch you right on top of your frilly, pink coverlet."

She cast him a sideways glance. "Don't you know me at all? What are the odds that I have a frilly, pink anything? I was raised by—"

"Aunt Griselda," he supplied, heaving a sigh. "I know. Considering my career, it's probably for the best that you're not a frilly pink sort of girl. But still, a man can dream."

She released his hand and opened a door at the end of the corridor, revealing a masculine room, all dark wood paneling and leather upholstery.

She led him to the room's back corner. The second he noticed the full-length painting hanging on the wall, he recoiled. "Is that your *father*?"

"It is," she replied coolly.

He gave a low whistle. "I'm surprised your brother didn't have it burned. Although..."

He frowned, then reached out to touch the pockmarks marring the layers of oil paint. He turned, and she marked the moment he noticed the bucket of darts in its custom-made mahogany stand.

He laughed. "Now I understand. My, but you Latimers are a vindictive bunch."

She took up a dart, gesturing for him to stand clear. Once he had stepped back, she threw it, neatly spearing her father in the throat. "And don't you forget it."

He came to stand behind her. "Is that why you wanted to show this to me? A warning not to step out of line?"

"Not at all." She selected another dart. "I merely wanted to gloat. It is one of the most treasured pastimes for every member of the Latimer family. I have won, and he has lost." She threw the dart, hitting her father square in the forehead. "Take that, you blackguard."

Harrington laughed. "May I?" he asked, gesturing to the bucket.

"Please. Are you good at darts?" She gestured to a scar in the wood paneling to the left of the painting. "Alas, Ceci is not."

Harrington tutted. "It's deep, though. At least she has enthusiasm, if not skill. Never fear. I am excellent at darts."

He made his throw, spearing her father neatly in the buttocks. He tried to make his expression solemn, but his lips were twitching. "For Aunt Griselda."

They took turns throwing darts, skewering the old duke through the heart, in his left nostril, and, in a shot that made Harrington wince, directly on the falls of his trousers.

He shook his head. "Remind me not to anger you. You mentioned that you had won." He seized her about the waist, pulling her flush against him. "Would you care to expound upon the nature of your victory?"

She stroked his chest. "Do you truly not know?"

His voice was a low rumble. "I have an inkling. But I would very much enjoy hearing you say the words."

She smiled. If there was one thing she had learned about her husband, it was that he liked nothing better than being told that he was good, that he was worthy, that he was loved. "In a word, the thing I won is you."

A sound of contentment rumbled through his chest. She continued, "I have married the ideal husband. A man who adores me. Who supports me in my every endeavor. Who makes me indescribably happy." She twined her fingers in the curls at the nape of his neck. "He was miserable for most of his life, while I am living happily-ever-after. Is this not the highest form of victory?"

He gave her a crooked smile, and when he spoke, his voice was a trifle unsteady. "If anyone won, it's me. You're everything I've ever wanted, Diana." He paused, hugging her close. "Are you sure we can't continue this conversation in your bedroom?"

She laughed. Indeed, she could feel something stirring beneath the placket of his trousers. "Completely sure. For the first time in years, you're on decent terms with my brother. Do you really want to throw that away?"

He heaved a petulant sigh. "I suppose not."

She decided to take pity on him. "Although."

He perked up. "Although?"

She leaned close to his ear. "I always used to daydream that a handsome man would steal me away to the orangery for a kiss."

"Your wish, my darling Diana, is my command." Without warning, he scooped her up into his arms. His eyes were bright. "Which way to the orangery?"

Their laughter mingled as he carried her through the door.

Keep reading for a preview of the next book in The Astley Chronicles series, *A Laird for Lady Lucy*!

~

Would you like to see what hijinks Harrington and Diana get up to in the future? Subscribers to my newsletter will receive a second epilogue short story so you can check in on their happily-ever-after. Sign up at courtneymccaskill.com/newsletter/ .

PREVIEW: A LAIRD FOR LADY LUCY

It was a marriage built on a lie.

After unexpectedly inheriting an earldom—and the Scottish castle that comes with it—Peter Ferguson finds himself besieged by distant relations eager to become the next Countess of Darrow. In an attempt to get rid of them, he announces that he is already married to the closest woman at hand, Lady Lucy Astley. Unfortunately for Peter, under Scottish law, a man and woman can legally marry by publicly declaring themselves to be husband and wife, meaning that his white lie is legally binding!

Accidentally yours.

Lucy's heart thrilled when Peter announced that she was his chosen bride. She has never lacked for suitors, but none of the men bringing her flowers ever seemed to see the real her. That is, until she was seated next to Peter at a dinner and discovered how thoughtful and attentive he could be. She's been trying to catch the sophisticated merchant's eye ever since, but she had thought her efforts were in vain… right up until Peter's declaration.

Some things are worth fighting for.

Lucy is heartbroken when she learns that Peter doesn't really want her. But word of their "marriage" has spread like wildfire, and Peter refuses to ruin Lucy by setting her aside. The guileless Lucy is about the last woman Peter pictured himself marrying. But Lucy is determined. Peter might speak nine languages, but Lucy is the one who knows about love and happiness. And she's going to show this stern businessman that what he really needs in his life is a little sunshine.

HISTORICAL NOTE

The description of the duel Diana read about between two German fencers that was, "as much a trial of endurance as of skill," comes from *Schools and Masters of Fencing from the Middle Ages to the Eighteenth Century* by Egerton Castle, originally published in 1885. Egerton lists several dozen German fencing manuals in his bibliography but does not specify which one is the source for this particular duel.

Harrington's enjoyment of flagellation was not uncommon during the nineteenth century. Flogging was such a widespread punishment at the schools of the time that virtually every upper-class English male experienced it firsthand, and some of them discovered that they found pleasure along with the pain. There were "birching parlors" in London. Once, Queen Victoria asked the Prime Minister, Lord Melbourne, for his opinion on corporal punishment. Melbourne, who was well-known for keeping mistresses who specialized in flagellation, replied solemnly that it had had an "amazing effect" on him.

Many of the events in the book—the 95th Rifles' return from Hanover, the Parliamentary Acts Harrington helped pass, the King's German Legion creating a light infantry division, and their being blown off course en route to Ireland and forced to maroon briefly on Bere Island—really did take place in 1806. But I wish to confess that I have played very fast and loose with the exact dates of these events in order to facilitate Diana and Harrington's love story.

ACKNOWLEDGMENTS

Many thanks to all of the "usual suspects"— my wonderful editor, Diana Bold; my indispensable proofreaders, Linda and Melinda; and my very talented, very patient cover designer, Bailey McGinn! I'd like to thank all of the wonderful readers on my ARC and Street Teams. And a particular thank you to Mireille G. for helping me translate the bit of French Harrington says to Diana to show off his skills. In case you're wondering, what he said was, "Are you perchance related to Giuseppe Bussandri, the leader of the rebellion in the Italian region of Piacenza? Because you are inspiring an uprising in the south."

This book is dedicated to V & J. I love you two bunches!

ABOUT THE AUTHOR

After reading *Black Beauty* for the 1,497th time, Courtney McCaskill was inspired to write her own stories. Reviews of her early work were mixed, with her fourth-grade teacher, Mrs. Compton, saying, "Please stop writing all of your essays from the point of view of a horse." Perhaps she is improving, however, as in 2024, her book, *The Duke's Dark Secret*, received the prestigious Maggie Award.

Today, Courtney lives in Austin, Texas with the hero of her own story, who holds the distinction of being the world's most sarcastic pediatrician. She is reliably informed by her son that she gives THE BEST hugs, "because you're so squishy, Mommy." In 2022, Regency Fiction Writers honored her with its Lady of the Realm award in appreciation of her volunteer work, both on its Board of Directors and as the Coordinator of the Regency Academe. When she's not busy almost burning her house down while attempting to make a traditional Christmas pudding, she enjoys rock climbing, playing the piano, learning everything there is to know about Kodiak bears, and of course, curling up with a great book. Visit her online at www.courtneymccaskill.com.

ALSO BY COURTNEY MCCASKILL

The Astley Chronicles

Book 1: How to Train Your Viscount

Book 2: What's an Earl Gotta Do?

Book 3: The Sea Siren of Broadwater Bottom

Book 4: The Duke's Dark Secret

Book 5: Let Me Be Your Hero

Book 6: Romancing the Rifleman

Book 7: A Laird for Lady Lucy (Coming Soon)

My Favorite Mistake: An Astley Chronicles Novella

The Weatherby Wallflowers

Book 1: A Wallflower Never Surrenders

Book 2: Snowbound with the Scoundrel

Book 3: One Bed for the Bluestocking (Coming Soon)

Book 4: How He Won His Wallflower (Coming Soon)

The Wicked Widows' League

Book 1: Scoundrel for Sale

Book 2: A Very Roguish Boxing Day

Other Books:

One Fine May (The Rake Review)

For more information, visit www.courtneymccaskill.com.

www.ingramcontent.com/pod-product-compliance
Lightning Source LLC
Chambersburg PA
CBHW050518110726
47899CB00005B/1506